MW01286054

Storybook Ending

Storybook Ending

A Novel

Moira Macdonald

DUTTON

DUTTON

An imprint of Penguin Random House LLC
1745 Broadway, New York, NY 10019
penguinrandomhouse.com

Copyright © 2025 by Moira Macdonald
Penguin Random House values and supports copyright.
Copyright fuels creativity, encourages diverse voices, promotes
free speech, and creates a vibrant culture. Thank you for buying an
authorized edition of this book and for complying with copyright laws by
not reproducing, scanning, or distributing any part of it in any form without
permission. You are supporting writers and allowing Penguin Random
House to continue to publish books for every reader. Please note that no
part of this book may be used or reproduced in any manner for the
purpose of training artificial intelligence technologies or systems.

DUTTON and the D colophon are registered trademarks of
Penguin Random House LLC.

LIBRARY OF CONGRESS CATALOGING-IN-PUBLICATION DATA

Names: Macdonald, Moira, author.
Title: Storybook ending : a novel / Moira Macdonald.
Description: [New York] : Dutton, 2025.
Identifiers: LCCN 2024041739 (print) | LCCN 2024041740 (ebook) |
ISBN 9780593851296 (hardcover) | ISBN 9780593851302 (epub)
Subjects: LCGFT: Romance fiction. | Novels.
Classification: LCC PS3613.A271426 S76 2025 (print) |
LCC PS3613.A271426 (ebook) | DDC 813/.6—dc23/eng/20250103
LC record available at https://lccn.loc.gov/2024041739
LC ebook record available at https://lccn.loc.gov/2024041740

ISBN 9798217046362 (international edition)

Printed in the United States of America
2nd Printing

BOOK DESIGN BY SHANNON NICOLE PLUNKETT

The authorized representative in the EU for product safety and compliance
is Penguin Random House Ireland, Morrison Chambers, 32 Nassau Street,
Dublin D02 YH68, Ireland, https://eu-contact.penguin.ie.

for Bruce,
beneath the moon and under the sun

Everybody allows that the talent of writing
agreeable letters is peculiarly female.

—Jane Austen, *Northanger Abbey*

It's all about developing a conversation
between the books. When they're placed side by side,
they talk to one another.

—Paul Yamazaki, *Reading the Room: A Bookseller's Tale*

Storybook Ending

1

April

The letter was a mistake. She was sure of it.

April often wondered if living alone gave her too much time to ponder. She had a tendency to overthink, telling herself stories for company, to fill up her otherwise unoccupied rooms. Her apartment, for example, was the source of many stories: It was a cozy one-bedroom on the third floor of a forthright-looking redbrick 1920s building, and sometimes April imagined a small family sharing it during the Depression, maybe with a sheet curtaining off a corner of the living room to give the parents some privacy. Or a woman living there alone in the 1940s, working an assembly line in a Seattle factory and waiting for her husband or fiancé to return from war. Or a *Mad Men*–ish single woman in the 1960s, a secretary in a bright dress who gazed at all the men who held the jobs she really wanted and wondered when her life would change. Each of them might have left their mark, in the faint scratches on the wood floors or the tiny chips in the bathroom tile or the ancient, yellowing shelf paper in the linen closet. Maybe some of them were still alive, living somewhere else, fondly remembering the years in that apartment on that quiet Seattle block with a springtime view of paper-pink cherry blossoms on the street below. Sometimes April imagined a reunion in the apartment, with people from different eras somehow magically sharing the same time and space. They'd probably all be horrified by how much she was paying in rent, and by the fact that she hadn't gotten around to changing the shelf paper. (Did anyone really change shelf paper?)

But right now, April was fixated on something entirely new, something far from those familiar, pleasantly faded walls. She had written the letter and taken it to its destination, and almost instantly regretted it.

Nobody ever seemed to write actual letters anymore, but April loved the idea of a handwritten, on-paper, non-email correspondence—handwriting, with its loops and swirls and angles, seemed to be a tiny map to someone's essence, or a portal to another time, like a Victorian novel written with a scratchy fountain pen. But she knew all too well that some letters should never be sent. Letters confessing a painful secret, perhaps; the sort better to be carried to one's grave or at least one's dotage, whatever that was. Letters that contain the written equivalent of a toddler's temper tantrum, a fury quickly dissipated but living on through angry scribbles on a piece of paper. Letters repeating gossip that may or may not be true—maybe especially if it's true. Or letters written late at night, beginning with "You don't know me, but . . ." and going on to express something that could only be described as a crush on a person one doesn't exactly know.

Unfortunately, the letter she had written was exactly that last type.

And while she hadn't actually *sent* it, it had nonetheless reached its destination: slipped within the pages of a book—Anthony Horowitz's *Magpie Murders*, to be precise—and dropped off in a pile at the used-books desk at Read the Room, the neighborhood bookstore just two blocks down from April's building, on a bright May afternoon that seemed to pulse with promise. At the store, a thirtysomething man whose name April didn't know, with a carelessly becoming beard and the kind of gentle smile that might inspire bad poetry, had the job of tending to the new arrivals of used books, sorting and checking through them.

He would, April was certain, find the letter and read it. He seemed careful in his work, like he might be the sort of person who would appreciate the mystery of an anonymous correspondent. Though very, very good-looking—surely he wasn't an actor, but he looked like he could be one—he seemed quiet and bookish and maybe even a little shy. She'd seen him politely interacting with customers, and once watched him patiently looking up a book online for an elderly man who seemed highly skeptical of computers. He seemed, in short, nice.

April was ready for nice. She was, officially, lonely. Working from home had seemed so convenient at first, but now it appeared to have become something permanent without her ever agreeing to it—and, as a person who tended toward introversion, she'd adapted to it maybe too easily. The other day, she'd been out for a walk—she made herself leave the apartment once a day no matter what, even in the frequent Seattle spring rain—and found herself getting far too enthusiastic over a sweater-clad dog whose owner hustled her pet away quickly. It worried April that she seemed to be getting out of practice in talking to people, but how could she practice? She just wasn't meeting anyone. Even her neighbors in the building all seemed just like her: quiet and solitary, rarely venturing out. April heard their music and footsteps and mysterious thumps, but rarely saw them—imagining their stories rather than knowing them.

She could, of course, have just walked right up to the bookstore man and said hello, like a regular person, but she'd hatched the idea of the letter late one night after watching a rom-com double feature, not long after she'd reread *84, Charing Cross Road*. Things worked out so nicely in the movies, and the letters in the book (between a bookshop employee, April noted, and a woman who loved to read) were so charming, and somehow in the middle of the night it all seemed like a good idea. Sometimes, April had reasoned, sitting at her desk in the darkness, you just have to throw something out into the world and see what happens. That morning, she'd quickly dropped off the letter in the book without giving herself time to rethink it. And now, as the late afternoon settled into a quiet, soft-sweater grayness, it wasn't easy to keep her mind on her work.

A buzz from her apartment's intercom interrupted April's thoughts, startling her. She was, as usual, not expecting anyone; her brother, Ben, was the only person in her life with a habit of showing up unannounced, and this afternoon she knew he was at an audition for a musical, despite not being able to sing. She crossed the room and pressed the button.

"Hello?"

"I have a pizza delivery for . . . Jackson?"

"Sorry," April said, "that's next door. Number 305." This wasn't the first time the pizza man had gotten it wrong. Mr. Jackson, a retired schoolteacher with whom April had chatted briefly a couple of times in the lobby or the hallway, ordered pizza every Thursday. She was uncomfortably aware of knowing this; maybe she had a little too much time to study her neighbors' habits.

"Thanks."

From her window, April watched the pizza man return to his car, a tiny two-door with an enormous plastic pizza slice on top. Maybe someone was waiting for him at the end of his shift— someone who had thought to preheat the oven for the pizza he would bring home, someone interested in hearing about his day and his adventures in pizza-delivering. Someone who hadn't had to leave a note in a book to meet someone. The little car drove away.

Anyway. The letter was done. And then what would happen, if the bookstore man did read it? Probably nothing, April thought, back at her desk and back to overthinking. Maybe grown-up women—April was thirty-three, an age that felt to her neither old nor young—working grown-up tech jobs from home shouldn't be imagining themselves as the not-blond heroine of a Nora Ephron movie. (April's hair was a very non-rom-com medium brown, though she liked to think she had a better haircut than Meg Ryan had in *You've Got Mail*.) Maybe boredom and solitude had led her to take a step too far. Maybe she really wasn't much of a writer. It wasn't even truly a letter, just a paragraph really, and maybe it had needed another draft—it was too short, not funny enough. April believed in rewriting, in trying to make things better. In the empty stretch of her evening, she feared the letter left in the book would be met with silence. It had perhaps been a crazy idea.

But April's life seemed in need of a crazy idea, to shake things up. Mostly she spent long hours in her apartment, working remotely for an online real estate company (a job that mainly consisted of writing cheery emails to potential home sellers) in the daytime and reading at night. She loved to read; it had always been her way of tuning out the world, of postponing troubles and escaping someplace else. As a child, her favorite days were trips to the library, when she'd stumble back into the car balancing a small mountain of books, reading on her bed until the afternoon light faded and her mother called her for dinner. She had loved Francie Nolan reading on the fire escape in *A Tree Grows in Brooklyn*; Jo March weeping over fiction while perched in a tree in *Little Women*; the All-of-a-Kind Family sisters, in their matching dresses and pinafores, making their own ritual trips to the library. April didn't have sisters in real life—she had Ben, but he was another story entirely—but books had given them to her.

These days, she was mostly reading mysteries, in which lone-wolf female detectives—all of whom, like herself, seemed to live alone in quirky apartments and have a strange assortment of mismatched food in their refrigerators—somehow always seemed to be stumbling into mysterious murders that they were able to figure out through nothing more than clever deduction. April imagined that she might be good at this, maybe just from reading all those novels—in the same way that, after watching all of *Call the Midwife* on Netflix, she was fairly certain she could deliver a baby in a pinch, as long as it wasn't breech—but the opportunity hadn't yet arisen. Maybe the letter was an attempt to create a little mystery of her own.

Like her mystery heroines, April didn't mind living alone,

despite the odd bump in the night that made her wish for another person in the room, at least for a moment. Sometimes the old building just seemed to need to stretch out its bones and make mysterious sounds, like little whispers from inhabitants past. Even in daytime, her apartment had pleasantly squeaky floors that seemed to remember other footsteps. When she was younger, April had dreamed of living in an apartment like this, somewhere all hers, filled with pretty leaded-glass windows and books. But now sometimes she wondered if this was really how adult life was supposed to be: this quiet stretch of days not too different from any other, this low-key contentment that never quite became all-out happiness. Long ago, she had thought that thirty-three was a ripe old age, and that by that time, she'd be happily settled in a rich, full life. There wasn't anything wrong with April's life, really, but she just always seemed to feel like she was waiting for something—for love, for a job that wasn't just OK, for busy gatherings with friends, for something unexpected.

As a regular at Read the Room (April had chosen the apartment several years ago not just for its vintage charm but also for its proximity to the bookstore; she'd long nurtured a fantasy of working in a bookstore someday), she had often surreptitiously watched the man at the desk, from a table in the café or from the corner of her eye as she browsed the shelves. He was handsome, but in a way that indicated that he didn't really know it—he was always absently rubbing his hand through his hair, leaving it whimsically askew. He seemed, from what she could observe, like he might have a sense of humor. She liked the way he laughed at his colleagues' jokes: not a big guffaw, but a soft, throaty peal, often chiming in just a bit later than everyone else. He wore no wedding ring, and he didn't seem to have any particular attachment to anyone at the store, at least from what she could see. Of course, she had no idea if any of these impressions were accurate (for all she knew, he was gay, or deeply involved with someone very impressive, or a total jerk, or maybe all of the above), or if he would in any way welcome her approach. But the only way to find out was to reach out, and April believed that the whimsy of sending a letter rather than directly approaching him might appeal. Well, she believed it yesterday, and it was too late to undo it now.

April closed her laptop for the day, pondered leftovers for dinner, and tried to focus on other things. Like why it was that whenever she saved up to buy some longed-for piece of furniture or décor, it never quite looked at home in her apartment, as if it was an early party guest waiting for the rest of the A-list to arrive. (She had a new armchair that wasn't getting along with the rest of her mostly secondhand furniture; it seemed to be keeping its distance, no matter how many throw pillows she put on it.) Or why she was receiving strange unknown texts from someone looking for their wayward son-in-law: "U need to come back. Gloria needs u. The kids miss u." Or whether it would be rude to ask her next-door neighbor in 303, who was taking tango lessons, to turn down the bandoneon music and maybe practice in socks after 10 p.m.

She texted Ben, just to check in:

How did the audition go?

He replied quickly, as he usually did.

Not great I guess they were looking for singers

April, snorting quietly to herself, typed "Well, it was a musical!" but quickly deleted it, sending a heart emoji instead.

The evening passed quietly, as evenings so often did, like links on an endless chain. A pretty chain, but one that maybe needed a pendant. Or something. Late at night, reading her latest mystery in bed, she kept thinking of the letter, sitting just a few blocks away on a counter in the store, a tiny corner peeking out from the pages of the thick red-and-black hardcover like a hand reaching out into the unknown. The nice thing about mysteries in novels was that they always got solved, though maybe not the way you thought they would.

2

Westley

People were always leaving things in books. It was part of Westley's job, as used-books coordinator at Read the Room, to riffle through the books accepted for resale and remove any flotsam, and he prided himself on doing this carefully. Dozens of the lost items that he'd found inside books were thumbtacked to the wall above the used-books desk: postcards depicting faraway beaches or glittering skylines, scribbled grocery lists, ATM receipts, magazine subscription cards, random brochures (there was one, all black and purple and curlicued typeface, from a "metaphysical supply shoppe" on the opposite coast, and Westley often stared at it, imagining its clientele), faded birthday cards, movie ticket stubs, overpriced arty bookmarks bought in museum gift shops. All of these pieces formed an accidental halo around the desk, ringing it in forgotten treasure.

Westley had worked at Read the Room for almost six years now, and some days he could barely remember how he had ended up at the store. It was as if he too had floated there unexpectedly, like all those cards and bookmarks, and had liked the feel of the air. He'd always loved books, even as a little boy; a good story always seemed to be better company than another person, and you didn't need to worry about saying the wrong thing. Being surrounded by books all day felt comfortable, like being among friends.

Westley was an only child, born to parents who made much of him: His mother, gasping at the beauty of her newborn son (in a tale Westley had heard way too many times and which always embarrassed him), named him after the hero of her then-favorite movie, *The Princess Bride*. As a result, Westley went through life having people say "As you wish" to him a lot (had *everyone* seen that movie growing up?), and he'd learned through no fault of his own that things tended to come easily to very good-looking people. Not that Westley thought he was particularly good-looking—his face in the mirror seemed like just a face to him, and he had no idea how to make his hair do what men in the movies seemed able to achieve without effort—but people were constantly telling him he was. He never knew quite what to say in reply.

Discovering Read the Room as a teenager had been a revelation to him. For a shy boy who didn't like attention, here was a place he could happily disappear, to browse the shelves and read in a tired but still cushiony armchair. Through his abbreviated college career and later, it was his favorite place to sit for hours with his laptop and a single coffee in the café. After years of using the store as his personal clubhouse, rarely speaking to anyone, one day he'd seen a "Help Wanted" sign in the window—on a day when he very much needed a new start. The sign had seemed so retro that Westley was thoroughly charmed—how could this possibly be how people found jobs these days?—and that was that.

To Westley, Read the Room was the perfect bookstore size: big enough to seem to be holding multitudes on its array of shelves, small enough to feel cozy on a rainy Seattle day, pleasantly barnlike thanks to a high ceiling and mellow wood floors that felt a little bit soft when you stepped on them, as if years of wear had turned the wood into carpet. Previously named BookLove (Westley liked the current name better), the store had been sitting on the corner in a quiet Seattle neighborhood for decades, on a street lined with trees and Craftsman houses not far from the university campus.

No one on the current staff had any memory of when the store was new, though occasionally longtime customers would reminisce about Read the Room's low-tech beginnings. Harry, an old-school gentleman with a cane who came in every second Friday to buy an old-school British mystery with a worn-soft twenty-dollar bill, always told whoever was assisting him that he remembered when the staff would just write down purchases on a yellow tablet. He always seemed faintly critical of them no longer doing so. It was the kind of place where a child's crayoned drawing of two smiling booksellers hung over the front desk, even though nobody remembered who the child was or when it was drawn (he or she was probably now old enough to work there), and in the evening, once the fragrance of baked goods had gone, its air smelled like old paper, coffee, and possibility. There was a small café in the back, with decent fresh pastries and perhaps too-creative sandwiches. Westley had never tried the marmalade-and-prosciutto panini; maybe someday.

It was, in short, a nice place to spend time, and Westley was contented there. He loved to read any kind of fiction, but particularly loved old books—the way that they would fall open to someone's favorite passage from long ago, like a ghost reader was gazing over his shoulder; the tiny tears at the top of the page indicating vigorous page-turning; the occasional whispered pencil marks or folded corners—and was happy to spend his days surrounded by them. But at thirty-five, he was uncomfortably aware that he wasn't particularly ambitious. Westley was always waiting for something to happen to him, and then wondering why nothing did. Maybe it wasn't enough to spend his days flipping pages; maybe there was something else he should be trying, something waiting for him that he hadn't thought of. Maybe he needed to find a way to make more money, to get his own place. But for now, the people at the store were pleasant (most of them), and there was always something good to read during slow times. Long ago, there had been a job that really mattered, and things there didn't work out. He didn't like to think about that time; it was a closed chapter. The books never asked any questions. His colleagues occasionally did, but Westley was good at pleasantly avoiding answers.

Raven, a fellow bookseller who today had on a T-shirt with the Louisa May Alcott quote "She is too fond of books, and it has turned her brain," suddenly appeared in front of the used-books counter. She had a seemingly unending collection of literary T-shirts that she wore as a sort of uniform; Westley could imagine her buying them in bulk from some extremely niche website. Raven looked irritated, which Westley had learned from experience was just her standard expression and didn't necessarily mean anything was amiss.

"Can you watch for used copies of *Magpie Murders*?" she said, in a tone that implied a carrying of great burdens. "Some book club called and wants as many of them as we can get, right away. I can order them but the system's backed up. As usual."

"OK. I'll keep an eye out for it," Westley said, waving an arm vaguely toward the boxes and shopping bags of book donations that he hadn't yet sorted. Though people weren't supposed to just drop off books without prior approval, it happened all the time, as apparently some people were willing to forgo the small financial recompense in order to not have their taste in fiction publicly scrutinized. He tried hard to be pleasant to Raven—and had, in fact, read and enjoyed the book; twisty mysteries were a particular favorite for him—so he added, "It was pretty good. Did you read it?"

Raven shook her head and a silence, faintly scented with awkwardness, ensued before she wandered off with no further comment. Westley and Raven had a bit of romantic history, if "romantic" is the right word, involving some minor making out back in the Self-Help and Memoir shelves during last year's holiday staff party. In an exceedingly stilted January conversation that

Westley hesitantly initiated, both agreed that it meant nothing, that they'd had too much free Chardonnay and made some bad choices, and that they would continue to respect each other as co-workers. It was now May, and the two of them were still talking as if they were rehearsing for a play. If that metaphysical shoppe had sold a product to erase unwanted history, Westley would have bought it instantly. He had vowed to himself to never again drink at a work event, and maybe make more of an effort to meet someone nice outside of work, though he wasn't at all sure how.

There was plenty of time to ponder such things; business was quietly steady but never downright bustling, except in the week before Christmas and on the rare occasions that Julia, the store's owner and manager, announced a weekend twenty-percent-off-everything sale to get some new customers in the door. Westley often wondered how Read the Room was surviving financially—things were challenging for brick-and-mortar bookstores in the age of Amazon—but Julia didn't share much information other than urging the staff to be nice to the customers and encourage them to buy good books. A steady stream of readers, many of them regulars who lived in the neighborhood, came through the doors, often with specific requests for something they'd heard of or read about. Not long ago, the store had a problem with customers coming in to research the shelves and make note of the titles, to purchase later for less online. But Julia developed a strategy that involved long, pointed stares at any customer writing down titles or snapping a smartphone photo of a book cover. This was hard for the more introverted among the staff—Westley wasn't very good at it—but Raven in particular enjoyed the challenge, staring with a laser-like focus that would make the errant customer visibly nervous. Oddly enough, shame seemed to work, and eventually the problem more or less disappeared.

The store had a handful of employees, but the ones Westley dealt with the most were the other full-timers (he was one of five, counting Julia, working a flexible five-day schedule); he'd learned, through years of working and listening, that each of them had some other passion project going on. Raven, for one, ran a yarn-dying business out of her apartment, and was always proudly talking about how she'd discovered a new blue. (Blue, apparently, had endless possibilities.) Andrew, who wore a blazer to work every day even in the heat of un-air-conditioned summer, was studying for the LSAT. Julia was constantly talking about her three grandchildren, who were all exceptionally bright and ador-able, or so she said. (She'd brought them in a few times for story hour and they seemed perfectly non-exceptional to Westley, but what did he know?) Alejandra was writing a fantasy novel set on a planet where everyone's hair was perpetually and visibly grow-ing, and she was often staring out the window, imagining her next chapter. Westley would watch her curiously, wondering what it would be like to create a world. He envied all of them, for having something they loved outside the store.

Read the Room sold both new and used books, and Westley was always surprised at the number of people who would show up with boxes and bags full of books for resale, hoping for a windfall. Nobody ever got much money—Julia, perpetually wor-rying about cash flow, preferred to give store credit rather than cash, winning people over by offering double the value in credit—for their piles of tired paperbacks, old textbooks, inscribed cook-books, and their copies of *Fifty Shades of Grey*, which everyone seemed to buy but nobody seemed to want to keep in their homes. Today's offerings, as Westley sorted through them, looked typi-cal: about a third of the volumes, if that, were acceptable for re-sale; the rest would be donated to the public library or returned to the customer, if they'd left a name. Used books make their way downstream, and it wasn't much fun to think about what hap-pened to the ones nobody wanted. Westley sometimes imagined a sad island somewhere far away, its lonely beaches stacked with worn-out mass-market thrillers and tahini-stained vegan cook-books.

The pile he was looking at now seemed destined for just such a place: It was a small, weary-looking stack of faded paperbacks, spines cracked and corners curled with wear. The only option for them was the recycling bin—even the library didn't want ancient paperbacks with pages as soft as old flannel sheets—but as Westley slid the pile toward him, he noticed one book in the stack that still seemed new and shiny, in an odd size for a paperback. He picked it up: *Shivering Timbers*, by Duke Munro, with a drawing of a man and a woman, both in khaki-colored uniforms, embracing in a forest made up of brushstrokes, with smoke wafting in at one corner. The author's name wasn't familiar, but there was something about the hopeful amateurishness of the book's design that touched Westley. He turned it over and read the back cover:

> *Can two firefighters in a remote outpost find love? Verity Sloane didn't become a firefighter to meet men: She did it because she loved the elements, especially water and fire. When the first woman at Rural Fire District #39B meets Will McEwan, longtime leader of the team, sparks fly—but what kind of sparks?*

Westley was about to toss the book into the to-be-shelved pile when the picture of the author at the bottom of the back cover caught his eye: a bearded, thirtysomething man in a plaid flannel shirt. He looked, oddly, rather like Westley himself. The brief bio described Duke Munro as "a beloved author of manly tales" who lived in the Pacific Northwest and enjoyed foraging, rock climbing, standing on the edge of cliffs (was this a metaphor, Westley wondered?), and sustainable cuisine. The book was published by a small press that Westley didn't recognize; maybe it was one of those self-publishing vanity presses, or maybe not—it was getting harder to tell these days. In any case, it was a romance novel.

For a man named after the hero of a famously romantic movie, Westley wasn't much for romance—or at least, that was what he told himself after his last relationship had gone so horribly wrong. He'd been single for a long time (the occasional misbegotten dalliance at a holiday party notwithstanding) and lived with housemates who were pleasant but mostly distant. A romance novel would typically be something he'd avoid, but he felt a sudden and strange connection with this author, who seemed like someone he could have known—was this story a life he might have had if he were not so cautiously tethered to this bookstore? Anyway, the book seemed like perhaps it might be something entertaining to read over dinner, which he usually ate alone, and maybe this could be the start of saying yes to things, since saying no didn't seem to be getting him anywhere. Westley tucked *Shivering Timbers* into his messenger bag, a bit furtively, though no one would have faulted him for taking home a used book; that was an unspoken perk of his job, of which he frequently took advantage.

Julia's voice distracted him from thoughts of Duke Munro. "Westley, can you come over here?" she called from across the room. "Quick staff huddle." Julia, who had spiky gray hair and a fondness for flowy thrift-store Eileen Fisher (she talked a lot about where to buy the brand at discount, despite nobody else seeming interested), frequently used sports analogies in managing the staff. He liked Julia and found her to be a fair and considerate boss, but could easily imagine her presiding over drills involving planks and push-ups.

Over at the front desk, the small number of full-time staff had gathered, looking mildly expectant but not terribly interested. "Hey, Westley," said Alejandra, gazing up from a box of new paperbacks she was unpacking. "Did you find that Octavia Butler book I left for you?"

"Yes, thanks," Westley said. He wasn't usually a big reader of science fiction, but he enjoyed hearing Alejandra talk rapturously about her favorites. "I'll start it this weekend." He would have liked to continue the conversation, but he'd run out of things to say.

Luckily, Julia was ready to start the staff huddle. Such a meeting usually meant that it was somebody's birthday, or a holiday was coming up, or Julia wanted to remind everyone to keep the shelves tidy. (For some reason Julia felt it was important to constantly announce this, even though the shelves were always tidy; Read the Room's wares bore an almost military precision.) Today, though, Julia's expression indicated that something more momentous was afoot. "Everybody here?" she said, appearing to do a mental head count.

"Yeah," said Andrew, who frequently announced his opposition to staff huddles on principle. "It's not like there's that many of us."

Julia didn't hear him, or perhaps pretended not to. "OK! I have an exciting announcement," she said, her voice bright. "We are going to be in the movies!"

The exciting announcement landed with the sort of dull thud that a pile of hardcover books makes on a counter. Julia ignored the silence and went on. "Maybe you've heard of Donna Wolfe? The director who really should have gotten an Oscar nomination for *Twelve for Dinner*, that movie about the cannibals?" The silence reigned. "Well, she is in town, and her new movie is partly set in a bookstore—and she wants to shoot some of the scenes here!" Julia paused dramatically and looked around for a response.

"Is her new bookstore movie like *You've Got Mail*?" asked Alejandra, gratifying Julia by displaying a bit of excitement. Alejandra, a film buff who loved to arrange "Books to Movies" displays at the store, had applied for her job at Read the Room in part because of her fondness for the Meg Ryan movie and had been immediately disappointed. She had once confided to Westley her tongue-in-cheek dismay that the staff at Read the Room did not gather outside of work for impromptu singalongs or solve problems with the addition of more twinkle lights. Having not seen *You've Got Mail*, Westley had no idea what she was talking about, or what "twinkle lights" were.

"Yes," said Julia, a bit crestfallen at the lack of excitement. "I mean no. It will be a very different movie. I mean I guess it will be, I don't really know anything about it."

"Why is Donna Wolfe making a movie *here*?" said Andrew, who liked to be the person who asked hard questions. He often seemed like he was practicing being in a courtroom, bearing down on a reluctant witness.

"Will we get to be in the movie?" Alejandra wondered.

"Will it happen during work hours?" Westley said.

"Will we get paid extra?" Raven asked.

"I don't know the answers to any of those questions," said Julia, whose enthusiasm was quickly fading under the light of their queries. "We'll find out soon. It's a bit last-minute. I think there was another bookstore that pulled out, and apparently somebody suggested to Donna Wolfe's staff that Read the Room has the look she wants, whatever that means. But they want to begin shooting here later this month, for a few weeks. It will be wonderful publicity for the store, so of course I said yes. There will be people from her crew visiting early next week, including a *location scout*." Julia pronounced the title carefully, like it was something exotic to be meticulously handled. "Please assist them in any way you can." Clearly irritated that her big announcement didn't catch fire, Julia waved her hands in dismissal. "OK, back to work. I'll have more details later."

Westley returned to the used-books counter, wondering what it might mean to have a movie shot at the store. He'd seen *Twelve for Dinner*, a satire involving cannibalism and dinner-party etiquette, and hadn't really understood it, but it had made a fairly big splash for an art-house movie. He quickly looked up Donna Wolfe online, making sure his computer was turned so that his colleagues couldn't see the screen. A number of stories and photographs turned up, with the filmmaker always in dark glasses—he wasn't sure if it was a vision problem or whether she was just pretentious. Wikipedia informed Westley that Donna Wolfe was in her late fifties, that she had made a number of films that had attracted critical attention if not huge audiences, and that she had "a striking visual sense" and "a gift for cinematic question-raising," which Westley took to mean that her movies were complicated and maybe not much fun. What she was doing in Seattle he didn't know, but a movie in the store sounded like an interesting distraction from his fairly mundane routine. At any rate, it would be *something*.

Turning to the next pile of book donations brought in that day, Westley was distracted by a lottery ticket falling out of the top book. This was a fairly common occurrence, and he paused to look up its number online to be sure the ticket wasn't worth anything—it wasn't; they never were—and in doing so forgot his usual process of riffling through the pages of the remaining books in the stack. All were mystery titles that he knew would easily sell, and he processed them in a familiar ritual, putting new price stickers on the back covers and setting the stack on the new-inventory cart for Raven to pick up when she next passed through. Pleased to have spotted a copy of the book Raven had asked for, he put *Magpie Murders* on top of the pile.

3

Laura

Driving was one of the few times Laura felt that she could truly be herself. At work, as a personal shopper at Waterton's department store, she had to project an image of sleek competence: a stylish blank slate on which clients could project their own images; a fount of fashion wisdom who could explain why enormous baggy pants or tiny backpacks or voluminously puffed sleeves were suddenly, weirdly chic. At home, with her seven-year-old daughter, Olivia, she had to be all-knowing and sure, answering endless questions while trying to convey a loving, grown-up single-parent stability.

But in the car on this May afternoon—alone, heading home from work and stopping on the way at Read the Room to pick up a book for the book club that she most definitely didn't have time for—Laura could just be. She could listen to silly programs or podcasts and giggle, or sing along with songs that reminded her of less complicated days, or appreciate the view of Lake Washington, which on bright days bordered Laura's neighborhood in dazzling blue and today looked like a rough, scratchy blanket of gray. Or she could revel in the quiet, and the fact that just for a moment, nobody needed her—not her daughter, not the babysitter, not her delightfully dramatic assistant at the store who was always wanting feedback on the arch of his brows or whether the color of his socks popped. Laura never minded traffic jams. In fact, she looked forward to them. Between parenting and work, it was a welcome novelty to have no one to talk to but herself.

Most importantly, she could cry in the car if she needed to. And she had, many times, particularly during the awful months long ago when her husband, Sam, was sick, and Olivia was a fretful baby, and life was so completely overwhelming that Laura was sometimes afraid to get up in the morning. She had been a widow for five years now, though it was a word that never seemed to sit right with Laura; it seemed to suggest a much older woman, ashen-faced and draped dramatically in black. Sam had died in his midthirties of a quick, vicious cancer, leaving Laura with a toddler and a broken heart. She and Sam were in their very early twenties when they met, and Laura had been certain that she'd happily grow old with him—but sometimes life, as she reflected far too often, doesn't give you what you expect.

Time passed; the toddler grew and Laura's shattered heart very slowly mended. . . . Well, no, it hadn't really mended and probably never would, but as the years went by it no longer hurt quite so badly. For a long time, Laura had thought she would spend the rest of her life in grief and mourning, bursting into tears whenever she'd see a man wearing the kind of baseball cap she used to tease Sam about, or hear a song they'd once enjoyed at a concert together. But the memory of Sam, over the years, had transformed from devastating pain to a quietly melancholy ache. Though he was still very much present in her life—particularly whenever she looked into Olivia's brown eyes, which were as meltingly serious as her father's had been—Laura found that over time the sadness didn't disappear, but it slipped further and further away. Now it was something she could see on an increasingly distant horizon, like a souvenir from a long-ago journey that was mostly kept in a drawer, brought out only on occasion. There were still reminders of him everywhere; the car, for instance, had been Sam's, with a Northwestern bumper sticker still attached. Despite intermittent engine problems and an ever-growing medley of stains on the upholstery, she couldn't imagine ever wanting another.

The damp spring air smelled like fresh leaves as Laura hurried into Read the Room, the outside aroma quickly replaced by that magic bookstore fragrance: like a fresh paperback, like delicious leisure time. There were, as always, an assortment of people sitting in the café and various chairs around the store, poking desultorily at laptops and looking as if they hadn't moved for hours. Not for the first time, she wondered if they ever actually left, and what kinds of lives they led with nothing to do. Obviously, they didn't have children. When the store was closed, she wondered, were those people still there, sitting in the darkness, mesmerized by their screens, quietly aging in place? They seemed as much a part of the atmosphere as the books on the wooden shelves, ever-present like extras in a stage production; you couldn't imagine the store without them.

Noticing a lull at the front desk, Laura stepped up, catching the eye of a woman in an ill-fitting T-shirt and equally ill-fitting bra, with a blue streak in her hair and dangly homemade earrings crocheted from yarn in colors that didn't quite match. Laura always noticed people's outfits, and even their undergarments; after many years working at the store, starting in the lingerie department (where she learned the precise art of assessing someone's bra size at a glance) and working her way up to personal shopping, she couldn't help it. Tempted to offer this woman advice on better-fitting underpinnings, Laura sternly stopped herself: It was important, she believed, to help only those who *ask* for assistance.

"Excuse me," Laura said to the woman, focusing on the task at hand but realizing belatedly that she wasn't sure of the book's title. "Do you have a copy of, I think it's called *Magpie Mysteries*? The author's name is, um, maybe . . . shoot, I don't remember."

Bookstore employees, it seemed, were never fazed by such queries; it was, Laura imagined, their superpower. "You must be in the book club. That's Anthony Horowitz, *Magpie Murders*," the woman said, not even hesitating. "Someone else from your club just called this morning. We don't have any new copies on the shelves right now, but I might have one at the used-books desk. Hang on just a sec; I'll check." She walked over to the far side of the store while Laura pondered a display of fashionable reading glasses at the counter as she waited, wondering if a pair of round frames would make her look charmingly retro or like Harry Potter's mother. A tiny mirror confirmed that the latter seemed much more likely.

After a wait that seemed unnecessarily long—had the blue-streak woman gone on a break?—the bookseller returned with a hardcover book in her hands. "Sorry about that," she said, sighing a bit. "My colleague at the used-books desk was taking forever for some reason. Anyway, somebody brought in this copy today. Cheaper than new, and it's in great condition. Would that work for you?"

"Perfect. Thank you," said Laura, trying not to stare at the woman's earrings, which were asymmetrical in a way that didn't seem quite intentional. Laura paid with a credit card, declined the offer of a bag, resisted looking at the cheery displays on the front table—how was it that the world could have so many books in it? How did all these writers find the time?—and was back in the car within two minutes and home within ten. Laura loved to take the drive through her neighborhood slowly—up a hill with a glimpse of the lake at the top, past Olivia's school with its now-quiet playground—but there was, disappointingly, no traffic this afternoon; Laura barely had a chance to hear her favorite public radio announcer intone the afternoon's headlines. It wasn't that Laura didn't love her child and her work—she felt extraordinarily, giddily lucky in both of them, as if the universe had noticed her tragedy and given her two incredible gifts in return—but she was always a little disappointed when a day didn't bring enough forced buffer time, like traffic stops or line-waiting. She couldn't imagine adding a book club to a life already overstuffed, but her best friend, Rebecca, a busy lawyer who nonetheless had time to read every buzzed-about book and answer every one of Laura's late-night phone calls, had urged her to give it a try.

As Laura entered her front hallway, Ashley looked up from the couch and her phone. Olivia called her Ashley Two to differentiate her from the previous babysitter, also named Ashley, who had to be dismissed when Laura discovered that she was parking Olivia in front of age-inappropriate TV programs and making semiviral TikTok videos in which she made fun of the items in Laura's wardrobe. Laura had never been able to look at her favorite sundress in the same way since Ashley One had called it a "Golden Girls mom sack." Ashley Two didn't seem to mind the moniker; she was a sweet, easygoing young woman whose only strong opinions seemed to involve her extremely particular diet, which consisted of a long litany of intolerances. "Hey Laura," she said in greeting. "Livvy's at Hayden's. I like that jacket. Is it new?"

"Thanks. No, I've had it awhile," said Laura, feeling mildly if unfairly annoyed that once again, she was paying a person to watch a child who wasn't actually there. Ashley's job was to collect Olivia at school on weekdays when Laura worked—Laura delivered her in the mornings and picked her up on Mondays and Tuesdays, her days off—and keep her appropriately safe and entertained in the afternoons or on weekends until Laura got home from work. (Laura often dreamed of getting weekends off, so as to spend them taking Olivia on adventures, but Saturday and Sunday were the store's busiest days. Maybe someday.) But more often than not, Olivia went next door after school to play at her friend's house, leaving Ashley to lounge on the couch posing for an endless series of selfies. Occasionally Ashley, who treated her employer with some reverence because Laura "worked in fashion," would ask for help choosing the best among them. They all looked exactly the same: all pursed lips and arched eyebrows and careful non-expression, like her face had somehow checked out for the day. "Did you tell her I'll come get her at six?"

"Yes. The grocery order came, and I put everything away. You need to buy more sunscreen; we're almost out. I made a salad and put a chicken in the oven for dinner. The fridge is making a weird noise. And Livvy needs a permission slip signed for her class trip to the solid waste facility," said Ashley, who tended to speak in lengthy outpourings of information. Laura's initial annoyance instantly disappeared; Ashley, despite her own food issues, seemed to enjoy puttering in the kitchen and often surprised Laura with Instagram-worthy homemade meals, gluten and all.

"Why are a bunch of second graders going to a solid waste facility? That's just the dump, right?" said Laura. She was often mystified by Olivia's school activities but had learned not to question them; it was best to not be one of *those* parents. Laura belonged to a Facebook group of parents for Olivia's class at school, and the conversation mostly consisted of rants about gluten-free food, something called "free-choice childrearing" (which seemed to have been invented by the parents of Olivia's classmate Ike, who every day was allowed to make his own decisions about everything and thus was often wearing shorts in January and snowsuits in June) and impassioned arguments about any field trip, no matter how benign. Laura kept her presence on the chat carefully neutral.

"Livvy's excited. She said she wants to see where the garbage goes." Ashley headed for the door with a sort of half-wave. "See ya."

"Thank you!" Laura called behind her. "See you tomorrow."

The door closed, and Laura looked gratefully around the quiet room. She and Olivia still lived in the two-bedroom townhouse Laura and Sam had rented just before the baby was born; though they had tried to save for a house, they hadn't managed to amass enough for a deposit before his illness, and acquiring real estate in an increasingly expensive city now seemed like an unlikely dream to Laura. Between her salary, Sam's Social Security benefits for his child, and a small inheritance from a great-aunt, Laura managed the rent and her household budget without much worry, pushing off thoughts of home ownership to another day.

The townhouse, on a quiet block near Olivia's school, was fine for now, though it wasn't quite the warm home Laura dreamt of; nearly everything in it was beige and plain and blank slate, from the carpeting to the walls to the few pieces of unadventurous furniture Laura had acquired over the years. Someday she'd hang quirky art on the walls and jazz things up a bit with some color, but all she'd managed so far was painting Olivia's room gumball purple at her daughter's insistence. The right moment never seemed to come.

Just now, though, she had a quiet home, a book in her hands, dinner already made (bless Ashley), and almost a half hour of nothing scheduled and nobody needing her. Maybe it was time to give this book club idea a chance and at least get started on the book, even if it seemed unlikely that she would finish it in time? Rebecca had sworn that the women of the book club were fun and that excellent snacks and decent wine would be served at the meeting. Laura hung up her jacket, grabbed a can of LaCroix from the fridge, and, shoes off, settled on the couch with *Magpie Murders*. But when she opened the book, a pale-blue envelope fell out. It read simply, "For You."

Hi,
You don't know me, but I've seen you many times in the
bookstore. Please forgive the intrusion, but you seem like
someone I would like to try to get to know; I love the way you look
at books like they're precious objects, and handle them so
carefully. I know nothing about you and maybe you wouldn't
welcome an overture like this? But I couldn't help thinking that
you might enjoy a bit of a mystery. If you're intrigued, leave a
note in the middle copy of The Hunger Games *in Young Adult*
and tell me your favorite book and where you most like to read.
I'll tell you more about me, too.
A

4

April

The letter was out there and there was nothing to be done about it. Maybe he'd seen it, maybe he'd tossed it into the recycling bin, unread. It had been a stupid idea anyway. April, at her desk trying to work, had been back to the store twice in the past four days, each time casually checking the middle copy of *The Hunger Games* (actually, she'd checked all three of them just in case anybody was rearranging things, ready with a story about needing a book for her niece in case anyone interrupted her). Nothing. Maybe it was time to try Tinder. The flannel-shirt man, whatever his name was, clearly wasn't interested, and the bold experiment had failed.

Then again, dating wasn't going so well either. Just last week, at her friend Janie's urging, April had met up at a neighborhood bar with a man named P.J., whose sister-in-law worked at a Star-bucks with Janie's cousin Tim. P.J., whose phone never left his hand for the duration of the date despite his consuming a beer and some fried cauliflower with the other hand, talked a lot about how streaming movies was absolutely superior to watching them in a movie theater (entirely wrong, April thought, but it didn't seem worth the bother to chime in with her opinion), disappeared into the bathroom when the check came, and said goodbye to April in a way that indicated he'd forgotten her name, if he ever indeed knew it. Going home to her quiet apartment was a relief, if a bittersweet one.

A notification pinged on her phone—a text, from a group chain of some of April's college friends that had been going for some years, which included Janie. Janie was April's best friend; well, she *had* been April's best friend; now she was usually too overwhelmed by two small kids, a husband, and a job to make time for April. All of the other friends in the group also had young kids, except April, and conversations once full of giggle emojis and excited plans to get together were now mostly baby-oriented. April opened the text, without the happy anticipation she once would have had.

You guys, does this look normal???

A photograph showing the contents of a diaper was attached. This was a bit much for April, who quickly closed the text window, but not before another reply had already popped up from another friend, asking for more details as to volume and texture. Well. Maybe it was time to put the phone away for a while.

Though reading made her world bigger, April's actual life had gotten rather small. Particularly her social life, which was pretty much nothing these days: killed first by the departure years ago of her boyfriend Josh, taking many of their mutual friends with him; second by the pandemic; and third by the frustrating fact that all of her remaining friends seemed to be at a stage in life where young kids or careers or both made things overwhelming. April had mostly given up trying to organize *Sex and the City*–ish drinks gatherings, as everyone seemed just too exhausted all the time. She loved her friends' kids, and kept careful track of all of their names (even the ones whose spellings she silently disapproved of, like Jaxon) and birthdays and developmental stages, but it was hard to take part in a group of which she no longer felt like a member. And that posted photographs that really should come with a "Not Safe For Those Without Kids" warning.

April particularly missed Janie, who'd once been a big part of her life; they'd been two nervous freshmen in a dorm together and went through college life side by side. She'd learned not to expect any answer these days when she texted Janie—something she did almost unconsciously, wanting to share moments of her life with the person who'd known her back when her life was in its early chapters. Lately, on the rare occasions that Janie had time for April, she was mostly invested in trying to fix her up with someone—misery, or at least exhaustion, apparently craves company. April loved Janie, remembering the goofball college student more readily than the stressed-out mom, and tried to be understanding when Janie kept canceling their lunch plans. She went on those dates orchestrated by Janie more often than not, out of loyalty to her friend and a desire to get herself in circulation, but her heart wasn't in it. It just seemed like too much work to dive into a relationship, hoping the water would be comfortable; safer to stay on shore.

A quiet knock on the door interrupted her thoughts. Peering through the peephole, April saw that it was her neighbor, Mr. Jackson, he of the weekly pizzas. She unlocked the chain and opened the door.

"Oh, hello there," said Mr. Jackson, sounding a little out of breath, like he'd just climbed a couple of flights of stairs. (Their building did not have an elevator. April had gotten pretty good at reaching the top of the stairs laden with groceries without panting, but she was a few decades younger than Mr. Jackson.) "I believe I've gotten some of your mail in my box. Are these catalogs yours?"

April, who tried hard to be meticulous about recycling, didn't receive many catalogs. These ones looked like they contained clothing more appropriate for a woman twenty years older. She flipped one over and read the address. "Oh, this is for 303, the woman next door to me over there," she said, handing the catalogs back and pointing at her neighbor's door. Feeling like she should say something social, she added, "I'm sure she'll appreciate getting them."

"Alrighty then," said Mr. Jackson, who both looked and talked like he was an older gentleman in a 1930s movie; he often seemed like he was wearing a hat, even though he wasn't. "Sorry to bother you. Enjoy your afternoon."

"No problem," April said, smiling and waving and immediately feeling awkwardly silly (why wave to someone standing two feet away?) before closing her door. She couldn't help eavesdropping a bit as Mr. Jackson tapped on the next door and had a not-particularly-brief conversation with the woman April mentally called Tango Lady—April's only knowledge of her, other than the tango practices she overheard, was that she was maybe sixtyish and wore a lot of dramatic black outfits and a faintly spicy perfume that often trailed her in the hallway—but she couldn't really make out the words. Maybe they were becoming friends. Well, why not? Somebody should.

Her phone—ignoring it was easier said than done—blinked with an alert; nothing important, just news of continuing spring rain. April, back at her desk, absently swiped through a few emails and checked her calendar (no meetings, no plans). By habit, her finger seemed to automatically fly through old voice-mail messages to find one from long ago, carefully saved. She pressed it. "Hi, sweetie," her mother's voice said. "Just checking in. I bought you some of those socks you like, and I'll bring them over later. Love you." It was the last message her mother had sent before her sudden, unexpected death, almost ten years ago. Enough time had passed that April could talk about her mother without getting tearful and could smile when imagining her mother's advice—but she often listened to the message, appreciating how it brought back her mother's perfume. Mom, who always used to talk about seizing the day, surely would have been cheering on the letter-in-the-book move.

April had spent her life in Seattle—she loved the city's dark winters and bright green summers, and had never yearned to live anywhere else—but didn't have a lot of family around. Her father lived nearby and checked in regularly but was busy in retirement with his golf and seniors' clubs. And there was, of course, her only sibling, Ben, who was three years younger and generally too obsessed with his own life to notice anything lacking in April's. Ben was always telling people grandly that he was an actor—you could almost hear the capital A—but in reality, he worked at a deli, made a lot of jokes about ham, and spent most of his time auditioning for roles that he did not get. The director was looking for someone a little taller, Ben would always say. Despite her instincts, April tried hard not to micromanage Ben's life for him, which was easy enough as he didn't listen anyway.

For several years now, April had worked for Picket Fence, an enormous online real estate company founded in Seattle by an eccentric heiress and now turned national. She'd gotten the job, despite not having tech experience, during a time of massive growth for the company and a moment of risk-taking in her own life, impressing an interviewer with her quick, confident answers to questions. The company's website listed homes for sale and numerous other services, including unique perks like special "make it your own" filters in which potential buyers could see images of their own furniture mocked up in the rooms of homes for sale (a popular feature, though it often resulted in odd-looking mishmashes). Company analytics had told April, however, that most people used the site to look up what their houses and their neighbors' houses were worth, and then presumably to brag about the numbers.

April's job title was "content associate," and her day-to-day work involved reviewing listings submitted by people who wanted to sell their houses on Picket Fence, and offering suggestions to make the homes seem more marketable. These suggestions were usually along the lines of "Maybe you could put that laundry away and try taking another picture?" and "Buyers like an uncluttered look," the latter of which she told people over and over. (She'd half-seriously suggested the company distribute T-shirts with the phrase, but nobody in the executive office answered her email.) April had seen many pictures dominated by people's collections of Disney figurines or scary antique dolls or souvenir snow globes. It was sort of touching, in a way, that people thought others would be charmed by their passions.

She didn't mind the work, really, though it wasn't the sort of thing you'd want to do forever. The pay and benefits were good, far better than at her previous job: shelving books at the public library, something that she'd thought would be a dream job (all those books!) but that ended up being tediously repetitive. Not that advising Picket Fence home sellers wasn't repetitive, but at least she could do it sitting down, and it was fun to see inside people's homes without leaving her own, to get a sense of how other people lived, what they thought was beautiful or useful or appropriate. Once April saw photos of a home with a large up-stairs open-plan bedroom suite that included a toilet, right out in the open without even a partition, a few feet from the bed. "It's European," the owner had explained in an email. April, who had been to Europe a couple of times and certainly would have re-membered if she'd ever seen a setup like that, had furrowed her brow and said nothing. The house sold quickly, like houses in Se-attle always did; presumably some walls went up, European or no.

Funny how having a full-time job with a big company once meant a special cubicle or office with your name on a personal-ized nameplate, a desk with drawers, a Rolodex (something April knew about because she loved spinning her mother's as a child), a landline telephone with extensions, a communal supply room with mail slots and extra pens and spare batteries and a Xerox machine. April was just old enough to remember all of these things—well, maybe not quite old enough, but she'd seen a lot of nineties movies—and the whole workplace concept just seemed so appealingly permanent, like a sort of mini-fortress against the world. Working at home, April had a laptop that she carried from room to room—sometimes working on the couch, sometimes propped up in bed, sometimes at the kitchen table. That was all she needed. It didn't feel like enough; there were days when she wished for an anchor, something to hold her down.

As April composed an email to a Picket Fence customer who was trying to sell a house in which every room was painted black (time for one of those "Buyers like a light, neutral look" messages), her phone lit up with a text from Janie.

Ok I'm sorry I haven't gotten back to your last million txts, miss you!!! Can you cm for dinner Sat? Ryan is bbqing and we're inviting his friend Stephen, who is single and is a camera operator for movies. Sorry I should have been more subtle about that but who has time to be subtle Zoe's teeth are STILL coming in and none of us are sleeping. Please come!! Xoxo

April thought for a minute and then replied.

Sorry, can't come Saturday. Hope Zoe's teeth improve and you can get some sleep! See you next week maybe? Love you. Xo

It wasn't that April was actually busy on Saturday. It was just that meeting Stephen the Camera Operator, just like Joshua the Barista or Tom the Emergency Room Nurse or P.J. Whoever He Was, seemed too exhausting to contemplate. It was easier to stay home and stream something . . . and hold on to the fantasy of the bookstore guy with the flannel shirts and the smile, just for a little bit longer. His job seemed a lovely haven of stories, on and off the page.

5

Westley

When Westley was a little boy, he'd loved to go places by himself. At an early age, he'd begged his mother to let him go to the park or the library alone; she'd reluctantly allowed it, after insisting on tailing him a few times to make sure that he made good choices. He'd loved quietly sitting on a park bench or a library chair and watching people, making up stories to himself about their lives. He was perfectly content with his own life—as a child, his home was uneventfully safe and pleasant, and he walked through his days in the bubble that good-looking and well-loved children occupy—but he was fascinated by other people. How did that young nanny in the park, wearily tending to toddler twins, end up in her job, and did she like it? Did the elderly librarian, the one Westley's mother said had been at her job as long as anyone could remember, have a room full of books waiting at home, or was it enough to spend her day among them? Did the man selling popcorn from a park kiosk still like popcorn?

The habit of telling stories to himself had stayed with him to this day; during quiet moments at work, he was always gazing at customers and wondering what was happening in their lives that brought them to the store at this moment. But on this Tuesday, there were no quiet moments. The store was abuzz, if "abuzz" meant that Andrew was dusting the dandruff off his vintage blazer and Julia was scurrying about straightening books on already perfectly straightened shelves and shooting dark glances at two small children whose mother was allowing them to share a croissant in Picture Books. A location scout was coming in, the staff had been told, to do whatever a scout does. Julia's excitement was such that Westley wondered if maybe there was more to this than she was saying. Julia did appear to be imagining the process as a glamour-filled one; she was clearly savoring the phrase "location scout" and impressively managing to work it into nearly every sentence she uttered. Westley, drawing on his sparse knowledge of old movies, was picturing a handsome, Cary Grant–ish person in a trench coat, wearing sunglasses and fast-talking as he dramatically pointed out things to a waiting entourage who gobbled up his every word.

As so often happens, the actuality of the location scout was rather less compelling than the idea. Just after ten, a middle-aged man in a leather jacket that seemed underwhelmed by its wearer came in, looking around with an expression both expectant and weary. Westley watched from his desk, curious as to how this element of the movie business worked. Seattle was, of course, a long way from Los Angeles, but if Donna Wolfe wanted to make a movie here, surely that meant something?

Raven greeted him from the front desk. "Can I help you find something?" she asked him, a broad smile widening her face. Since she so rarely smiled at all, the effect was a little startling, Westley thought, like a rusty gate opening with some reluctance.

"I'm supposed to meet . . . Julia Nakamura," the man said, consulting his phone for the name. His skeptical tone implied that he wasn't entirely certain that the meeting was a good idea, but that he was nonetheless determined to see it through.

Julia, appearing out of nowhere as if conjured up by a Hollywood special effect (she had an uncanny way of sneaking up on people that had often startled Westley), introduced herself enthusiastically and they shook hands. The location scout's name, disappointingly, turned out to be Al. The glamour was leaching from the visit with each moment.

"Can these shelves be moved?" Al asked Julia as they walked through the store, not waiting for her to answer.

"Does that window have a shade?"

"Is there a quieter way to make coffee?"

"Does the store have air-conditioning?"

"Why not?"

"Is there any flexibility to the way the café is laid out? Could you, say, move the counter over here?"

"Do you have any books in brighter colors?"

"Are there other employees we could use as background? Maybe, I don't know, younger ones?"

Upon passing by the used-books desk, Al paused and gazed at Westley, who was pretending to look up something on the computer in order to avoid eye contact. Unfortunately, he hadn't realized that Al could see his computer screen, which was Westley's personal email and was currently showing a display of summer khakis from the Gap. (Westley had, earlier, been trying to unsubscribe, slowly coming to realize it is impossible to extricate oneself from an email relationship with the Gap.) Feeling Al's stare, Westley looked up, smiling sheepishly. "Hi. Uh . . . can I help you?"

Al stared for rather longer than Westley thought was called for. The silence felt awkward. Finally, Al spoke: "Would you . . . excuse me, what's your name?"

"Westley. Westley Richardson." There was a pause. There was always a pause when people, specifically people of an age to have gone to movies as an impressionable youth in 1987, heard Westley's name.

"Westley like in *The Princess Bride*?"

"Yes."

"He was the one always saying, 'As you wish,' right?"

"Right." Westley, through sheer force of will, did not roll his eyes.

"Excellent," Al muttered, as if to himself. "I love it. Westley, have you ever been in a movie?"

This was an unexpected question. "No?"

"Would you like to be in one?"

"Well, I'm not an actor . . ." Westley said, confused.

Al smiled patiently. "No, no. I mean as background, doing your job here. Maybe a line or two. You just have . . . the look."

"The look?" asked Westley, smoothing his soft flannel shirt self-consciously and hoping his beard didn't have toast crumbs in it.

"Precisely. We'll get you a contract. There'll be a small payment, permission to use your likeness, et cetera, you'll read all the details. Shooting starts in two weeks. You don't need to learn anything, just do your job." He held out a buff-nailed hand for Westley to shake. "Thank you."

Julia, watching all of this with a rapt expression, let out a silent shriek while Al's head was turned; this was, Westley noticed, the most excited he'd seen Julia since the day years ago that one of her tweets was liked by Roxane Gay. All right, so he'd said yes—well, he hadn't really, but that didn't seem to matter—and he was going to be in a movie. Strange; he'd been looking for something to happen and now it had.

6

Laura

It had been almost a week now, but Laura couldn't stop thinking about that note, written in small, plain handwriting on pale-blue paper. She'd tucked it away in her nightstand drawer where Olivia wouldn't find it—her daughter would surely insist on reading it aloud, sounding out the hard words and asking too many questions—but nonetheless it preoccupied her. Had someone really been watching her, on the rare occasions when she had time to browse in Read the Room? She didn't think she looked at books as if they were precious objects; really, she was usually in a hurry when she went to the bookstore to choose something for bedtime reading with Olivia, or to pick up whatever bestseller Rebecca was talking about. She had always loved to read, and often dreamed of a less-busy life in which she could surround herself with books. Could it really be possible that somebody out there was paying close attention, noticing something about her that most people didn't see? It didn't seem likely—but there was the letter, sitting in the drawer.

All day at work, making her way through the store's selection of formal gowns for a client who was attending a wine gala and wanted something the color of merlot, Laura pondered the possibilities. The most likely scenario, of course, was that the letter was intended for somebody else and all of this was a mistake.

But, in replaying the moment to herself, Laura remembered that the bookseller with the blue-streak hair had gone across the store to pick up the book and had been gone for a little while. It was easy to see the front desk from the used-books area; maybe somebody there saw her and wrote the note quickly, slipping it into the book that she'd asked for? Maybe he'd seen her in the store before and had the note ready? Or maybe the blue-streak woman had written the note? No, *that* seemed quite unlikely; her entire manner with Laura had conveyed brisk, sincere disinterest. Of course, maybe the note had been in the book for ages. But no, the bookseller had said it was a used book that had only just arrived, and surely the store checked the pages of new inventory before selling it?

And maybe, deep down, she wanted to imagine that the note was for her, despite her better judgment. Laura hadn't had a romantic relationship, or even a date, since Sam's death five and a half years ago. She told herself this was because she was too busy between taking care of Olivia and trying to do her best at her job, but she knew that wasn't entirely right. Dating someone else would mean stepping through a door, leaving her memories of Sam on the other side of it. There was a part of her that was still holding on to him, not quite able to accept that he was gone—she still sometimes found herself unconsciously picking up the crackers he liked at the supermarket, or remembering a joke to tell him when he got home. (In dreams, occasionally, Sam came back to her, looking like he did before his illness, laughing fondly at her shock at seeing him again. She'd wake up alone, trying desperately to hang on to the vision as it slipped away.) Laura hadn't thought about romance in many years.

It might be time, though, to step through that door; Rebecca had been gently urging her to think about it for the past year or so. Maybe this letter—the kind of whimsical act that Sam would have appreciated; she could imagine him enjoying a movie with this plotline—was a sign? Or maybe it was a potential disaster.

Love didn't always bring a happy ending, as Laura knew too well. Clearly, she needed another opinion.

"So, does Livvy still like the tutu?" asked Rebecca, on the drive to the book club meeting that evening. She took her fairy-godmother role with Olivia quite seriously and was always dropping by with something adorable that she'd found online or seen in a store window.

"Oh my God," said Laura. She had in fact had a standoff with her daughter over that very tutu the night before, in which Olivia had insisted that an enormous tulle pouf would make an excellent nightgown. "She adores it. I think she's going to wear it every day for the rest of her life. Thank you again!" She paused, watching Rebecca driving, and jumped in with a question: "Um . . . do you ever feel like your life has become a movie?"

"All the time," said Rebecca cheerfully, not moving her eyes from the road. "Not a good movie, though. Like, one where I'm played by Adam Sandler or somebody and everything keeps going wrong and in it my ex-husband turns up and says I owe him alimony. Which he just did, by the way. I guess his money's running out."

"He didn't!" Laura gasped. Rebecca had been married years ago to an impossibly handsome man who'd abruptly fallen out of love with her when he came into his trust fund and decided, foolishly, that he could do better. Despite Laura's urgings to try dating again, Rebecca was on an extended break from relationships, which gave her more time to lovingly micromanage Laura.

"He did! I guess he heard about my last promotion. I'm going to have one of the real sharks at my firm get back to him. He'll freak. It'll be fun. Anyway, why do you ask?"

"What's that movie where Meg Ryan has a bookstore and a really bad haircut?"

"That's *You've Got Mail*."

"Right. I think I'm in the sequel. Minus the haircut."

Rebecca snorted. "There is no sequel to *You've Got Mail*. And you know I never liked that movie. The Meg Ryan character was really mean to her boyfriend."

"Tom Hanks?"

"No, the other one. I forget his name. But what did he ever do to her? Just because he doesn't send her dopey emails about bouquets of pencils? Who wants a bouquet of pencils? And she's mean to her boyfriend in *Sleepless in Seattle*, too! She dumps him for a guy she doesn't even know! Why does everyone think Meg Ryan's characters are so loveable?"

Laura loved Rebecca, whom she'd met in a college English class, for many reasons, not the least of which was her ability to instantly engage with any conversation topic and to remember the details of every movie she had ever seen. "There *is* a sequel to *You've Got Mail*," she said, taking a breath, "and I'm in it. This week I bought a book at that bookstore Read the Room, and someone at the store had left a note in the book. And it's sweet; it says hi, I like the way you look at books, I'd like to know more about you. How weird is that?"

"Wait, so it's for you? Like, from someone who works there? How do you know?"

"I don't. But when I asked for the book, I had to wait awhile, and maybe someone who handles used books put the note in? I know I've seen a guy at that desk, but I've never really looked at him."

"OK, so maybe it's that guy," said Rebecca, clearly already formulating a plan of attack. "Who is he? Are you going to answer it? What are you going to say?"

Laura sighed. "I don't know. What would I say? That I have a kid and a dead husband and nothing but Go-Gurt in my fridge? And that I'm super boring and not Meg Ryan?"

"Do not tell him any of these things. You are not super boring. And he knows you're not Meg Ryan. Tell him that you love vintage coats and peacock blue and *Moonstruck* and . . . what's that book you were going on about the other day?"

"*All the Light We Cannot See*. Why did it take me so long to find that book? It's so good!"

"Don't change the subject! But yes, tell him that. And sure, tell him that you have an amazing kid. That's part of who you are." Rebecca paused. "You're seriously thinking about replying, aren't you?"

"Maybe I am? I don't know," Laura said. "It's just weird. I don't even know who this person is. It's probably just a mistake."

"You need to check this out," said Rebecca. "I mean, at least go back to the store and scope out the employees. It could be anyone, right?"

Laura laughed, though not happily. "Right. Some sad pathetic guy, who smells of mildew and has bookstore dust all over his clothes."

"Or he might be nice! And cute! You always assume the worst."

"Well, I have reason for that," Laura said quietly. There was a silence as Rebecca pulled the car into a suburban driveway. "But I mean, obviously this note isn't for me, right? I shouldn't even be thinking of replying to it. It's for somebody else and I got it by mistake. And that's the end of it."

"Fine," said Rebecca, turning off the ignition in a dramatic fashion. "If you say so. I'm not going to try to change your mind." (Laura did not believe this for a second.) "I'm just going to say one thing, OK? I knew Sam, and I loved Sam, and I *know* that he would not want you to be lonely. He would want you to meet someone nice and be happy. He would definitely think that five and a half years was too long to keep your heart closed off like this."

"That's more than one thing," said Laura, who knew that Rebecca was right.

Rebecca, sensing that she'd made her point, quickly moved on. "OK. That's all I'm going to say. So, the one hosting the book club is Kylie; she's a paralegal, and the others are. . . ."

"Never mind, I'll pick up their names as I meet them," Laura said. "All your work colleagues are a blur to me. I'm just here to maybe get a new client or two." This was the argument Rebecca had used to ultimately convince Laura to hire Ashley for the evening and come to the book club—that a few of her fashionable colleagues might have use for a personal shopper. "I'll be charming, I promise. But I'm done talking about the note."

Rebecca, however, was not done talking about the note. The book club was eight women from Rebecca's law office, all of whom squealed at Rebecca's arrival despite presumably having just seen her at work that day. They moved in with hugs, offers of various pink-hued cocktails and cracker/cheese trays, and wild enthusiasm over meeting Laura, who quickly gave up on remembering names and noted what they were wearing instead.

Kylie, dressed in what looked like silk paisley pajamas (was this what she normally wore at home? Laura wondered, impressed), ushered the group into the living room. "Sit, everyone!" she said, waving her hands in the general direction of the furniture, which was 1950s-mod. "I'm so excited to have you all here for our book club! I guess we should start by going around and seeing if everyone liked the book?"

"Wait," said Rebecca, holding up a hand and rapidly swallowing a too-big chunk of cheese. "I have one other order of business first, if you ladies don't mind. So, my friend Laura here is in need of some advice."

Laura felt her face turning red, frustrated at having not actively forbidden Rebecca from sharing this story. "No, really, that's not necessary," she said halfheartedly, knowing that once Rebecca had an idea, there was nothing to be done but follow it through.

Rebecca ignored her and went on. "So, the other day when Laura went to the bookstore to pick up this book that we're reading, she had to wait awhile at the front desk before they brought the book to her. And then later, when she opened the book at home, she found a note in it."

"What kind of note?" asked a woman in Lululemon joggers.

"A note that expressed interest in getting to know more about her," said Rebecca dramatically. "Not in a creepy way, but an endearing, kind of charming way. Obviously, it's written by someone who works at the store who left it in the book. Now, Laura here thinks the note is a mistake and isn't for her. Because she is an amazing human being who has had some really hard things happen to her, and now she's afraid to believe that something nice might be right in front of her. But can I get a show of hands? If you got a really sweet anonymous note in a book, asking you to write back, would you answer?"

Every hand in the room, except Laura's, shot up. "Totally," said a woman in a J. Crew sundress Laura had coveted at the mall last month. "What's the harm?"

"I would," said a woman in vintage Levi's and slightly pilly cashmere. "Better than meeting someone in a bar, right?" A chorus of groans and agreement greeted her.

"I would too," said a woman in a knockoff Chanel business suit who clearly hadn't had time to go home from work to change. "What's the worst that can happen? You'll get a great story out of it."

"I would too," said Lululemon. "Why are you hesitating, Laura? This seems really fun!"

Laura felt a bit overwhelmed by all these strangers egging her on. "Well . . . it just seems too weird? But I guess I could maybe go to the store and look around a bit? See if I can figure out who left it?"

"Yes! Do it!" said J. Crew enthusiastically, to general approval around the room. She started a chant, "Go Laura, go Laura, go Laura, go Laura . . ."

Laura looked over at Rebecca, who was enthusiastically joining in the chant. "I am *never* coming to book club with you again," she said quietly.

THERE WAS NOTHING ELSE TO BE DONE: LAURA WAS GOING TO have to investigate. Maybe all those enthusiastic women from the book club (most of whom, as it turned out, hadn't actually read the book and seemed more interested in gossiping about colleagues Laura didn't know) were right—it couldn't hurt to poke around at the bookstore just a bit. It was certainly the most interesting thing to happen to her in a long time. Generally, Laura got her romantic thrills from hearing Ashley talk about her boyfriend Zach, who was starring in a self-produced web series about a man who woke up one day to find that he was a cat. (Zach had never heard of Kafka. Laura had once tried to tell him about *Metamorphosis*, but Zach had just looked at her in his soft-focus way and muttered something about magic and inspiration and fan fiction, and Laura, feeling very old, gave up.) Ashley and Zach lived together, and Ashley was convinced that Zach was going to be rich and famous someday, as soon as Hollywood discovered *I, Cat*, a level of devotion that Laura found rather sweet.

On her lunch hour the next day, grateful that her hair was having a relatively low-frizz moment, Laura drove from downtown to Read the Room; traffic was easy midday and the drive was short. Entering, she looked around the store. It was a welcoming place on a spring afternoon, with laden shelves and lazy ceiling fans making slow circles. It really was charming, Laura thought, noticing the details of the store as if for the first time; perhaps she had been taking for granted the joy of having a bookstore nearby. Growing up, she'd fantasized as a child about being trapped in one overnight, eating leftover scones from the store café and happily scanning the shelves by moonlight. Now she appreciated the book-cover posters on the walls, the handwritten recommendations in tidy handwriting tacked below certain books on the shelves, the way nobody there seemed to be in a hurry; bookstores, it seemed, create their own time zone.

A couple of staffers huddled at the front desk, opening cardboard shipping boxes full of shiny-covered hardback books. One looked up, but Laura nodded and quickly looked away, walking purposefully toward General Fiction as if she had a title in mind.

And then—*aha*. There he was? Maybe? At the desk where the used books were sorted sat a man: a handsome man, in his thirties, wearing a plaid flannel shirt unbuttoned over a blue T-shirt and jeans. Laura, accustomed to reading people based on their attire, quickly noted that it was a casual look and a bit rumply, but the blue was a flattering shade. Somebody, maybe, had been giving this man good advice, or maybe he just had good instincts. He had a light-brown, close-trimmed beard and mildly unruly curly hair not unlike Laura's own, and he frowned slightly, adorably, when looking at the computer on his desk, like it was worrying him in some way. If someone made a photo calendar of "Handsome Men of Independent Bookselling," he'd be one of the primo months.

But he most definitely did *not* look like someone who would send an anonymous note to a fortyish single mom, Laura sternly assured herself. A man who looked like this didn't have to write notes. A man who looked like this probably had notes sent to *him*. But . . . who else would have had the opportunity to slip the letter into the book? There was only one chair at the desk, and clearly it was his; obviously it was his job to sort and check the books. Could it be possible that he'd been observing her from his desk on her visits to the store, and written the quick note once he saw how to get it to her? This seemed crazy, but sometimes couples met in weird ways. (Ashley and Zach, for example, loved talking about how they met through a Craigslist "Missed Connections" ad. Ashley was not, in fact, the woman Zach had placed the ad to find—she was actually nowhere near the Starbucks on Seventh Avenue where Zach had been charmed by a woman who helped him wipe up a spilled latte—but had seized the moment and replied to the ad anyway "because I thought he sounded so awesome," as she explained to Laura. Luckily for Ashley, the actual woman never responded, and Zach seemed happy to shift his sights elsewhere.) Was it possible that life could actually work this way, with cute booksellers leaving anonymous notes expressing possible romantic interest in random single moms? It was a dizzying thought, and Laura abruptly shook her head, as if the sudden action might bring reality back.

"Can I help you find something?" The man looked up and spoke to her, no doubt in response to Laura's staring. He had a soft voice and blue eyes, and he looked as if he might smell good in a slightly woodsy way, but Laura wasn't close enough to verify. He really was just ridiculously good-looking, like he might play a rogue lawyer or a male secretary in a Netflix series.

"Um, no, just browsing, thank you," Laura said automatically. Was there a spark? Did she imagine it or was there the teeniest emphasis on the "you" in his question? She blinked, feeling a little foolish.

"OK," said the man. He smiled—was it acknowledgment of a secret between them? Or just a polite staff-customer interaction? Maybe there was something knowing in that smile? Was that how this worked? "Let one of us know if you need any help." He turned back to the piles of books on his desk.

Flustered, Laura made a quick turn away and ended up in Mystery/Crime Fiction, where she grabbed a random paperback (which turned out, coincidentally, to be a thriller about a stalker) and bought it without really looking at it, feeling that she somehow needed to justify her presence at the store. Back in the car, she exhaled, feeling strangely off-balance and, maybe, just a little bit thrilled. She fished her phone out of her purse and pressed a name.

"Hey," said Rebecca, sounding a bit breathless. "I'm doing my fast walk. What's up? Did you go to the bookstore?"

"Yes. I'm just in the parking lot now," Laura said. "There *is* a guy at the used-books desk. He's cute. He's *really* cute. I'll go out on a limb and say he seemed straight."

"Did you talk to him?"

"Not really," Laura said, taking a deep breath. "I mean, I did a little bit, but he's clearly into the letter-writing thing. I've decided: I'm going to write back. Maybe it's a mistake, maybe I'm opening myself up to something really stupid, but I want to believe that somebody has reached out to me. He seems nice. And I want to reach back."

"I've been thinking about this ever since you told me," said Rebecca. "I want to believe it too. But I'm a little worried that I was pushing you the other night. Are you sure you're ready for this, Laur? This is a big step for you."

"I think it might be time," Laura said. "I think . . . I want to try. I'm going to run in before work tomorrow and leave a note."

"OK," said Rebecca. "OK. I'm with you. I got you."

"I know," said Laura quietly, to the friend who had been there the whole time five years ago, bringing soup and running hot baths and dealing with details and just listening. "I know."

Rebecca quickly got practical, as was her way. "How are you going to get the note to him?"

"His letter said to leave it in the middle copy of *The Hunger Games*, in the Young Adult section of the store. I'm telling you, this is a movie."

Rebecca laughed. "Right? Why do you suppose he chose that book? It's about Jennifer Lawrence and a bunch of teenagers fighting to the death or something! Does he not know that they have a romance section in that store?"

"I haven't read it," Laura said. "Maybe he's got a weird sense of humor? Anyway, I have to get back to work. Call you later. Love you."

"May the odds be ever in your favor," intoned Rebecca.

Laura, who had not seen the movie, ended the call, puzzled.

TO: donna@donnawolfefilms.com
FROM: al.watson12@freemail.com
SUBJECT: Bookstore

Hey DW; I think Read the Room will work fine. Decent light, enough room for setups, some character in the building. The owner is very excited about the store being in a movie so will be happy to work with us for whatever we need; she doesn't mind that we're fast-tracking because the original location fell through. And there's a bookseller who looks like a Seattle version of Andrew Garfield, and he's willing to be on camera. So we're good to begin in May.

TO: al.watson12@freemail.com
FROM: donna@donnawolfefilms.com
RE: Bookstore

But how does it *smell*?

TO: donna@donnawolfefilms.com
FROM: al.watson12@freemail.com
RE: Bookstore

Like we can afford it.

7

April

This was definitely going to be the last time that April checked the Young Adult shelf at Read the Room. Absolutely. It had now been more than a week, and she was an adult woman with a career to plan and a life to get on with, and if the handsome flannel-shirt guy at the book donation desk wasn't on board, that was fine. She would Move On. She had options. She was going to read Proust and volunteer at the neighborhood food bank and maybe get a kitten and an unexpected piercing and try kombucha (once she figured out what it was). Life had so many possibilities! Or so she repeated to herself on her way to Read the Room for one last, final, definitely-not-going-to-think-about-this-ever-again check. And there, inserted neatly into the middle copy of *The Hunger Games* (she'd chosen the title mainly for the readiness of multiple copies and for the relative quiet of the Young Adult corner), was a note.

April carefully looked around, but there was no one there to see her collect it, or to hear the tiny, delighted giggle with which she slipped the folded paper into her pocket. The handsome used-books guy was gathered in a group near the front desk with other employees while an excitable-looking gray-haired woman seemed to be instructing them about something. It didn't seem right to read it then and there, so she left the store quickly and walked home, the note seeming to rustle promisingly with every step. There was something thrilling about collecting something secret, just for you, in a place bustling with other people who had no idea what was going on. Maybe she just imagined it, but the birds seemed to be chirping more happily today, creating a hopeful soundtrack. It was a bright, beautiful May afternoon, and the flowers in the street's well-tended gardens seemed to smile at April as she passed, with the windows in the neighboring apartment buildings seeming to hold delightful mysteries behind their curtains. Finally home—it was only two blocks, but the walk seemed to take forever, with the note in her pocket seeming to be singing alluringly to her—she had barely closed the door behind her before grabbing the paper and opening it.

Hi A,
I was so happy to get your note. I've never gotten an anonymous handwritten note before but I love the idea—so much nicer than social media. It sounds like we both love to read. I don't have as much time to read as I would like, but my favorite book is probably The Great Gatsby, *or maybe* The Remains of the Day, *both of which I've reread a lot, and my favorite time to read is late at night, in bed, with just one lamp on and quiet so deep it seems to wrap around you like a blanket. Not that I get very much time like that; life is busy. But what about you? I'll be checking the middle copy of* The Hunger Games *for a reply, and I really look forward to hearing back from you.*
L

Just seven sentences, written in small, tidy printing on a plain piece of soft-yellow notepaper, but April read them over and over, charmed and dazzled and wondering how to reply. This was not the kind of relationship she was used to, when you met somebody through a friend, or at a bar when out with a group from work, and things went on well until they didn't. This felt not-unpleasantly tingly, like the kind of really good mystery novel where you had no idea what was coming next and you have no choice but to keep turning pages.

April had had only one previous long-term relationship: her college boyfriend, Josh. It had ended badly after four years, when they had quarreled over who should pay more rent on their apartment. They hadn't really moved in together on purpose, but things just seemed to happen; they'd been two of eight residents in a big rental house near the university, but their various housemates graduated and moved on, and somehow April and Josh ended up getting an apartment together without giving it too much thought. Sometimes life was good: April, who at the time was working at the public library, enjoyed having someone to come home to and buying groceries for two. And she thought she loved Josh, who was a good conversationalist, recognized a lot of literary references, and had a way of holding her hand in the movies that charmed her, even if it did make it harder to eat popcorn.

But they couldn't live on charm, and eventually an increasingly cranky Josh, who was trying to get funding for a startup that would help startups get funding (the business plan never made any sense to April), became incensed when April insisted on splitting expenses fifty-fifty. It wasn't fair, he claimed, to equate April's salary with his "soft money," an expression he seemed to use to describe money he didn't want to spend, and he left one day in a huff, leaving behind only a stray Foo Fighters concert T-shirt in the wash. April now used the T-shirt for dusting, feeling simultaneously vengeful and indifferent as she did so; years had gone by and she didn't really miss him specifically, just the company.

But now here was L, with his blue eyes and his cute way of piling up books on the counter so that their corners aligned nicely. This talking about reading cozily in bed, she thought, seemed promisingly flirty. Leo, maybe? Lawrence? Logan? Larry? No, definitely not a Larry. Lenny? Liam? So much possibility.

Here, at last, was a mystery she might solve, one in which she actually had a stake.

Automatically—old habits die hard—she reached for her phone, to tell Janie about this development, but paused midtext. Janie was busy. It was a lot to expect someone with two tiny kids to be constantly available. Maybe try her again later, April mused; maybe in the evening after the kids' bedtime. Maybe tomorrow. For now, she had the note, and that was company enough.

April's thoughts wandered as she handled some routine emails for work.

TO: bluebanana@freemail.com
FROM: aprild@picketfencehomes.com
SUBJECT: Listing #503367B

Hi! Thank you so much for listing your house with Picket Fence. We offer a free advisory service to help sellers maximize the potential of their listings. Here are a few thoughts on your online presentation and photos.

1) Maybe wash the dishes and put them away, and then take another picture of the kitchen?

2) Your collection of foot photographs is definitely interesting, but we always advise clients that art is subjective. A blank, neutral wall will appeal to more buyers than an art collection that may not be to everyone's taste. (Also, you may want to fill in those holes in the wall and repaint.)

3) There's a dark spot on the carpet in the living room. If you can't get that spot to come out, maybe a throw rug would help?

She felt oddly fond of these unknown sellers, bravely sharing their home with the world, taking a leap of faith that maybe someone might love it, foot photographs and all.

Variety.com | Home > Film > News | May 13, 2024 8:30 am PT

Production to Begin on Donna Wolfe's Surrealistic Bookstore Dramedy; Local Actor Cast in Lead

BY MARCEL GEORGE

Writer/director Donna Wolfe, a veteran of the indie scene whose latest, *Twelve for Dinner*, got a decent chunk of art-house box office in 2021, is poised to begin a location shoot for her new film, *Shelf Consciousness*, a Charlie Kaufman-esque dark comedy/drama set in a bookstore. The plot involves a young man who is troubled when his girlfriend doesn't return home after a trip to a bookstore and finds upon looking for her that she's been pulled through a portal into the world of a book on the shelf.

Wolfe, who has spoken recently in interviews about being on a "search for authenticity" in her films, plans to shoot both in Los Angeles and Seattle, the latter primarily to get location shots at a bookstore. Though normally based in Los Angeles, she says she has grown tired of "the usual locations" and wants to branch out to another city, moving to Seattle before production begins in order to "immerse myself in the culture."

Wolfe has chosen Kelly Drake, a Seattle-based theater actor, to play the lead role. He is making his film debut. Discovered during local auditions, Drake has "a face made for classic movies," Wolfe said.

Drake flew to Los Angeles to shoot scenes earlier this spring. The Seattle shoot will begin in late May.

8

Westley

Now that Read the Room was getting ready for its close-up—
filming would start in less than a week—Julia was determined that it would be shipshape. Normally, booksellers
could look forward to a bit of downtime during their shifts, to be
spent perusing the new books and reading up on what was expected to be a big seller that season. But now all were expected
to spend every minute of spare time making the store look
movie-star perfect. Julia's stress level was high—Westley wondered if it was possible that her hair was even spikier than usual,
due to anxiety?—and the staff had no choice but to comply. Mysterious cleaning products kept appearing at the front desk or at
Westley's workspace, with an unspoken but clear message attached.

Though Al had told Julia not to change anything in the store,
she wanted to make sure that bright movie lights didn't expose
anything too weary-looking, and thus gave clear orders in daily
staff huddles: Long-unneeded overstock on high shelves was
carefully dusted, windowsills were elaborately wiped down, bul-
letin boards were cleaned of ancient yellowing notes flapping on
thumbtacks, and the fiction shelves—particularly Science Fiction/
Fantasy and Romance, where the most well worn of the used
books tended to congregate—were scrutinized meticulously and

the shabbiest paperbacks removed. Alejandra had covertly hung twinkle lights, which Julia just as covertly took down.

Donna Wolfe herself, not deigning to remove her sunglasses, had stopped by the store, allowing Julia to give her a tour (it was a quirk of Donna's personality, Westley observed from his desk, that everything she did had the feeling of her extending a personal favor) and sharing a few details about the movie, which Julia breathlessly passed on to the staff. It was, she said, a dark and sophisticated surrealist comedy starring Kelly Drake, whose performance as Frank-N-Furter in a recent production of *The Rocky Horror Picture Show* had been described as "wickedly erotic" by the local alt-weekly. It would only be a handful of shooting days at the store, as most of the film had already been shot in Los Angeles.

Frowning at a broom left out by the front counter, which Andrew hastily whisked away, Julia had once again gathered the staff. "They'll be shooting here at night for perhaps a week or two, and in the afternoons on Mondays," she said. (Monday was the store's slowest day.) "Next Wednesday will be the first day. We'll be closing a little early on shooting days. I will post a sign on the door. The crew will be bringing in lights and other equipment, but they have assured me that they will be careful not to damage anything. And they won't be moving the books. I have been clear to them about that. Nothing on the shelves is to be touched."

"Do we get to be on camera?" Raven asked.

"Well, no," said Julia. "They're bringing in actors to play booksellers. Except for Westley. Al, the location scout, has asked him to be in the movie as a background character."

"Why Westley?" said Raven. There was a long, awkward pause. Westley tried not to look at anyone.

Andrew rolled his eyes at her. "Um, maybe because Westley looks like someone who should be in a movie? Unlike the rest of us?"

Raven, who Westley suspected of secretly harboring a fantasy of being discovered, looked offended. She took out her phone and stared, a little too intensely, at a possibly imaginary incoming text.

Julia went on. "We'll close at six on Wednesday. I'll be sure that we announce this on the store website and you can certainly let any regular customers know about the change in hours. Any other questions?"

Andrew raised an eyebrow. "Um, why are we doing this again? Isn't it going to be a lot of work?"

"Never mind," Julia said. "I just . . . think it will be good for the store." Her tone implied very faint hope, rather than the excitement she'd expressed when first announcing the plan, which seemed to have rapidly translated into stress.

Westley went back to the used-books desk, trying not to feel embarrassed about having been singled out by the filmmakers. The movie scout had chosen him; that wasn't his fault, and his colleagues shouldn't hold that against him. He'd never done any acting really, though he had taken a small role in his high school's production of *Our Town*, and the drama teacher had encouraged him to try for something bigger next time. (She'd told Westley to go watch Paul Newman in *Our Town*, saying that Newman was an example of an actor who overcame extreme good looks. Westley, embarrassed, dropped drama as an extracurricular activity, opting instead to hang out at the outer circles of the chess club, pretending to be interested.)

It was long ago, but Westley remembered enjoying being on stage, stepping out of his own life and pretending to be in someone else's, feeling as if a special light was shining on him. He might have tried more acting, maybe with a different teacher, but college came quickly and ended quickly, after Westley flunked his first three classes. Though he loved to read—particularly novels in which he could disappear into a time and place very different from his own life—writing papers didn't come naturally to him, and after numerous nights spent staring anxiously at blank computer screens and wondering how other people always seemed to know what to say, he just gave up, and his annoyed father didn't want to pay tuition anymore. Westley didn't want to stay in college badly enough to argue about it, or to take out loans; he'd thought about majoring in English but really just wanted to read, which he could do without being in school. A few restaurant jobs followed, one of which was the job he didn't like to think about, and then Read the Room. All of them seemed like things he'd found by accident, never by plan.

Just like this. But this movie thing wasn't really acting, Westley told himself—it was just being himself, in the background. Which he thought he could probably manage. He'd been doing it his entire life.

Alejandra

The best thing I ever found in a book was a tiny work of art: a book-mark, cut from thick art paper, painted in soft watercolor blues and greens that seemed to ripple under my gaze, with a small handmade yellow tassel attached. It was just the prettiest little thing—well, I shouldn't say "was," I still have it and I use it all the time—and I love to imagine somebody with a paintbrush, lov-ingly creating it, maybe to go along with the gift of a book. The world is full of free objects that work just fine for bookmarks— we give away logo bookmarks at the store with every book pur-chase, and they're perfectly nice—but I like to think that there are people out there making special ones, that somebody cared enough to craft something lovely for the sole purpose of marking a page.

Working in a bookstore when you're trying to write fiction is something I feel lucky to be doing. Writing is hard; not waitressing-on-a-double-shift hard, but nonetheless really chal-lenging. It's something I make myself do when I'd rather be read-ing, and it helps to look around at work and see all of those books around me, each of them representing an author who Got To It. (And, not incidentally, found an agent and a publisher, two things still on my to-do list.) But it does inspire me, even on days when Julia is driving me crazy with her reminders to dust the shelves. I like Julia, to be clear. But she is, well, a lot.

My latest book is science fiction and definitely on the quirky side. I have no idea if anyone will be interested in it once it's finished, but it's mine; something on this earth that wasn't there before, something I made, like that bookmark. It's not my first book; I've played with other genres, and most recently finished something experimental that I think might work but I'm waiting to get some feedback on it. People are always surprised that I've written so much, but I've always wanted to be a writer, and even when it's challenging, it's what I love to do. I like to play with words the way Raven plays with yarn, but hopefully to better results. (OK, that was a little mean of me. Raven's actually decent when you get to know her—I think she likes people to think of her as intimidating. Her yarn jewelry is kind of weird, though.)

As a kid I was always making up stories, which I would laboriously write down and then read to my grandmother, who was learning English and loved to hear my stories about birds who could talk and streets that suddenly shifted, so you couldn't walk a straight line if you tried. I loved to walk around my block, or farther after I got a little older and was allowed more freedom, looking for something to fascinate me or for a little root of an idea. I wondered if the flowers talked to each other; if the roses in Mrs. Steele's garden were scornful of the daisies in the grass next door. I wondered how long the birds on the power lines had been sitting there, and if they were waiting for something in particular to happen. And I wondered if there were neighborhoods on other planets that looked like mine but operated in different ways. I guess that's what initially led me to science fiction. I loved thinking about a world that had different rules. What if we could see people's hair growing? Or look right through their skin to see their hearts? That's the gist of my current novel. It's fun making this stuff up.

I work five days a week at Read the Room, living with roommates so I can get by on the pay, which is decent as bookstore pay goes (Julia's a very fair boss; I've talked to people at other local indie bookstores and we're definitely paid on the higher end) but still doesn't go very far in this expensive city. I enjoy helping customers find books, whether they want something specific or come in looking for suggestions, and I have lots of regulars who'll come back and tell me how they liked what I recommended, which is pretty much why I wanted to work at a bookstore in the first place. But mostly I like it because it's a quiet job, giving me space to just think. I've learned to do this while staring at the shelves in Science Fiction/Fantasy, so Julia thinks I'm caught up in rapt alphabetization.

And of course, sometimes I sneak a few looks at Westley. This has to be done very carefully. I think he and Raven have some sort of weird romantic history, because sometimes I see her looking at him kind of sadly, and she gets very possessive if she thinks a customer is flirting with him. And Andrew quietly watches everything; nothing gets by him, and I don't really want him knowing my personal life. Not that I have one, really; I just work in the store and work on my book and sometimes go for a beer with my roommates when they're not driving for Uber or delivering for Amazon or whatever their current gig is. My life feels OK, but it seems like things haven't really gotten started yet; like I'm waiting for something or someone.

Westley intrigues me because he seems like that rare combination: movie-star handsome (in an admittedly low-key, flannel, Seattle kind of way) and genuinely nice, though he's so quiet it's taken me a while to find this out. He caught me crying one day in the café—it was the anniversary of my grandmother's death and I was missing her—and he bought me a scone and offered to fill in for me at the front desk for as long as I needed. We haven't really talked much since, but I would like to get to know him more. Maybe someday I'll get the nerve to ask him out.

I once wrote a character who is a little bit like Westley, and one who is a little bit like me. In that story, they ended up together. But that's what fiction is, right?

9

Laura

Waterton's was the fanciest store in town. In business since before World War II, it occupied an elegant, faintly Art Deco building that had been sleekly updated in recent years but was still redolent of old-school perfume; an anomaly in downtown streets studded with angular skyscrapers and posh-looking condominiums so new you could still smell the fresh paint. Laura had worked at Waterton's for many years, ever since she and Sam arrived in Seattle almost two decades ago. She'd always loved the store, particularly the main-floor accessories area just before opening hours, when all the handbags and jewelry and scarves seemed to sparkle like treasure in the quiet light.

Not that she ever shopped there much. Even with her generous employee discount, most of the Waterton's goods were too pricey for her budget, and while she'd occasionally buy outfits for work on sale or save to make a special purchase (like that ill-fated sundress criticized by Ashley One), she mostly saw the store like a museum of fashion—for looking and enjoying, not for taking home.

Laura loved her job. Her work was, she often thought, maybe a bit like how an artist approached a painting or collage: You look at a client and think about color, and line, and mood. Most of her customers were women over forty (Laura was herself in that category, just barely) with money to spare, often from the tech industry or from some glamorous-sounding, mysterious occupation like corporate PR, and had little time for or interest in shopping. As a child who had spent countless hours making new combinations of outfits for her Barbies (she had figured out at a very early age that matchy-matchy accessories, despite being what came with the dolls, were a no-no), Laura could never understand why people wouldn't want to shop for themselves, given the generous budgets her clients all seemed to have, but she was happy to help them figure out what looked best on them and what made them comfortable. It was thrilling for her to help a client get out of her fleece—why did so many women in the Pacific Northwest wear fleece of some sort? And such blandly sensible, boring trousers and shoes?—and into something that made her look in the mirror and light up. It was a kind of magic, Laura thought, how the right color and shape could transform a person, and she loved the challenge of figuring that out for every client who walked in.

Today had been an unusually busy Saturday; she'd had no time to think about the note she'd left or whether the bookstore man had responded, in a morning filled with back-to-back clients, all of them in search of professional-but-not-fussy office wear. (The profession of personal shopping would cease to exist, Laura often thought, if more women realized the magical properties of a well-fitting dark blazer and good earrings.) And now, after a quick desk-salad lunch, she had potentially a much more exciting appointment: The film director Donna Wolfe's assistant, sounding harried, had called yesterday requesting an appointment for her boss, who was attending a banquet in town and needed something "formal creative" to wear. Laura, who had immediately looked up Donna on IMDb, hadn't quite made it through *Twelve for Dinner* on Netflix after Olivia had gone to bed (the cannibal stuff was a bit much for someone who normally watched rom-coms at night while browsing through fashion blogs). But this promised to be rather more interesting than talking yet another tech exec out of shoes that fastened with Velcro.

Sydney, Laura's assistant, popped his head into her cubicle, just as Laura had gulped down the last of her lunch. "Your appointment's here, luv," he said, in the downstairs-at-Downton-Abbey accent he had been affecting for a while, despite not actually being British. Today Sydney was wearing a button-up shirt with wide stripes, a pinstriped skirt worn over matching slim trousers, a floral scarf wrapped around his head, and sparkly burgundy sneakers. Laura envied how an assistant had the freedom to play with fashion (and with his voice, for that matter); her job, she felt, required that she radiate a very classic, upscale simplicity, so that clients focused on their clothes and not hers.

"Thanks," she said to Sydney. "Nice sparkle. You didn't buy those sneakers here, did you?"

"Ha ha ha!" Sydney's laugh was theatrical but nonetheless genuine, as was the sudden disappearance of the accent, which tended to wander late in the day. "You're so cute, Laura. Like I could shop here on what they pay me."

Laura smoothed her hair, checked her lipstick, and headed into the personal shopper area, which the store grandly called an atelier but was basically an elegant lounge where clients sipped champagne (it was a fairly cheap brand bought in bulk; part of Sydney's job was to make sure no one ever saw the label) on sofas while perusing racks of clothing brought to them. It was a quiet afternoon and only one of the sofas was occupied, by a tall woman in her fifties with a pageboy haircut, dark glasses, and an all-black ensemble. Laura noticed that, rather than gazing at a cell phone as most clients did, she was scribbling something in a dark notebook, contributing to her retro look.

Laura approached her with a practiced professional smile. "Hello, are you Donna Wolfe?" she said, reaching out a hand. "I'm Laura Barry, and I'll be working with you today."

The woman stood, the way one would if about to take a bow, and extended a pale, antique-ring-laden hand to Laura. She was wearing an asymmetrical jacket that seemed to twist around her body—it wasn't clear to Laura just how it fastened; maybe it was magic, or something clever involving magnets—and a scarf that resembled a very expensive snake. Laura wondered where these garments came from; certainly there was nothing in Waterton's that was this avant-garde. Maybe she bought them while shooting in Europe?

"Lovely to meet you," the woman said, offering up the brief sentence like it was a grudging gift. "Yes, I am Donna Wolfe." She paused modestly, perhaps casting her eyes downward—the glasses made it hard to tell—clearly hoping that Laura would say something.

Laura knew her cue. "Of course. The filmmaker. I know your work well," she lied. (Well, maybe not a complete lie; seeing half of one movie had to count for something, right?) "We're thrilled to have you here at Waterton's. I understand you're looking for something to wear to a formal event?"

"Yes," said Donna, seeming a bit disappointed in Laura's reaction, but determinedly soldiering on. "I'm being given an award by the American Women in the Arts, which is having its national meeting here while I'm in town shooting my new film. It will be a dinner event at the Olympic Hotel. I would have chosen an ensemble myself, but I've been terribly busy lately. There has been much chaos in pre-production."

"I can imagine," said Laura soothingly, though she didn't know what "pre-production" might be, or why it might be chaotic.

"You were recommended to me," Donna continued, "as somebody who understood"—she paused rather dramatically, as if waiting for an audience to gather before finishing the sentence—"the importance of individuality. I do not wish to look like anyone else attending this event. I'm sure you can understand."

"Of course," said Laura, mentally imagining Donna as a movie character played by Meryl Streep and wondering which of her clients had recommended her. She was actually quite pleased with the outfits she'd pulled in advance for Donna, all of which were elegant and unusual and not one of which was a standard formal-dinner gown. She raised a hand to signal Sydney, who was hovering like a fashionable hummingbird. "Could you please bring the rack for Ms. Wolfe?" she asked him. He sprang away—Sydney, who studied ballet in his off-hours, enjoyed a dramatic spring—and quickly returned with a rack hung with garments.

It was hard to read Donna's expression, as she still had her dark glasses on, but the corners of her mouth drooped, like a curtain suddenly sagging off its rod. "Hmm," she said, riffling through the rack, occasionally surveying an outfit at arm's length as if she didn't want it to come any closer. "This is . . . not exactly what I had in mind."

Laura, who prided herself on being good with picky clients, was dismayed; she could feel her professional smile fading just a bit. "What about something like this, with heels or ankle boots?" she said, holding out a voluminous tulle skirt and short tweedy jacket, to which she had whimsically pinned a silk corsage.

"Oh my dear," said Donna (who had the voice, though not the skin, of a lifelong smoker). "I am not attending my own art school graduation. I'm afraid this won't do at all." She looked away, eyebrows delicately raised over the dark glasses, as if the tulle was someone else's misbehaving child that it was more tactful to ignore.

"Can you be a little more specific about what you had in mind?" Laura asked, trying to remain upbeat. She had won over difficult clients before. "Sometimes it takes a few tries to find just the right thing."

Donna was not interested in conversation; she'd clearly already mentally checked out of the appointment. This was the worst kind of client: those who know exactly what they want but won't say what that is.

"I'm afraid I have no more time today," Donna said. "Please have your assistant call my assistant to arrange another appointment later in the week. I don't know if I'll be able to make the time, but we shall try. Thank you." She picked up her voluminous leather shoulder bag and swept out, leaving a faint amber perfume and much confusion in her wake.

Laura and Sydney exchanged glances. "That was *awesome*," Sydney said, grinning broadly, his faux-Cockney forgotten. "Is she for real, or is there a camera here that I don't know about?"

"There's *nothing* here that you don't know about," said Laura. "Yeah, she's kind of a lot. She's a movie director. Maybe they're all like that? She's in town for a movie, shooting at that bookstore, Read the Room."

Sydney's impeccably tweezed eyebrows shot toward the ceiling. "No way! I thought that name sounded familiar. Didn't I tell you that I'm working on that movie? My friend Maverick got me a gig as a costume assistant."

"Is Maverick the one with the ear tattoo?" Laura had met a few of Sydney's friends on an ill-advised night of clubbing a year or two ago. Sydney, she'd realized at the time, had extended the invitation out of genuine concern that Laura had no social life; touched, she'd accepted, realizing too late that her years of ear-splitting music and cheap drinks were behind her. The evening was a bust, but it seemed to have cemented an unlikely friendship with Sydney, who now often had to be forcibly prevented from trying to fix up Laura with all of their presentable straight male clients. Of which, luckily, there weren't many.

"The very one. I don't know what a costume assistant on a movie does, but I guess I'll make sure the outfits are clean and pressed and ready to go. And maybe see Kelly Drake in his underwear."

"Sounds like fun," said Laura, realizing gratefully that she hadn't thought about the letter for hours. Maybe she'd stop at Read the Room later. Just to see.

10

April

April, who had various social media accounts but rarely posted anything on them (she mostly used them to look at pictures of people's pets and to keep up with the constant stream of updates on Ben's adventures in local theater), felt these days as if she had slipped backward in time. It is a very strange feeling to be carrying on an anonymous, handwritten correspondence during a time when everybody you know is accustomed to posting their every move and emotion online. While working she was constantly distracted by thoughts of L: What books was he sorting now? What kind of coffee was he drinking? Was he, maybe, thinking about the note, which had been sitting face-up on her desk for four days? About her? What should she reply? It had been many years since April had thoughts like this, and she was almost embarrassed by them—she seemed to have slipped back to junior high, wondering if a cute boy liked her. She felt both thrilled and scared in equal measure. Life had gone off-script, and all she could do was try to follow along, enjoy it, whatever happened.

Work. She had to work.

TO: bluebanana@freemail.com
FROM: aprild@picketfencehomes.com
RE: Listing #503367B

Hi! The new kitchen photo is much better, thank you. But that dark spot on the living room carpet is still a problem. If you don't have a throw rug, maybe you can move the sofa?

The sofa looked like scientific experiments involving fabric-eating substances had been performed on it, but whatever; something needed to be done. A notification suddenly lit up the top of April's computer screen—her company's internal message system, cutely called Picket Fence Coffee Breaks. It was a reminder of the all-hands virtual meeting for the Seattle staff, coming up in just a few minutes.

Picket Fence's founder, Sophie McBride, was a charismatic speaker, with an origin story that included a stint in standup comedy until she famously thought (according to her bio on the company website), when preparing to sell her grandmother's house, that it would be helpful to have an accessible database of all properties and their assessed value, whether or not they were for sale. As it happened, Sophie's cousin was a software engineer, and the company grew from a two-person operation in Sophie's mother's basement to a vast conglomerate. Sophie was now a local celebrity who was currently on her fourth husband—her prenups made frequent headlines in *The Seattle Times*, particularly the latest one, as she'd married a local journalist—though she wasn't much older than April. The too-regular all-hands meetings were a mixture of jargon and comedy; it sometimes seemed as if Sophie was still honing her act and might one day go back to standup, not that she needed the money. Everyone always laughed uproariously at Sophie's jokes (there would be cascades of "lol lol" in the chat box), as if they were worried their stock options might be canceled if they didn't. (In reality, Sophie's comedy was not great; a bootleg YouTube video of her former standup act, circulated surreptitiously by employees, showed a heavy reliance on tampon jokes.)

April clicked on the link, bringing up a video image of Sophie at her desk in the office, which was all glass and chrome and softly elegant lighting. (Rumor had it that Sophie had brought in an Oscar-nominated cinematographer to supervise the lamp arrangement in her office, for maximum onscreen flattery. April had no idea if this was true but Sophie did indeed look almost alarmingly dewy.) On the wall behind her was a famous bit of company lore: a framed front-door key, from the first house sold on Picket Fence years ago.

It was exactly time for the meeting to begin, but Sophie, who currently had a net worth of something like $800 million but prided herself on being down to earth, liked to keep things casual. She was visible but having an animated, muted conversation with someone off-camera. Three long minutes went by before Sophie laughed showily, waved a sparkly-nailed hand in dismissal at whoever she was talking to, and clicked on her audio, elaborately brushing her hair back from her face and tossing her head.

"Hey, Picket Fencers!" she said. "How's everybody? Everyone having a good Monday?" Sophie had an unnerving way of speaking during all-company video meetings as if she were in a crowded room with an audience, leading some sort of pep rally or spin class, rather than at her desk like a television anchor. Perhaps in her mind, there was a cheering crowd responding to her questions. "So, this'll be a quick one today, but I just wanted to introduce our new marketing slogan to everyone," she said. "As you all know, we've been working with new marketing partners, and now we have a new logo and slogan that I'd like everyone to be using. Add it to your email signatures, wear it on the T-shirts that will be messengered to your homes, dream about it at night, and remember that this is now our new message." Sophie's image faded, replaced by a corporate logo in a sunny yellow with the company name encased in the outline of a house and the words "Welcome home" below it.

Really, April wondered, that's the best you can do? A group of experts got paid to come up with *that*? Was she really going to have to wear the T-shirt? (April, in general, did not approve of garments with words on them.) But this kind of market speak was pretty standard for Picket Fence meetings. April mostly attended the all-hands meetings because (a) they were mandatory, and word was that managers checked to make sure you'd logged on, and (b) she always hoped Sophie might say something personal about her rather interesting life, which she unfortunately never did. April wondered what it would be like to be astonishingly wealthy, to have the optimism to marry your fourth husband before you were thirty-five, to feel the weight of an enormous company on your shoulders. Sophie never seemed quite real to April; she was like a fictional character from a not-yet-finished novel. "Welcome home" seemed like an awfully flat slogan, but maybe Sophie knew what she was doing. Save for a few of those marriages, she usually did.

Losing interest in the meeting, April sent her latest email, sipped her coffee, and thought, with some envy, about L's job. He looked at books all day—books that people once wanted in their homes, but no longer did—and decided which ones were worth reselling and which should be discarded. Not too different from her own job, really. His seemed so much nicer, though: a workplace to go to, one that smelled pleasantly of fresh paper and just a bit of dust, and with unlimited books there for the borrowing. And it was a job where you could talk to people, and maybe help them find a wonderful book and leave them feeling a little happier.

After lunch—the same yogurt-and-fruit routine she'd been doing for ages—and rather more staring into space than Sophie McBride would approve of, April finally took out a sheet of pale-blue notepaper (from a box she was now ready to admit she'd bought specially) and wrote carefully, in her best handwriting.

Hi L,

I love to read too; mysteries mostly these days, because I love the feeling you get at the end, when everything is figured out and the world makes sense again. Funny how really all mystery novels are the same—a puzzle to solve, a solution by the end—and yet starting a new one always feels like such an adventure. Hard to say which book is my favorite; it's like saying what meal is your favorite, when so many are so delicious and so very different. I've been on my own a lot lately, maybe too much, and I like disappearing into a complicated plot, where everyone has their own motives. It's like being in a movie where you're the silent central character, observing everyone. But I'm getting a little tired of solo observations, so it's especially nice to be connecting with someone.

I do envy your job. It must be nice to spend your day curating, choosing what people will love and what they won't. Maybe one day we can meet in person and you can tell me more.

A

11

Westley

Despite being named for a character in a beloved film, Westley didn't really watch movies very often; when he did, it was usually an adaptation of a book he'd liked, or a mindless action movie if he was feeling restless. (He rarely watched romances, not even *The Princess Bride*, which his mother had proudly shown him when he was a small boy, and which left him so embarrassed that for six months afterward he had insisted on being called Kevin.) When not at work, Westley spent much of his time either reading in his room—he was currently making his way through Patrick O'Brian's *Master and Commander* novels, enjoying the bracing sea air the pages conjured up—or out walking. Even in the frequent Seattle rain, he enjoyed long walks of at least an hour, every day, looking at the houses and the people in his neighborhood and imagining what their lives might be like, both now and when the neighborhood was new.

It was a welcome respite from his home, a nondescript, three-bedroom midcentury rental house that he shared with two other people. Westley liked his housemates, who were both perfectly nice and reasonably considerate, even though Cory didn't always respect refrigerator-shelf boundaries and Jillian had one of those piercing voices that could be heard through walls, particularly when she was on her phone complaining about something, which was often. But they were always just *around*, lounging in the living room and making sandwiches in the kitchen and generally taking up psychological space. Though he frequently took refuge in his bedroom, it was small and cramped, and there seemed to be something defeatist about hanging out alone in your bedroom when you weren't sleeping. Until he could afford his own place, he coped by getting outside, where walking the city streets felt expansive and freeing, like there was nothing but possibility and space quivering around him. Seattle was, he thought, the kind of city where every neighborhood felt like a different person, and he enjoyed figuring out who that person would be.

And today as he walked to Read the Room (it was a pleasant forty-minute stroll from his house, and on this warm May morning he didn't even require Gore-Tex), he thought of Duke Munro. *Shivering Timbers* had turned out to be rather more interesting than he'd expected: Munro had a clever, playful way with language; pleasantly over-the-top in a knowing, funny way. And while the book's plot was a standard boy-meets-girl romance, it was brisk and wry, as if a refreshing wind was blowing through it. The two firefighters, Verity and Will, were likable and funny and Westley had surprised himself by sitting up late in bed and reading the whole thing, hoping that the two might end up together and that the Big Fire in the book's final act didn't cause too much damage. Its ending had surprised him; it was exactly what he hoped for and yet somehow unexpected, as if Munro had somehow found a magic way of making a formula feel fresh. Before he had to leave for work, he had tried looking up more books by Munro online over breakfast, but found only a quaintly ancient-looking author website—maybe made by the author himself long ago?

The first day of shooting the film would begin this afternoon, and things quickly started looking different at Read the Room. By 2 p.m., the small parking lot was already full of vans and people unloading mysterious-looking equipment, and a trio of young men in dark jeans and T-shirts were taking a smoke break near the store's front entrance, something Westley knew would send Julia into apoplexy. As he stepped inside the door, he could already see her having an animated conversation with a man holding an iPad. Westley moved closer, the better to eavesdrop.

"We were told that the books would not be moved!" Julia said with some agitation to the man, who was mostly ignoring her and looking at his iPad as if it held some secret to be revealed. In the past few days, Westley had noted that Julia was becoming increasingly stressed out about the shooting process, as it had become clear that many of the promises made by the production company were not going to be honored, and that nobody on Donna Wolfe's team seemed particularly concerned about it.

"The shelves are too high," he replied without looking up. "We need to clear off what's piled on top, to let the light through and reduce the clutter. Otherwise the scenes won't look right."

"But I have customers here! The store is open! We were assured that nothing would be done during working hours!" Julia was now a little red in the face.

"If we're going to begin shooting by five, we need to do this work now. We'll try not to bother your customers." The customers, for their part, seemed fascinated by this exchange, and one had his cell phone out taking pictures of the disruption, to be posted later with the hashtags #bookstoremoviedrama #readtheroom. Behind Julia, several people were already working at clearing off the top of a shelf, where overstock books were stacked. Julia flung her hands in the air and walked off in a huff, the sort of dramatic exit that might have worked well in a movie—that is, if she hadn't brushed up against a stack of used paperbacks and sent them flying. Alejandra, watching from the front desk, hurried over to pick them up, stifling a giggle. Julia disappeared behind the "Staff Only" door, letting it slam behind her.

Thinking it best to remove himself from the situation, Westley headed over to his workstation at the used-books desk, slinging his messenger bag over the back of his chair. Somebody had cleared off the counter, stacking the used books on the floor behind it with no regard for order. As Westley began picking them up, the man with the iPad suddenly materialized in front of him.

"Can you please keep this counter cleared off?" he said, eyes on his screen.

"I'm sorry, but this is my workspace," Westley said, polite but annoyed. "I can't do my job if I can't stack the books here."

"Well, we'd like a more uncluttered look." The man's eyes lifted from the iPad and he saw Westley, seemingly for the first time. His eyebrows raised, and he suddenly looked interested. "Oh, *you're* the one Al was talking about," he said, offering a hand to shake. "Westley, right? Joe Byrne, production manager. You'll be in the background of what we're shooting tonight. Somebody from wardrobe will come talk to you."

Westley suddenly felt self-conscious. "Isn't what I'm wearing OK?" He had on his usual jeans, plaid flannel shirt, and plain colored T-shirt, basically the same outfit he'd worn for years, ever since a long-ago girlfriend told him what colors looked good on him and helped him match up the shirts and Ts. He'd made a point today of wearing the best ones in his rotation; fresh from the laundry rather than the floor.

"Oh, you're likely fine. Gayle will just want to take a look at you, maybe a smidge of makeup."

That sounded a bit extreme. "Are the actors coming in tonight?"

"Yes, Kelly will be here." Joe was suddenly distracted by a waving trio across the store, who looked like they were arguing with Andrew about moving a table display. "Excuse me. Maybe just clear off the counter before we start shooting? Thanks."

The movie business was, it seemed, stranger than fiction. A theatrical-looking woman, wearing an apron with multiple pockets from which protruded brushes of all sizes, hurried over to Westley, standing rather closer than seemed necessary. "Hi," she said, her dark-rimmed eyes darting over his face. "I'm Gayle. I do makeup. You look . . . fine, really. Really good. Really. You've got excellent pores."

"Thanks," said Westley, not sure what the appropriate response was to that. She seemed a bit stuck, scrutinizing his face like she was carefully proofreading it, so he stepped backward. "Hi," he said awkwardly. "I'm Westley. I guess I'm going to be on camera."

"Yes," said Gayle, eyeing Westley's forehead as if a secret code might be engraved there. "Can I have you scooch down just a bit, so I can reach you better? I don't know if you'll be on camera today, but I just want to give you an idea." She fished what looked like a palette of face-toned powder from one of her voluminous pockets, eyed it critically, then whooshed a brush over one of the colors and applied it to Westley's face, like batting away a fly. She hummed a bit while she worked, clearly enjoying herself. A few different sized brushes and different colors followed, then she held up a small mirror to Westley's face, satisfied. "How does that look to you?"

It was uncanny, as if he was gazing into a magical looking glass and seeing himself perfected; his skin flawless and his eyes somehow bigger and bluer. "That's great, I guess," Westley said. "Thank you. Gayle, was it?"

"Yes. Westley, right?"

"Yes."

"How do you spell that?" Clearly Gayle was not a *Princess Bride* fan, or maybe she just wanted to stretch out the conversation.

"W-E-S-T-L-E-Y." She was still staring at him, in a way that felt discouragingly familiar to Westley. As usual, he didn't know what to say. "Well, OK," Westley said finally. "Thanks again. I guess I'd better get to work."

"I'll send over Inez," Gayle said. "She'll take a look at your hair."

"My hair?"

"Don't worry," Gayle said, winking at him in a way that was rather disconcerting. "I think your hair looks great."

"But I'm just going to be in the background, right? The cameras won't really be noticing me. Is all this really necessary?"

"Just enjoy it," Gayle said. She seemed surprised by his reaction. "Lots of people would love to be on camera."

12

Laura

Things were quiet at work on this Wednesday afternoon, and Laura worked through lunch and slipped out by 4 p.m., waving a quiet good-bye to Sydney. He responded with a none-too-subtle wink, clearly assuming she was off to some romantic tryst. Someday she'd tell him about the note, but not yet; it seemed like too many people (Laura winced, thinking of the book club) knew already. The drive to Read the Room felt like going to another world—leaving the bustle of downtown for quiet residential streets, with kids in athletic uniforms walking home in scattered groups on the sidewalk. It was a pleasant day, unexpectedly warm for late May, and Laura wondered why she'd bothered with a jacket; summer weather in Seattle seems to sneak up on its residents, like a welcome dinner guest who nonetheless arrives at the wrong time. Laura loved this tree-lined neighborhood a couple of miles from her own, though she was sure she'd never be able to afford a house here; the homes neatly lined up on these blocks were large and old and looked like they probably had fireplaces and maybe wood-paneled libraries. Maybe someday.

Read the Room's small parking lot was busier than usual, with an assortment of focused-looking people milling around in a purposeful way, rather than the normal vague wanderings of customers. Entering the store, Laura felt a different mood from the usual tranquility. The lighting seemed brighter than usual, and people were bustling about carrying books and looking harried. A gray-haired woman in Eileen Fisher (circa 2014, to Laura's practiced eye; sage-green recycled rayon and a nice choice for her, if a little voluminous) was standing near the door, eyes closed and lips murmuring, her clenched hands seeming to beat out a calming rhythm. The booksellers at the front desk were agog.

"What's going on?" Laura asked one of them, a young man in a blazer who was intently watching the action. The bookstore phone rang in the background; nobody seemed to notice.

"They're shooting a movie here today!" he said, seeming to shake himself like a wet dog in order to snap out of his trance. "We'll be closing early, by five. Is there something I can help you find?"

"No, thank you," said Laura. "Just browsing. It's that Donna Wolfe movie, right?"

"Yes. It's called *Shelf Consciousness*," he said. "You know, I saw *Twelve for Dinner* and I didn't think it was all that? But nobody asked me. Kelly Drake is in this one, though. He's here right now." The bookseller pointed to the back of the store, where a handsome man with elaborately curled hair posed for still photos, managing to mug for the camera between elaborate glances at his phone.

"Oh, right," said Laura, trying to look unruffled. "Yes, I know someone working on the costumes. And Donna Wolfe is a client of mine." Never mind that she was a client of barely a few days' duration; it was fun, Laura thought, to be part of the scene in a tiny way, making her feel vaguely proprietary about the movie. It seemed odd that Donna Wolfe was making a movie in a cute neighborhood bookstore—her vibe seemed to tend far more toward dark, artier places—but Laura didn't know anything about the movie business. Maybe she was making some sort of dark satire of *You've Got Mail*, in which case this charming store would be just the right place. The blazered bookseller, losing interest in Laura, turned away to answer the store landline, just as it stopped ringing. "Read the Room. Hello? Hello?"

Laura made her way to Young Adult, where the three copies of *The Hunger Games* sat on the shelf like quiet sentinels. Casually glancing around—no need, really, as with all of the commotion no one was paying the slightest bit of attention to her—she slid the middle copy out and quickly riffled its pages. A folded slip of paper fell out; Laura hurriedly slipped it into her purse and replaced the book, feeling like she was committing some sort of minor literary crime. Walking quickly away, she rounded a corner—and walked right into A, who was shelving some books. Maybe life was, indeed, a rom-com. Or maybe . . . could he have been watching? Was he trying to run into her?

"Oh, excuse me!" said Laura stepping back, flustered. "I'm so sorry!"

"No, I'm sorry," he said politely. Was he gazing at her with interest? "My fault; I should have been paying attention. Did you find what you needed?"

Ah, Laura thought, quickly putting two and two together. He was asking, clearly, about the note. He was good at this. OK, she could play this game too. "Yes," Laura said, in what she hoped was a coolly enticing tone, layered with nuance. "I did."

"Great," he answered, looking . . . puzzled? Intrigued? "OK. Take care. Excuse me." And off he went.

It was an odd little interaction and not entirely satisfying, but there was something charming about feeling like she had a secret with this handsome stranger. Maybe he was speaking to her in code, indicating that he preferred to keep things on the downlow for now? Maybe booksellers weren't supposed to flirt with customers? Maybe . . . well, bottom line was that Laura had absolutely no idea how people started up relationships nowadays.

She and Sam had met as undergraduates, at a party thrown by college friends, where they bonded over books and slapstick comedies and old musicals and were pretty much inseparable from there; their friends would laugh about how the two of them met when they were practically kids. It was true: Sam and Laura had basically faced adulthood as a team, progressing through their twenties in tandem, moving to Seattle together and building a life from scratch. Laura had watched with sympathy as her friends tried to meet life partners through websites and blind dates and introductions, knowing how lucky she was that love had dropped into her lap. But luck ran out sometimes, and so here she was, sleeping alone and leaving notes in a bookstore for a man whose name she didn't know. Laura had no illusions about ever being in love again, with the bookstore guy or with anyone else. There wasn't another Sam out there, she was sure of that. But maybe it would be nice to have just a little, simple, dinner-and-a-movie relationship. Laura suddenly remembered sitting at the kitchen table with Sam not long before Olivia was born, late at night after he'd made her a grilled cheese sandwich to satisfy pregnancy cravings, talking about their lives. If a friend of theirs had been in this situation, Sam would have loved hearing about it and would have been full of advice. If only she could ask him now.

13

April

Picket Fence had nearly a thousand Seattle-based employees, almost all of whom worked remotely. Because of this, April had no reason to believe that Sophie McBride, the company CEO, would have any idea who she was. Thus, it was a little startling to receive an email directly from Sophie—well, surely written by an assistant, but it was from Sophie's actual email—inviting April to a Picket Fence Meetup that afternoon at five. Picket Fence Meetups were one of Sophie's supposedly innovative ideas: regular gatherings of five or six employees, who would join Sophie for a beer at a nearby brewpub and talk about how much they liked working at Picket Fence. (Or they could talk about what they didn't like, but rumors flew at the occasional PF social events, such as baseball games and movie nights, that those who complained would have it counted as a black mark against them at employee review time.) In her six years with the company, April had never been invited to a meetup before, but she knew that attendance was mandatory and that Sophie's expense account would provide generous food and drink—and that really, maybe, it would be a pleasant change to get out and meet some people without it being stage-managed by Janie.

The big win though, she thought, was that it might provide a bit of distraction from the bookstore situation, where April's latest note had been picked up but nothing new had replaced it. April, who was now in the habit of swinging by the store every afternoon just to check, reminded herself that it had only been a couple of days since she'd left it. Maybe getting out and meeting some actual people in person, not online or on paper, might be just the distraction she needed; perhaps there was a friend at Picket Fence whom she hadn't met yet. April fussed a bit over her outfit (meaning actual trousers, rather than leggings), put some product in her hair, and dug a pair of rarely worn earrings out of a drawer. It was nice to have a reason to make an effort.

Arriving a few minutes early at Gastronome, one of those interchangeable downtown places where beer was served in mason jars and every menu item seemed to include avocado or kale or both, April spotted Sophie at a tall table gazing at and occasionally lovingly fondling her phone, accompanied only by a young, worried-looking male assistant standing nearby with an iPad. April had expected her to sweep in late with an entourage, so this was a surprise. As she approached the table, Sophie looked up with an expectant, what-can-I-do-for-you expression, her abundant blond curls catching the light from the window. (Her spot at the table did seem chosen to offer the best backlighting.)

"Hi," said April, trying to seem coolly outgoing, like casual beers with the CEO was something she did all the time. "Sophie, right? I'm April Dunne. I'm a content associate, here for the meetup."

"Oh yes, of course!" said Sophie exuberantly. "So nice to meet you! Sit down! Would you like a beer? Shall we get a pitcher to start? And we'll get some appetizers too!" She looked pointedly at her assistant, who immediately waved to an aproned server and placed an order. It was uncanny how quickly the assistant moved, like he was a bot programmed to attend to Sophie's every need the moment she thought of it.

April sat down, a bit uneasily, wishing the beer was already there. It had been simpler to imagine going out than to actually do it; she hadn't really thought about the possibility of having to make small talk with the person who was, ultimately, her boss. Though Sophie wasn't far from April's own age, she seemed to live in a different world, and April suddenly worried about saying the wrong thing, about the company or about her job—was the guy with the iPad taking notes? "I guess the others will be here soon?" she said, regretting the question-mark tone of her voice too late.

"Oh yes!" said Sophie cheerily. "I never know who's coming. Edward keeps the list. I just like to meet the people who make Picket Fence what it is. Tell me: Do you like your job? Are you happy? Is there anything we can do to make your job easier?"

April glanced furtively at the doorway and was relieved to see a few unmistakable tech bros—polo shirts, ill-fitting khakis, unruly hair; you could almost see the key cards on lanyards around their necks—shuffling in, looking confused and vaguely alarmed at the prospect of a large table occupied only by two women. All of them looked like guys she'd dated at some point, though she'd never actually met anyone in this group. As for Sophie's questions, it seemed best to be vague. "It's good! I'm doing fine. Um, I can't think of anything but thanks for asking. How are you?"

Sophie laughed showily, displaying some expensive-looking dental work, like how a standup comedian might respond to a comment from an audience member. "I'm good! It's crazy! Picket Fence just keeps getting bigger and bigger, thanks to all of you!" She waved to the tech bros, beckoning them over, flapping her hands to indicate that they should sit down. "Welcome! Sit! Tell me your names!"

The guys looked at one another, not sure who should begin. "I'm Derek," one said, finally. "I work in IT."

"Rob. Software dev."

"Rishi. Also in dev."

"I'm Will. Marketing."

"Welcome!" Sophie trilled. "And this is . . ." She looked, attractively and blankly, at April, who obligingly filled in her name despite having just provided it seconds ago. "April! But shouldn't there be one more?" Sophie asked her assistant, who checked something on his iPad and murmured an answer. "Ah," she said. "Thank you, Edward. The sixth person can't come. She had to go to the ER with a ruptured appendix. I suppose *that's* an excuse I'll take!" She laughed, looking around for a reaction. Everyone dutifully joined in, with forced heh-hehs. The beer pitcher was passed around and quickly emptied; Sophie waved to the server requesting another. The four men all seemed to be extremely interested in the contents of their beer glasses. April was reminded that maybe there was a reason she rarely dated co-workers, or even hung out with them. (Rob looked alarmingly like one of her recent Janie fix-ups, who had talked nonstop about nineties television and confessed, toward the end of the date, that he was trying out a new system of having his day clothes double as pajamas and that his current outfit was on day three.)

"So!" said Sophie, the only person at the table who seemed comfortable with the event. "Let's go around the table and I'd like each of you to share your favorite thing about working at Picket Fence! And your least favorite thing too. I want to hear the good and the bad! That's how we move forward with integrity and get better and better!" It was fascinating, April noted, that whether addressing an entire company or just a small table of people, Sophie's delivery was made up of equal parts cheerleader, inspirational speaker, and infomercial pitchwoman, with that ever-present dash of standup comic as an echo of her past.

Sophie pointed at Derek, beaming. "OK, you start us off!"

Derek gulped his beer, looking mildly panicked and like he was afraid he might burp. "Um . . . I guess what I like best is, um, being free to do my job and use my own judgment? I like being able to work from home? And my least favorite . . . well, I kind of miss the free Cokes that I got when I worked in the office at Microsoft."

"Edward! Are you getting this?" Sophie said, listening raptly as Edward busily tapped on his iPad. "Great! Thank you, Derek!

We are thinking about a pilot program where we send soft drinks to people's homes, and maybe other things too! You can order whatever you like, and we'll deliver it! Kind of like Amazon but free to employees!" Sophie seemed to have an exclamation point permanently embedded in her sentences. "OK! How about you . . ."— she leaned toward Edward, who whispered a name in her ear—"Rishi!"

"I guess the best thing is my co-workers, who are all smart and awesome and really funny on Slack," Rishi said. "And the worst is maybe that I still can't afford to buy a house in Seattle, even with a full-time job and stock options."

"OK! I hear you!" said Sophie, with a laugh that had a touch of braying to it. "We are working on this! We want all Picket Fence employees to be able to buy a house if they want one. A special program is in the works! Edward, you have that down, right?"

"Yes," said Edward, with a tight smile. April had heard a rumor that being Sophie's assistant was a revolving-door sort of job; it was always a young man, and he rarely lasted more than a few months, but anyone surviving in the job for a year was guaranteed a very cushy position in HR. Clearly Edward was playing the long game. "Should I order some avocado nachos with kale chips?" he said.

"Oooh, yes! Now, April, your turn! Tell us what you love and don't love about working at Picket Fence."

Though April had had a moment to think about it, she still felt uncomfortably on the spot. "Well," she said slowly, "I like the idea of helping users find a place to call home. I like looking at the houses on the site and figuring out how best they can reach the perfect person for them. I like imagining the people in their homes, after they're sold, making it their own."

"Oh my!" Sophie's reaction was as if April had told a particularly good joke. "Ha ha! I hadn't realized you were such a poet! That's so lovely! And what is it that you don't love about your job?"

This one didn't take April long; she knew exactly what it was. "I miss the office. I think something's lost when we all work from home full-time and don't meet each other, and don't get energy from each other. All the communication apps help, of course, but I think most people work better when we're around others. It can get . . . a little lonely at home." She stopped, worried that the last sentence might have been a bit too personal.

Derek, Rob, Rishi, and Will were all staring at April, oddly, as if she'd suddenly begun speaking in a language they didn't understand. Sophie, sensing the awkward quiet, jumped in. "How interesting! It's always been my philosophy that it's more efficient for people to work in their own spaces. Isn't that, of course, what we do at Picket Fence—find people their own spaces? What do the rest of you think?"

The four men looked uncomfortable. "I, um, like working from home?" Rob offered tentatively, like he was testing out the phrase. The other three, still mesmerized by visions seemingly floating in their beer, vaguely nodded, not really looking at each other. It was obvious, April thought, that they weren't accustomed to being around fellow employees; they were like the unsocialized dogs she had once seen in an online video: When brought to a dog park, they had no idea what to do in the presence of others like them, but just stood around awkwardly, not knowing how to mingle.

Will, the marketer, seemed the most at ease of the four, though even he seemed like he'd rather be somewhere else. "I think we all understand," he said smoothly, "the pressures Picket Fence is facing, and the difficult decision, when looking at metrics and trends, to drastically reduce the communal office space. We're all, of course, invested in creative solutions and the wellness and well-being of both our employees and our bottom line." A word salad, April thought, big enough for a meal.

"Exactly!" said Sophie, waving her beer glass so that some foam slopped out around the top. "I couldn't have put it better myself! And what do you all think of our new corporate slogan, 'Welcome home'?"

Silence. Elaborate beer-sipping. "I like it?" Rishi offered, tentatively. Quiet nods all around.

Edward gently cleared his throat, looking nervous. "Sophie, I'm afraid it's time to go," he said. "You have a dinner at the Wing Luke Museum tonight, and then an after-party in SoDo. You said you wanted time to change, so we'd better head out."

"Right!" Sophie beamed at the five employees while extricating herself from her barstool; a complicated exercise that involved a lot of showy leg unwinding. "Thank you all for coming! Have a great evening and order whatever you like; it's on me, Edward has already taken care of the tab. Appreciate all your great work! Keep it up! Bye!" And just like that, she was gone, in a poof of blond hair and citrusy perfume, like a vivid TV show that suddenly switched to a bland commercial.

The server arrived with a second pitcher of beer and a plate of nachos. Before April could even offer to pour, the four men were already checking their phones and climbing down from their stools. "Sorry, gotta go, need to finish a work thing," said Rishi, not making eye contact.

"My Uber's here," said Will, who had not seemed to order one.

"My wife's expecting me," said Rob, who was not wearing a wedding ring.

"Um, I have to go walk the dog," said Derek, who didn't seem like he was very good at making up excuses. Leaving plenty of space between them, the four awkwardly made their way out of the bar, heading off in various directions.

From the empty table, April watched them go. The whole meeting had taken maybe ten minutes. She wondered why she'd looked forward to it. April poured herself a beer and toasted the empty table; sometimes, being on your own wasn't so bad.

14

Westley

Making a movie, as it turned out, was a very slow process. On the first night of shooting, Westley had to be carefully scrutinized by the wardrobe department, which turned out to be a very dramatic person named Maverick who had safety pins stuck all over their clothing and who grandly pronounced Westley's flannel shirt "iconic." Westley wasn't at all certain whether his shirt had just been praised or insulted, but at least he didn't have to change clothes. Then Gayle, again standing rather closer than was perhaps entirely necessary, had to brush his face with powder, this time in order to "minimize shine," she said (was he unnecessarily shiny? Was this something to worry about?), and the hair person, Inez, had put some sort of product into his hair that smelled weirdly sweet, like he was walking around in the middle of a dessert buffet. It was all very unfamiliar, and Westley found himself getting, unexpectedly, a little bit nervous and maybe even excited. Maybe this was what he needed: something that he hadn't done a million times before, something where he didn't know the beginning, middle, and end.

Finally, things seemed ready to begin, and a woman inexplicably wearing a fedora—she was, Westley thought, maybe an assistant director? If that was a thing?—instructed him to stand at his desk, to which somebody had added a picturesque hodgepodge of framed photos and kitschy knickknacks, the sort of thing Westley would never have owned. "Just do your job," she said.

"You mean, sort the books?"

"Yes. Try not to move very much, and don't make any noise. The microphones pick up everything. And don't look at Kelly."

"But, how do I do my job without moving? You can't sort books without . . ." It was too late. The fedora had moved on.

It didn't seem possible to do his job without actually picking up the books—just what did she think his job was, anyway? Did the sliding of a book across a desk count as actual noise?—but Westley tried to comply, staring intently at book covers as if something enticing was written there. It was hard not looking at Kelly Drake, who had been stationed just a few feet from the book counter and who had that actorly way of seeming to generate his own lighting effects. Westley had earlier been briefly introduced to Kelly and had offered a hand to shake, but the actor seemed lost in his own world and didn't respond.

Westley, who had been searching online for any news that he could find about the film production, had read about what a coup it was for a local actor to get a plum role in Donna Wolfe's latest film. Word was that Ethan Thompson, who had gotten some Emmy Awards buzz last year for playing a librarian who solved crimes in the popular Netflix series *Death in the Stacks*, had been signed for the role but dropped out at the last minute, and the filmmakers decided that it would be great publicity to do a Seattle talent search. The truth was, it seemed, that they knew that no other big name would do it for the pittance that Ethan had agreed to be paid, because Donna had somehow convinced him that doing a low-budget film at this moment in his career would make his currency skyrocket. But Ethan had bailed after being offered the role of a second-string superhero in a lesser Marvel Comics movie, causing Donna to make some caustic remarks on social media about commercialism versus art.

It was disappointing to find Kelly so unfriendly—Westley had never met a professional actor before and was mildly curious about what it was like—but it was probably inevitable; maybe actors had some sort of preparatory process that couldn't be interrupted by pleasantries. Kelly, dressed in a jeans-and-plaid-shirt costume not unlike Westley's own clothing, was extremely handsome in a chiseled sort of way, with a chin that looked copied from classic statuary. Even his hair looked like it was carved from marble.

Westley tried to keep his eyes away from the actor and on his own "work," as instructed. In the distance, he could see a surprisingly rapt-looking Raven standing near the doorway: an extra, positioned at the front desk, had been styled to look remarkably like Raven, right down to the blue streak in her hair. (Apparently the location scouts who visited Read the Room in advance were very thorough, or maybe Donna Wolfe was trying to achieve some sort of meta-realism.) The fake Raven, though, wore much more makeup and a very sweet smile; she was Raven as if reflected through softer glass.

"Action!" yelled somebody, startling Westley, who hadn't realized that yelling "action" wasn't just something people said in movies about moviemaking but an actual thing. Donna Wolfe, in her dark glasses and a garment that looked weirdly like a black toga, watched intently as Kelly took a few steps down an aisle of books, looking around furtively. Westley, who hadn't been given a copy of the script, didn't know exactly what was going on but it seemed like maybe something important was hiding among the shelves.

"Cut!" yelled that same somebody.

Donna Wolfe—she was one of those people of whom it was impossible to think without using both names—strode over to Westley's desk, her clothing floating out behind her like a sail. "My dear," she said in a voice that rasped like an old-school pencil sharpener, "do not look at the camera. Just do your work. Be yourself."

"I wasn't looking at the camera," said Westley, surprised.

True, he had been peeking a little bit—who could blame him?—but he'd been consciously making sure that his head was down, pointed toward the books.

"We can see your eyes. Keep focused on your work. You are lovely."

He wasn't sure how to respond to that. "OK."

"Can I get some water?" Kelly yelled out. A young woman instantly appeared with a bottle of water with KELLY written on it in dark marker, and another dabbed Kelly's face with a powder puff after he'd taken a few sips. The lack of air-conditioning at Read the Room had been a sore point with the staff for a long time. Normally they'd have a few fans going (although it was still May, temperatures had risen dramatically in a way that alarmed rain-conscious Seattleites) but the subsequent noise and breeze was pronounced unacceptable by the film crew. Already somebody had had to dry off Kelly's armpits with a portable hair dryer between takes, and there were many complaints about the store temperature, to which Julia listened with a set jaw. After Kelly was repowdered and his hair elaborately recalibrated and repositioned, he resumed his initial pose.

"Action!"

Again, Kelly stepped down the aisle of books; again, he looked furtive and frightened. Westley, keeping his eyes intently on his desk, wondered not for the first time exactly what was going on in this movie. Why would anyone be afraid in a bookstore?

"Cut! Thank you! Take a tight five, everyone."

Westley, grateful to leave his post, hurried over to Raven—not that she was his favorite person but at least she was someone he knew, something familiar. "Kind of amazing, right?" he said.

"I guess. It's a shame we had to close tonight, I've been turning people away over here. I don't know how much they're paying us to close the store but I doubt that Julia was much of a negotiator." Raven seemed determined to be entirely negative about the experience, even though she wasn't actually on the clock at the moment and therefore wasn't missing out on any work hours.

"Do you know anything about the plot of the movie?" Westley asked. "Other than that it's a magic bookstore or something?"

"Nobody's read the script, but apparently the location guy told Julia that in these scenes, Kelly Drake's character has lost his girlfriend, and he thinks she's disappeared into a portal at the bookstore."

"Why would he think that?"

"I guess she was able to send him some sort of message? Like, she's turned into a book and the books have become people? That person at the front desk is apparently Jane Eyre in the present day. It's pretty high concept."

"Huh. OK." Westley pondered this a bit. He did, occasionally, daydream about books coming to life—maybe he'd seen too many fantasy movies as a kid—and this plot sounded oddly appealing.

"You should ask the costume and makeup people if they know any more. When they come to fix you up," said Raven a bit wistfully. "It must be kind of fun to be part of it." Westley noted that despite herself, she seemed excited, which made him feel a little guilty for being so unenthused. It was surreal, Westley thought, to be watching a version of their own work life, in which everyone looked shinier and prettier than their real-life selves.

"Places, please!" yelled whoever it was—Fedora, maybe?—whose job it was to yell.

Westley assumed his position at the desk. He tried to look like someone else.

15

Laura

It was important to Laura not to be the kind of parent who was always offering trips to the ice-cream parlor, or the toy store, or the water park. Her temptation with Olivia was often to overcompensate, feeling regretful that her daughter had only one parent—a harried, too-often-tired working mom—and had missed out on the adoring dad she should have had. (Sam had been devoted to Olivia from the moment of her birth and was always making up funny songs to sing to her as he bounced her. Laura sometimes wished she'd thought to ask him to write down those songs, but in other ways she was glad she hadn't; she knew she'd never be able to sing them the same way. There was one, she remembered, that rhymed "girls" and "curls" and "tilt-a-whirls.")

But Laura often had to remind herself that the little girl with Sam's brown eyes had no recollection of him—she wasn't even two years old when Sam died. Olivia of course knew that there had been a Daddy long ago and she was especially fond of a picture in her room of Sam holding her as a chubby-cheeked infant, but there was no wistfulness in her occasional questions about her father. Sam was, to her, just a pleasant abstraction, a story she enjoyed hearing. This was difficult for Laura, but she told herself firmly that life would be much harder if Olivia had sad memories of Sam. It was better to have only one of them griev-ing, only one of them thinking of how much fun Sam would have had with a bright, happy seven-year-old who loved books and playgrounds and silly knock-knock jokes. For Olivia, life with just the two of them was perfectly normal.

But as this summerlike afternoon stretched out on Laura's day off, the townhouse felt hot and stuffy, and Laura couldn't stop thinking about that pale-blue slip of paper on which a hand-some stranger had confessed to feeling lonely and suggested that, maybe, they might meet in person sometime. This made Laura feel simultaneously thrilled and panicky—were things moving a little too fast?—and so an expedition to the neighbor-hood ice cream shop after fetching Olivia from school seemed like a good distraction.

Olivia, who always refused booster seats even though she was short for her age, gazed up at her mother from behind a kid-sized sundae. She took elaborate bites with a too-big spoon, pull-ing it out of her mouth with a soft mound of ice cream still on it, which she inspected avidly as if it might hold some surprise ex-tra treat.

"Ashley Two is *lactose intolerant.* So she can't have ice cream," Olivia announced with some satisfaction, the sort that small children express when a grown-up has to endure some arbi-trary rule of deprivation that doesn't apply to them. She said the phrase carefully, like she'd practiced it, which she probably had. It amused Laura how much Olivia adored Ashley, whose youth and blond prettiness made her the closest thing Olivia had en-countered to a Disney princess in real life, albeit one with multi-ple piercings.

"Yes, that's too bad," Laura said automatically. She was very familiar with Ashley's dietary restrictions. There were special shelves in the fridge and the cupboard just for Ashley's snacks, which were very organic and soy-forward and often looked as if they were made from dust particles. Ashley was very particular about keeping track of her inventory and letting Laura know when things needed replenishing, along with the more recognizable food eaten by Laura and Olivia. (Laura had learned early that one way to induce a good part-time babysitter to stick with the job, especially if you couldn't pay lavish wages, was to keep them well fed with whatever mysterious foods they liked.) "She does have to be careful of what she eats. I didn't know you knew what 'lactose intolerant' was."

"Ashley Two told me," said Olivia, proud of her knowledge. "It means you can't have ice cream. Or string cheese. Or Go-Gurt. If she eats any of those, she gets really sick. I don't want to be *lactose intolerant*. It sounds icky."

"It probably is kind of icky," Laura agreed. "But you don't have to worry about that. Did you and Ashley have fun at the park yesterday?"

"Yes," said Olivia decisively. She said most things decisively, from her very first word ("there," pronounced "dere" and accompanied by pointing) at ten months. Laura often marveled at how she could have produced a creature of such absolute certainty, when she herself so often wavered. That Olivia had emerged from her body and yet was so different from her seemed like a tiny, beautiful miracle every day. "Zach came to the park with us," Olivia went on. "We had a race to see who could get to the swing set first, and I won."

"That's nice," Laura said. She privately thought Zach was a bit of a dimwit—he had once used the phrase "for all intensive purposes" in her presence—but he was sweet with Olivia and told her charmingly corny dad-jokes. And anyway, who was she, a pathetic person ridiculously awaiting unsigned notes from a stranger, to judge anyone's relationship?

"Do you think Ashley Two and Zach will get married?" Olivia asked. "Can we go to the wedding? Can I get a new dress and pretty shoes? And have flowers in my hair?" Olivia had never been to a wedding but had watched a few carefully selected rom-coms with Laura, and frequently staged elaborate matrimonial celebrations with her stuffed animals. She eyed Ashley and Zach with the curiosity of someone whose ultimate dream was to see a wedding dress worn in real life.

"Oh, I wouldn't get too excited about that just yet," Laura said. "If they had a wedding, I'm sure they'd invite us, but they seem a little young to be getting married. I think Ashley's only twenty-two or something."

"That's *old*," said Olivia decisively, chasing a trail of chocolate syrup with the edge of her spoon.

"Only to someone who's seven."

Olivia made a face, which was made impossibly cute by the ring of ice cream around her mouth. Or so it seemed to Laura. Parenthood, to her, was a terrifying level of duty and responsibility, made easier by the fact that her child was clearly the world's most adorable little person. Laura sometimes felt surges of love for her daughter that were so strong they almost seemed visible, like golden ribbons happily tethering her to Olivia forever.

Olivia was still pondering weddings. "Do you think you might get married again, Mommy?" she asked. "Would you wear that same dress again? And the same thing on your head?" Olivia was quite familiar with her parents' wedding pictures. Her father was, to her, like a character in a beloved old movie or storybook, an image to treasure.

"It's called a veil," said Laura, taking a deep breath before going on. (She believed in always addressing Olivia's questions, even when she didn't really know the answer.) "I don't know. Getting married is a pretty big deal. I'd have to meet somebody perfect. And you'd have to really like him. And he'd have to fit into our lives, yours and mine. I just don't know if someone like that is out there. Maybe someday, but right now I don't know anyone I'd want to marry. I'm happy enough with just you around." She paused, realizing she'd left out what was probably the most important part of the question to Olivia. "And no, I wouldn't wear the same dress again. I'd get a new one."

"Hayden's mommy got married again," Olivia said, taking another deliberate taste of her sundae. (Laura had heard a great deal of play-by-play, from Olivia by way of Hayden, about Hayden's parents' divorce, which seemed to involve both of them buying their son a lot of gifts. Laura had had to explain to a faintly envious Olivia that no, Laura couldn't get divorced, because you have to be married to be divorced.) "She got him a babysitter and went away to somewhere called Das Begas. Where's that?"

"Las Vegas," Laura corrected absently. "Really? That's a place people go when they want to get married in a hurry. It's kind of far from here."

"They went on a plane," said Olivia, "and she had a white dress and sparkly shoes. I saw a picture. Hayden's new stepdad is nice. He has a motorcycle. Can you marry someone with a motorcycle? Then we'd have one to go for rides."

"I don't think so," said Laura. She could not imagine handsome A, from the bookstore, on a motorcycle; he seemed more the public transportation type. Could he possibly be the kind-stepfather type, though? Would the three of them maybe sit in this ice-cream parlor someday enjoying a treat? But this was not a speculation she was going to enter into with Olivia; not today, anyway. "OK, finish that up," Laura said, whose own dish of ice cream had vanished long ago. "I think we need to stop by the bookstore on the way home. You need a new book, don't you?"

Olivia, who loved Read the Room and its cheerful children's corner, readily agreed. Yes, it was important to stop by the store today, Laura rationalized. For Olivia.

16

April

A pril had lately gotten into the habit of sitting with her laptop in the Read the Room café in the late afternoon. The café, a large sunny room in the back of the store that smelled of coffee and warm cinnamon, was called Charlotte's Web, and the menu took offbeat inspiration from the book; you could, for example, order a Fern's Falafel Wrap or Templeton's Tuna Salad. Regardless of the misplaced barnyard energy, it was nice to have a change of scenery at the end of a workday and enjoy a latte and maybe a scone, and watch the people streaming in and out. It reminded her of the Saturday-lunch tradition with Janie that she'd had for a long time, at this very café, a tradition that had slipped away somewhere around Janie's second kid. Janie kept saying they should start it up again, but never seemed to have time. But April didn't mind being alone at Read the Room; she had, in fact, always had a fantasy of working in a bookstore, surrounded by books and people who loved them. She enjoyed watching other people do so in real life, imagining the customers' lives and how the books they chose would make them feel.

On her way to the café, April had eavesdropped as a silver-haired woman at the front desk—she always seemed to be at the store, and April had wondered if she was the owner, since she had a faintly proprietary air—listened intently as a customer described wanting a novel she'd heard reviewed on NPR, maybe last week or the week before, and she didn't know the title or the author but it was something about a road trip and a misplaced inheritance and a chemical peel gone terribly wrong. The bookstore woman had instantly nodded, walked to a nearby shelf, and handed over a volume to the delighted customer. It was, April thought, a remarkable skill to have, like having an entire online catalog in your head, available to access anytime.

Things were quite busy in the store today—maybe some sort of ad was being filmed, as there seemed to be a lot of cameras and dark-clad people about—but she'd managed to get a table in the café that afforded a view of the used-books desk, and thus a view of L, her bearded note-writing man. He was quiet, April observed, and seemed to mostly keep to himself. Maybe he was thinking about what to write in his next note? It was so strange, she thought, to sit and gaze at the person she was writing to; he didn't yet know her identity and would have no idea why the woman at the café table was gazing at him. Today even the store seemed a little different: brighter somehow, and busier, with people bustling around equipped with clipboards and iPads who didn't seem like bookstore patrons. Even the café seemed more crowded than usual, with people gazing at the activity.

A text popped up on April's phone.

Hey!!! I have big newz!!

It was her brother, Ben, whose habit of deliberately misspelling things in texts annoyed April to no end (though, strangely, she didn't mind it so much when her friends did it). She turned over her phone. Ben's news, which she would spell correctly when replying to him, could wait. Probably it involved him needing her to lend him some money. It usually did. Right now she was busy; she had a mysterious admirer to stalk. In a G-rated, harmless, Hallmark-movie sort of way, of course.

"Excuse me," a young woman said to April, interrupting her

gaze. "Do you mind if I share your table?" She gestured around the full café. "I just have a fifteen-minute break."

"Oh, sure!" April said, sliding her laptop over to allow some room. "No problem. Do you work here?"

"Yes, in the bookstore," the woman said. She put her coffee cup on the table, as well as a notebook with a pen tucked into the wire spiral binding, placing it face down. "This movie's brought a lot of people in. I don't know why. Not much to see."

"Oh, a movie?" April asked, intrigued.

"Yes." The woman rolled her eyes a bit. "My boss is all excited about it, but the customers seem more interested in the cameras than in buying books."

April, accustomed to sitting alone, was intrigued by this woman, who had dark hair, watchful eyes, and a casually friendly manner. "Are you writing something?" she said, indicating the notebook. "I'm sorry, I don't mean to be nosy."

"No, that's OK," the woman said. "Trying to write something. Some days go better than others. Today's pretty busy anyway; I don't think I'll get much writing done."

"What's the movie about?" April asked, enjoying this conversation with a bookstore stranger. Not the right bookstore stranger, but one with proximity to *her* stranger, nonetheless. If this were a rom-com, they'd become instant friends and do a fun shopping montage together. In real life, a brief chat was pleasant enough.

"We haven't read the screenplay—at least I haven't—but it's apparently something about a magic bookstore. I love that idea. Bookstores are kind of magic anyway, don't you think?" The woman looked at April earnestly, having asked the question in a way that felt charmingly conspiratorial.

"I do, actually," April said. She wasn't usually one for entering into imaginative confidences with strangers, but there was something about this woman that felt cozy and appealing. This was so much better than stilted small talk. "I do think magical things happen in bookstores. All those books on the shelves. Maybe they have lives, after everyone's gone and the store is dark."

"I always wondered that," the woman said, turning over her notebook and jotting something down quickly. "I think they do."

"I always wanted to work in a bookstore," April said. "Is it fun to work here? My name is April, by the way."

"I'm Alejandra," the woman said, taking a sip of her coffee. "It is. I love working here. I like being around the books and kind of listening to them. And my colleagues are nice." She watched and smiled knowingly as April gazed across the room, intrigued by the sight of Westley narrowly rescuing a teetering pile of books from toppling over. "Not a bad view from here. Pretty cute, right?"

This was an actual girly moment; something far too rare for April these days. "Definitely!" It felt a little too spot-on to discuss L (what if Alejandra also liked him? This seemed too problematic to contemplate), so April abruptly changed the subject to something safer. "What else do you know about the movie? Is it a big deal? Anyone in it I might have heard of?"

"Do you know who Kelly Drake is? He was here yesterday! I saw him right before we closed. He absolutely looks like a movie star," Alejandra said. She looked ready to say more, when her eyes caught sight of the woman with gray spiky hair, who seemed to be hyperventilating while talking to two black-clad people trying to move a bookshelf. "Oh no," Alejandra said. "My boss is freaking out again. I'm sorry. I need to go help her out. Nice to meet you, April, and maybe I'll see you again in the store?" She scooped up her notebook and hurried off.

April did know who Kelly Drake was; he'd been on the cover of several local magazines and profiled in *The Seattle Times* as a sort of bad-boy hometown heartthrob a while ago, after some exuberant onstage stripping during a local performance of *Hair* went viral on Instagram. ("I was just in the moment," he had said at the time; curious how "the moment" always seemed to occur when there were cameras nearby.) He'd even had his face on the side of a bus recently, looking thoughtfully healthy on a PSA for flu shots. He was indeed very cute, in a carefully assembled way, and was probably the closest thing Seattle had to an up-and-coming movie star. April didn't see any sign of him today but allowed herself to gaze a bit longer at L—Leonard or Lloyd or Lincoln or whatever—at work, looking at his computer and stacking books in tidy piles. Looking up, he noticed April watching him and nodded politely before turning back to his computer.

How long, April wondered, should she play this epistolary game? He hadn't yet responded to her second note, though he'd definitely picked it up about five days ago; she'd been checking. Maybe she had been too forward suggesting they meet? Maybe he just couldn't decide what to say. Should she just walk over and initiate a conversation and move things along? No, she would not. Odd as it was, April was actually enjoying the slowness of their interactions; the very old-school, analog way in which they were communicating. She wasn't in a rush. Maybe L was enjoying it too.

April took one last sip of her coffee, having made it last as long as possible. Sitting in a café drinking coffee felt so different from drinking it at home; here, you were part of a world. It was as if the smell of the books on the shelves—that dusty, faintly yeasty odor of stories—was infused into the liquid somehow. After the strangeness of the Picket Fence happy hour, this felt more comfortable; a place where she was part of a story, where she belonged, where an ending was coming soon. Maybe even a happy one.

TO: All Read the Room Staff
FROM: julia@readtheroom.com
SUBJECT: Movie shoot

Good afternoon, everyone. I'm sending this via email to make sure that all staff, including the part-time employees, see it. As you will have noticed, the movie people have begun their work and things are rather more disruptive than I had guessed. So we are going to need to implement some temporary new rules, effective immediately and applying to everyone:

1) Do NOT help any of the movie people move any books, or shelves, or any of the store fixtures. I appreciate that all of you want to be helpful, and that there is a certain glamour factor to this film shoot. But I will not have the store's meticulously organized books and displays disrupted. I have told them repeatedly not to touch the books, as was our initial understanding. Please do not undermine my instructions. If you are asked to help with moving anything, report it immediately to me, no matter how busy I am.

2) Movie crew members are no longer allowed to use the staff restroom, after an unfortunate incident that I would prefer not to describe. Do not give them the key. They can use the restroom in the café, or they can go down the street to the gas station, and if they complain about this, tell them actions have consequences. Or refer them to me.

3) In general, send any questions about the filming to me. Do not agree to do extra work for the crew. As I have already had to explain to some of you, being nice to them will not get you a role on camera. There are union regulations involved.

4) Those who are interested may stay in the store to watch the filming when your shift has ended, but please be sure that your presence is not disruptive. This means: do not offer them suggestions on how to make the movie better. I have already received complaints about this. Those of you who have done this know who you are.

Thank you for your attention to these matters. It's my hope that the movie shoot won't go on much longer. Unfortunately I can't seem to get a specific date out of the production manager, who has taken to avoiding me. I will keep trying. In the meantime, please continue to do your jobs with as much joy as you can.

Julia

17

Westley

Westley had always known, though he didn't like to acknowledge it, that women found him attractive. (So did men, but he never knew how to respond to that. When a guy got flirty, he usually just invented an excuse and walked away.) Bookstore customers were always asking him for his advice on romantic novels—or erotic novels, for those especially bold—and gazing deeply into his eyes when doing so or touching his arm in a way that seemed rather more intimate than necessary. Just today, a woman in the café was staring at him over her laptop and looked flustered when he caught her eye. He generally tried not to catch unknown women's eyes, for exactly that reason. His housemates' female friends frequently found excuses to engage Westley in conversation, usually asking about his name (yes, it really was from the movie; no, he didn't really like it) or what it was like to work in a bookstore, while elaborately playing with their hair. They never seemed particularly interested in what he actually had to say.

Even at work, it could be a problem. The situation with Raven continued to be uncomfortable months after their brief fling (or their "mutually handsy French kissing in a dark aisle during a party after too much wine, enough to knock a few hardcover Self-Help books off the shelf"). Nothing had happened between them since that ill-fated holiday party, but sometimes Westley happened to catch Raven looking at him, with an expression that might have been longing.

And now, whatever it was that women responded to had caused him to end up in this movie, in a pointless background part that was probably going to be cut out anyway, and it was really just a bother. He was selected, he knew, because of what he looked like, and his looks were a lure he often didn't want.

Though women were always approaching him, and Westley had dated many, he'd only been in love once, briefly and passionately and very, very wrongly. It was a long time ago, at the job he didn't like to talk about or even think about—but nevertheless, it was often on his mind, a terrible mistake he'd made long ago that haunted him. He'd worked at Mad Hatter, a quirkily elegant downtown restaurant owned by an old high school friend of his, Mark. Though their friendship had gone dormant for a while— Mark had gone to some faraway prestigious college, while Westley had wafted around Seattle wondering what his next step would be—they'd reconnected when Mark returned to town after graduation to work for a tech company. (Westley often wondered, uncomfortably, why nobody had ever offered *him* a job in a tech company, particularly during a time when everybody else in Seattle seemed to be doing just that.) The job had proved lucrative, and Mark was soon able to realize his dream of opening a restaurant, offering Westley a job as a server.

Westley worked there for several years, enjoying the warmth of the atmosphere and the theatricality of the setting. Waitstaff at Mad Hatter had to wear natty shirt-vest-trouser combinations along with fanciful hats; it was the most formal Westley had ever dressed, and he was surprised by how much he enjoyed it, like putting on a costume before an anticipated performance. Though he typically wasn't comfortable with strangers, he was surprised by how much he enjoyed chatting with regular customers, getting to know their likes and dislikes, appreciating their compliments on the food. All the while, he was learning from Mark about flavors and cooking techniques and proper plating (a word he hadn't previously known existed). It turned out to be a dream job, and he'd worked his way up to being the restaurant's manager, hoping to maybe become a partner in the restaurant someday—until Mark's fiancée, Bridget, joined the staff as pastry chef.

Though Westley didn't like to dwell on what happened next— he tried hard not to think about it, picturing it behind a door that he had shut tight and locked—it came to mind too often, particularly on lonely nights in his room or quiet days at work. In short order, he and Bridget had fallen hard for each other—she was petite and short-haired and sardonic and charming, and eyed Westley as if he were the most delicious of macarons—and carried on a discreet but passionate affair for about a month. It was like nothing Westley had ever experienced; he thought about Bridget all the time, wondered what she was doing, didn't feel alive unless he was with her. It was as if, in her presence, he became somebody more vivid, somebody more confident; as if she had really seen, somehow, the person he could be.

It was wrong, he told himself every day, and a terrible betrayal of his old friend. But he couldn't stop himself, believing the vast sweep of his feelings for Bridget to be, finally, love—the sort he'd only heard of before meeting her, the sort in the face of which a person believes themselves powerless. And then one day Mark found Westley and Bridget in the pantry, on an afternoon when they had thought Mark was meeting with a supplier. Just like that, Westley lost a lover, a friend, and a job. It was as if the string holding up his life was suddenly slashed with a sharpened kitchen knife, leaving him abruptly dropped to a hard and unwelcoming ground.

It had been many years now, and Westley had had plenty of time to mull it over and to feel genuinely awful about what he'd done to Mark, a friend who'd trusted him and who'd maintained a stony silence throughout Westley's tentative attempts to connect and apologize. He'd given up trying to get through to Mark and had made a point of never trying to contact Bridget again; he had heard vaguely through an acquaintance that she had moved to California for another job. But he would sometimes still think about her late at night, guiltily reliving their stolen hours together as if they were scenes in a movie that he loved to rewatch. He knew that he and Bridget were never meant to be, but he wondered if he'd ever meet someone right for him—someone with whom he felt comfortable, someone who didn't make a fuss over his looks or his name but saw the person he was, shy and unsure and perpetually waiting.

Though he was frustrated by the slow pace of the movie—and by the fact that despite having an incredibly unimportant role, it still required more effort than he was accustomed to—at least it was a distraction. At his desk, Westley tidied his book piles and tried to focus, to send away all unwelcome thoughts. Things hadn't gone terribly well in filming yesterday, and Westley was determined to do better today. How hard could it be, really, to just hold still and not look at a camera? But the director, Donna Wolfe, had made things even more difficult: After staring at him for some time yesterday, she had announced that he was going to have a line to speak. It wasn't much of a line—"Over there, to your left," after an actor/customer asked for directions to the Biography/Memoir section—but it turned out that there were endless ways to speak a five-word line, and none of them seemed quite right.

"Over *there*, to your left." (decisively)

"Over there, to your *left*." (phrased as a slightly judgy correction)

"Overtheretoyourleft" (a sort of actorish mumble)

"Over there, to your left?" (phrased like a question)

He'd tried all of these variations, and numerous others, whispering in the mirror of his bedroom at home, but apparently he hadn't been quiet enough as his housemates had clearly overheard. Cory had winked broadly at him this morning—Westley had never brought home an overnight guest, and obviously his housemate had the wrong idea—and Jillian kept looking behind him expectantly during breakfast for someone who wasn't there. Westley hadn't shared the news of the movie with his house-mates, since he was a bit embarrassed at being singled out to play a role. Maybe he'd tell them later, when the movie came out. If it ever did. For now, he let them think what they wanted.

At Read the Room, Julia was just ushering out the last of the late-afternoon customers; the store was closing early for filming again, and people were reluctant to leave, craning their necks to get a peek at the flurry of camera setup. "Thank you so much for understanding about the movie," Julia was saying. "I'm very sorry, no, you can't stay to watch. We'll be open again at nine to-morrow."

Westley watched as a curly-haired woman, whose grade-school-age daughter was showing her a book from the featured Early Readers shelf, answered her ringing phone while gesturing that her daughter needed to put the book back. (They were al-ready carrying a Read the Room shopping bag; the little girl had apparently spotted another book on their way out.) The girl ran back to the children's section but hesitated, not sure where to put the book; Westley, whose desk was nearby, caught her eye. "Hi," he said, pointing to his counter. "You can just leave that here if you like. I'll put it away."

The little girl walked over to the counter, gazing at Westley with a serious, sizing-up expression. "Hi," she said. "Is this your store?"

"No," Westley said. "I just work here."

"Do you like books?"

"Yes, I do." It was nice to get a question so easy to answer.

"Have you read *all* the books in this store?" Eyes wide, she waved an arm at the laden shelves behind her.

"Some of them," Westley said conspiratorially. "Lots of them, really. What about you?"

She smiled, delighted with the exchange. "I've read a *lot* of them," she said. "I can read chapter books now."

The mother, near the door, finished her call and looked up, seeming a bit startled to see her daughter chatting with Westley. "Olivia," she called, "we need to go!"

The little girl—Olivia, a name from Shakespeare that Westley had always liked—gave one last, longing look to the book she was holding and placed it on Westley's counter. "Bye," she said, running off toward her mother, who took her daughter's hand and led her to the parking lot. They looked alike; the child a small copy of her mother, with the same mop of dark-brown curls. Westley was pretty sure he'd seen them in the store before; just two of many regulars.

Even as the door closed on the last book-buyer, the bustle of the movie had begun again. A crew efficiently coiled a maze of extension cords down the bookstore aisles, positioned lighting instruments, installed track on which the camera would roll. Kelly Drake emerged from the makeshift dressing room that had been created in a corner of the café; it had attracted, during business hours, a glut of customers casually hanging around peering at the wardrobe racks, hoping to maybe catch Kelly without his shirt on. The actor was now camera-ready, in that odd way that Westley had noticed: looking like himself, but more so, every detail in his face subtly emphasized with makeup, his hair meticulously arranged like a bouquet of dark flowers, his outfit carefully nondescript but perfect. Kelly was staring at his phone, clearly not liking what he was seeing.

"Places," yelled somebody, startling Westley. The process of shooting the movie felt like the meetings of a club of which he wasn't really a member. Other than Donna Wolfe and Al and Joe and the assistant director, a slightly overwhelmed-looking young woman named Erica (she was the one always wearing a fedora), he didn't know anyone's job title or real name—just that there was a small army of efficient people who knew how to move things forward.

Westley positioned himself at his desk, ready to deliver his line: In the absence of any direction, he'd decided to emphasize "there." Kelly, still staring at his phone, didn't move.

"Kelly?" said Fedora anxiously, scratching her head under the hat and looking a bit flushed. She was young and a little scared of Kelly, who had yelled at her and everyone else earlier about his latte having too much foam. "Can we ask you to take your place, please?"

Ignoring her, Kelly pressed some buttons on his phone and held it to his ear. "Ramona!" he said. He seemed not to care that he had an audience, Westley thought; in fact, he seemed to be projecting for their benefit. "Yeah, I just got the email. What do you mean, they've moved production up? I'm not available! I'm stuck here in Seattle, doing this bookstore movie!"

Everyone in the store seemed to freeze, like some sort of special effect had kicked in. All was silent as Kelly listened to his phone; Westley leaned in, hoping to hear, but couldn't make out the voice. "Of course I want to do it! It's a national spot!" Kelly said. "Tell them I can't come until July. Like we agreed. Isn't this what I pay you for?"

More silence. "Ramona, I am literally on the set right now," Kelly said. "I can't talk. You need to fix this. . . . OK. Call me later." He handed the phone to the harried assistant who constantly shadowed him and registered the crowd staring at him. "What? Can't a person take a phone call?"

Odd, Westley thought; Kelly Drake wasn't *that* famous; he was just a local guy who'd gotten lucky. What made him think he could behave like such a diva? Westley remembered the day that an actual famous actor who lived in Seattle had come into the store to buy a book for his wife. He couldn't remember the actor's name, but recalled that Alejandra, who was a huge fan of his films, had made a fuss and insisted on having him pose for pictures, and the actor, an older gentleman with a couple of long-ago Oscar nominations and a friendly twinkle in his eye, couldn't have been nicer. But Kelly had been pretty much a jerk to everyone throughout this process, as far as Westley could see. Weren't there plenty of other talented young actors out there who wouldn't behave like that? That kind of behavior at Read the Room might lose you your job, or at least get you a talking-to from Julia.

Gayle, the makeup person, hurried over to check Westley's face for shine, and flirtatiously flipped a brush over the tip of his nose. Westley barely noticed. "Places!"

18

Laura

Laura couldn't stop thinking about the note. How did A (Alex? Andy? Arthur? Aidan?) know so much about her? *It must be nice to spend your day curating, choosing what people will love and what they won't.* Laura had, in fact, often thought of her job as one of curation, though her title was simply "personal shopper." The clothing was the art—or, at least, it tried to be—and her job was to sort through the chaff and find just the right thing for a client: something that the person would respond to and feel happy wearing; something that wasn't necessarily the latest fashion, but that made them feel like themselves, just more so. She had in fact just last week found a perfect garment for one of her favorite clients: a sunshine-yellow, full-skirted halter sundress that made Cicely, a modestly dressed paralegal by day and a flamboyant lounge singer by night, pirouette with joy. It was a feeling of satisfaction that went far beyond the modest salary and commission Laura earned—knowing that someone out there was walking a little lighter, believing they looked great.

But how did Aaron or Andre or Alan know about Laura's job? Had he been researching her online? Maybe he'd gotten her name from a credit card purchase at Read the Room? That was probably it; he could easily have found Laura if he had her name, as she was right there on the Waterton's website under "Personal Shopping Team." The black-and-white photo was rather more glam than Laura usually looked—the Waterton's cosmetics staffers had really done a number on her brows and recommended a dark lipstick that made Laura look like a film noir heroine—but she was more or less recognizable.

"Tell me a story, Mommy," said Olivia sleepily, tucked up in her pink-and-purple sheets. This was a nighttime ritual for them, following whatever book they were reading aloud, ever since Olivia had been old enough to understand fairy tales. It seemed to help her settle down and go to sleep, and Laura enjoyed the quiet time with her, even if the storytelling on demand was sometimes challenging.

"OK," said Laura softly. "Close your eyes now. So . . . once upon a time there was a beautiful princess named, um, Fifi Annabella, and she was incredibly smart and was the best chess player in the kingdom."

"What was she *wearing*?" Olivia murmured. This was a favorite query. Laura felt an odd sense of pride in her daughter's love of artful clothing, somehow magically passed along.

"Oh, she has an enormous closet full of beautiful clothes, and right now she's wearing a purple sparkly ball gown with a full skirt and elbow-length sleeves and silvery trim, except it's short and she's wearing jeans with it, because it's important for princesses to be able to climb trees if they want to. And she loved to read books of fairy tales, but one day . . . um, she found a note in one of her books." (Nighttime storytelling often owed a debt to whatever had happened to Laura recently; she loved sharing her life with Olivia this way.) "A prince had left the note for her, and said he wanted to meet her, but he didn't tell her his name."

"Why not?"

"Maybe he's shy? Even princes can be shy. Anyway, she figured out who he was because of the special prince symbol on his notepaper, and so she looked him up on, um, Royal Facebook.

She invited him to the castle for an all-you-can-eat ice cream party, and they became really good friends."

"Did they get married?" The question was barely audible as Olivia was half asleep now, sweetly slipping away.

"No, because you don't have to get married to live happily ever after. Which is what she and the prince did. And they had twelve cats and lived in a treehouse and wore wedding dresses and ate ice cream every day and were very happy. The End." Laura smoothed Olivia's hair and kissed her forehead. "Good night, baby. I love you. Sleep well."

Olivia, a faint smile on her face, made no reply. Laura tiptoed out of Olivia's room and closed the door behind her. In the living room, Rebecca was waiting. She'd come over for a glass of wine and to inspect the latest note.

"OK, she's down," Laura said. "I don't want her knowing about this yet. Unless something major happens. So, I guess he could have found me online, right?"

"Of course he did," said Rebecca impatiently. "Everyone's easy to find these days, and you're super easy because you shop at that bookstore all the time, right? He probably knows everything about you." She gazed at the pale-blue paper again, which was starting to get a little soft with handling. "Interesting choice of paper. It seems like something a woman would pick. Maybe he thought you would like it? He has nice handwriting. Really small and tidy."

"Well, he seems really organized, from what I can see of his desk at work. Neat. But not like an obsessive neat freak or anything like that. Just like he knows where things should be."

"That sounds promising," said Rebecca with a wicked grin.

Laura blushed and wished she hadn't. Although she and Rebecca talked about everything, she didn't feel ready to talk about what it might be like to sleep with someone who wasn't Sam. Not yet. "I didn't mean *that*!"

"I know," said Rebecca. "I know, sorry. Let's get back to this virginal Jane Austen–ish situation you have going on here. So, this is the second note from him, right?"

"Yes. The first one just said hi and that he liked the way I looked at books. Do I look at books in a certain way?"

"I haven't noticed. Sure, why not. Maybe you do? Are there different ways to look at books?"

"I mean, I like books? And I like browsing in the store when I have time, and when Livvy's not whining at me to buy her something. Which is, like, never. But it seems like a funny thing to notice. Like he's really been watching me and thinking about me. But why? Why would a guy who looks like that look at me?"

Rebecca took a sip of wine and examined Laura with narrowed eyes. "Well," she said affectionately, "you are kind of a hottie. For your age, I mean."

"You mean *our* age," said Laura, with the kind of giggle that sounds more like a snort. Laura had always thought Rebecca was beautiful—she had shampoo-commercial long dark hair and a way of wearing elegant, expensive clothing as if it was something she'd just tossed on. "Speaking of hotties, what happened with Colin and the alimony?"

Colin was Rebecca's ex-husband, who looked like a younger George Clooney but who was nonetheless a snake. Laura had spent quite a lot of time trying to wish terrible misfortune on him, after he dumped Rebecca a few years ago, and apparently her messages to the universe were being heard—Colin, panicking, had run through his trust fund and was trying to siphon money from his well-off former wife.

Rebecca waved a hand dismissively. "He will be getting *no* alimony from me. I sicced one of the partners on him. Threatened to sue him, threatened to seize his assets, threatened all sorts of things. I'm not actually going to do any of it, but it scared him pretty good. Jerk. I can't believe I ever thought he was a nice person. I think I was blinded by that face."

Laura reached out and squeezed Rebecca's hand, lifting her

wineglass with her other arm in a toast. "To the end of Colin. May he know what it is to be poor. And may he lie in bed every night regretting that he ever let you go."

"Indeed," Rebecca clinked her glass. "Poor sap. Anyway, stop changing the subject! Tell me more about Bookstore Guy. Is he as pretty as Colin? Please say he's not."

"Different," Laura said. "Totally cute, though. And he does seem nice. He spoke to Olivia when we were in the store yesterday— I was on the phone, and he helped her put a book away or something—and I couldn't hear what he said but it seemed sweet."

Rebecca went on, pondering the situation in her analytical way. "I think you should just talk to him. Say hi, say you want to take this to the next level—which is, actual in-person contact. Meet him! Learn his actual name! Go crazy!"

Laura shook her head. "He's making this very slow and deliberate on purpose. See how short that note is? This is how he wants to play it. And I kind of like it. It's a game. I'm OK with things being slow." Her gaze flickered toward a framed photo on a nearby shelf, of her and Sam laughing together at their wedding reception. The posed wedding pictures had long ago been put away (though Olivia loved to occasionally get them out and leaf through the album, gazing at her mother in a filmy gown with the handsome, bespectacled dad she couldn't remember), but Laura was deeply attached to this candid black-and-white shot taken by a friend. In it, neither she nor Sam seemed aware of the camera, only each other.

Rebecca noticed. (Rebecca noticed everything, a very satisfying trait in a best friend.) She nodded sympathetically. "This is hard. I know. But you're not being disloyal to Sam. I know I keep saying this, but don't you think he'd want you to be happy?"

"Well," Laura said slowly, "yes, but he'd want me to be happy with *him*. But, ultimately, I guess you're right. He would."

"Even in a weird, letter-writing way?"

"Especially that way. Remember how he wrote me all those

letters, when he was away on that internship before we were married? Handwritten letters in the mail, every day? With little drawings on them? He'd like this."

Rebecca nodded. There was a pause, the kind friends have, when silence takes as long as it needs to. Rebecca looked at Laura, her eyes soft.

"You sure you're ready?"

Laura, suddenly feeling a tear welling up, blinked hard and nodded. "Yes. And no. But there's only one way to find out. Maybe it's time? If it's ever going to be time? I don't think this guy is going to be the next love of my life or anything, but maybe he's a step that I need to take."

"OK," said Rebecca. "So you do it your way. Take it slow. What are you going to say to him next?"

"I don't know! I need to think about it." Laura changed the subject. "Did you end up buying that plaid Vivienne Westwood jacket I set aside for you at the store? It would be great for court, with a dark pencil skirt." Rebecca was always complaining that the lawyers at her downtown firm didn't dress as well as TV ones; Laura often tried to help.

"It was more than a thousand dollars! How rich do you think I am?" Rebecca sputtered.

"Richer than me!" Laura raised her glass, laughing. Just for this moment, everything was perfect.

19

April

In the movies, particularly rom-coms, women often have adorable brothers; handsome male doppelgängers who turn up at just the right moments in their attractive cable-knit sweaters and elaborately floppy hair, offering manly advice, familial support, and boyish charm. April's brother, Ben, was not that sort of brother. He was charming, sure, when he wanted to be, but mostly he was just boyish, and usually not in a good way. Ben was nearly thirty, and yet he never seemed to have grown up. He clung to a dream of being an actor, even though he'd never been cast in a professional production and barely seemed to be getting work in community theater. He mostly showed up at April's when he needed to borrow some cash, wheedlingly calling her "sis," a habit she suspected he'd picked up from the sitcom scripts he studied online. She usually acquiesced if it wasn't too much money, out of a sense of duty to her only sibling and a faint feeling that their mother would have wanted her to help her brother out (Ben didn't like asking their father, who never handed out money without a lecture), and tried not to resent the fact that Ben didn't work as hard as she did. She had always been the older sister, the responsible one.

April did work hard at being supportive of Ben. She had even attended the low-rent dinner theater production of *Waiting for*

Godot that Ben was cast in last winter. It was in a drafty warehouse in an industrial neighborhood south of the baseball stadium, and "dinner theater" was rather too grand a name for what it actually was: The food, which came in cardboard boxes, tasted like cardboard boxes. The play was lengthy and took place in various locations throughout the building, with the audience herded somewhere new for every scene, shuffling their feet and carrying their sad boxes of food with them. The constant moving around, April thought, wasn't actually a bad idea; a couple of the audience members looked like they might have dozed off otherwise. Ben was proud of the production and April tried to praise his performance—playing Lucky the servant, he had hardly any lines—without completely lying, which was something of a challenge. "It felt so . . . real" was the best she could come up with. She didn't comment on the food.

But it wasn't just a sense of duty to their mother that kept April in Ben's pocket. Ben, however frustrating he often was, was company.

Today, April had spent too much time trying to eavesdrop on Mr. Jackson and Tango Lady, who seemed to have struck up a friendship and were having a mysteriously low-voiced chat in the lobby when April returned from a walk. It was a distraction from Ben's latest text. When she'd finally followed up with his irritatingly spelled announcement of "newz," it turned out to be that he was planning a trip to London so he could listen to "regular blokes" and work on his British accent. And, of course, he wanted April to help him out with the plane ticket. Clearly it was time to do something that April always struggled to do with Ben: say no. She started to tap out a reply, then sighed and pressed her phone to call Ben's number.

He answered quickly. "Cheerio, mate!" he said in what appeared to be a terrible Australian accent, like Hugh Jackman on a bad day.

"I thought you were working on your British accent?" April

said, not bothering with a greeting. "That was sort of Australian with a side of Valley Girl."

"Thanks a lot," said Ben. "I'll have you know that I am working on an entire smorgasbord"—he rolled the word around, like it was a cough drop in his mouth—"of accents. That is what actors do."

"Right," said April, who'd heard all this before. "OK, fine. Just wanted to talk to you about your text. If you want to go to London, that's totally fine, knock yourself out, have a good time. But I'm not going to help you with the money for that. That's something you need to do yourself."

"Oh, come on!" said Ben. "You know I'll pay you back."

"I certainly do not know that," said April, who knew in her bones that hell would freeze over, thaw again, and liquify before Ben would ever pay his debts to her. She made a point of only lending him sums that she could live without.

"Well, you know I will. When some real work comes in. But in the meantime, I need to keep my skills up. Did I tell you I've got a movie opportunity? They need extras for an indie movie that's shooting at some bookstore. I think it's that one right by your place. I look like someone who would hang out in a bookstore, don't I?"

April paused, wondering if Ben had ever voluntarily been in a bookstore. "Sure," she said patiently. "Why not? That sounds promising. But to get back to the point: I'm not going to finance a London vacation for you. I'm happy to help you with rent or grocery money when you get stuck. You know that. But it's not fair for you to ask me for money for extras like overseas vacations. You should be supporting yourself. You're almost thirty years old, for God's sake."

"Well, not everybody can land a cushy tech job," Ben said, sounding like he was pouting a bit. You never could quite tell if Ben was expressing a real emotion, particularly on the phone. He may have just been, in this case, imitating Jesse Eisenberg in *The Social Network*.

"Never mind my cushy tech job. You need to have a plan," April said.

"I have a plan! You just don't approve of it. Because you're boring."

He was definitely pouting. April, a little hurt, was ready to end the call. "Calling somebody boring is not a great way to get them to lend you money," April said. "I need to go. Talk to you later. Love you." Darn it, she hadn't quite meant for those last two words to slip out. But she did love Ben, more than she would admit, despite how he aggravated her. He was still the baby brother that she'd wanted more than anything as a child.

"Love you too, sis. Bye."

Moving quickly before she lost her nerve, April closed her laptop, slipped on some shoes, and headed out the door, walking the short distance to Read the Room. It was time for action: She was going to ask L for coffee. Ben was right—she was boring but she had the power to change that. The late-afternoon light seemed promising, like the neighborhood was getting ready for its close-up.

Though the parking lot was full and the store brightly lit and bustling, April was greeted by a sign on the front door: "Closed Early for Filming—Reopening Tomorrow." Ah, this was the movie the bookseller had been talking about, the one Ben had mentioned. A bit relieved to be off the hook—the coffee invitation would have to wait for another day—April peered in the window, where lighting instruments made the store a shinier, happier version of itself. She recognized Kelly Drake by his impeccably coifed wavy hair, standing in an aisle with his head bent over his phone. Suddenly the store's front door opened unexpectedly, and April was nearly knocked down by a tall woman dressed in a vintage-looking business suit, her wide-legged trousers flapping in her haste. She either didn't see April or chose to ignore her as she hurried outside, stabbing at her phone with a long, ringed finger.

"It's Donna. Donna Wolfe. What do you *mean* Kelly Drake is

not available?" the woman hissed into her phone. Donna, whoever she was, had the kind of voice April associated with soap-opera villains. Intrigued, April got out her own phone and pretended to be busy on it while she eavesdropped.

"I don't care that it's a national spot. He is committed to *my* film. In Seattle. Which is shooting *now*. You need to fix this. NOW." The whole conversation sounded like a movie script, the sort in which a Katharine Hepburn–type talked fast and brooked no nonsense. April would not have wanted to be the person on the other end of the conversation, who she imagined to be holding the phone very far from their ear.

Not that it mattered what that person was saying; Donna Wolfe was having none of it. "That is not my problem," she said, with the confidence of someone accustomed to people being terrified of her. (April made a mental note to try to use this tone, and this phrasing, with Ben the next time he asked for money.) "Just fix it. Now. Good-bye." She stabbed at her phone, exhaled, adjusted the peplum on her jacket, and marched back through the front door, never giving the slightest hint of having noticed April, who watched in awe. This woman, whoever she was, had moxie, a word April was fond of for its old-school vibe. April slowly walked back home, savoring the moment and briefly forgetting about coffee with L, about the note in the book; it was as if, just for a second, she'd become part of a story bigger than herself, one in which the heroine was in charge.

Andrew

The best thing I ever found in a book was basically an entire novel on one small piece of paper: a list, written in the spidery handwriting of someone not young. It had names on it (Eileen, Sybil, Justin, Clare) and reminders ("winter clothes," "new movies") and curious observations ("fields of pumpkins," "squirrels banging on windows"). I took it home and stuck it in a mirror frame in my bedroom, and I think about it a lot: who wrote it, why the list was so random (the word "rain" appears, by itself), why there's something strangely haunting in its phrasing. I'll never find out the answers—there's no way I could ever track down who wrote it—and I kind of like that. Generally I approach life in a methodical way, like it's full of problems that can be solved if you just make the effort, and I found something moving in this reminder that life is full of mystery. I hope whoever wrote it is still out there, making lists and then losing them in books. Maybe someday I'll find another.

Anyway, I don't know why everyone got so excited about the movie. So far it just seems to have created more work for everyone. A few years ago, when I was new at the store, Julia agreed to let a local crew come in to film a few scenes for a commercial—it was for a glasses retailer, and I guess they wanted to show a book-filled atmosphere for their visually corrected customers?—and it was a complete fiasco. Even though it was just one day, it was way more trouble than they said it would be and the crew made a real mess and left permanent marks on the wood floors. They sent flowers the next day but that didn't go very far. Julia was apoplectic at the time, but now she seems to have completely forgotten about that. She's being very strange about this whole thing; I wonder if there's something she's not telling us? Is the store in trouble or something? She has seemed particularly stressed lately, and she mumbled something the other day about sending someone undercover *to The Book-Up—our competition, a neighborhood away—to see if any of our regulars have started going there instead.*

The rest of the staff seem pretty into the whole movie thing; Raven and Alejandra, especially, seem to think that a movie shoot is glamorous, no matter what. Me, I can do without it. It's kind of fun to peek at Kelly Drake though. I've never seen an actor up close. I would love to ask him what moisturizer he uses—his skin is truly amazing—but he doesn't seem particularly friendly.

I've been at the bookstore for almost three years now, but I don't think I'll be here much longer. I'm taking the LSAT this summer and hope to apply to law schools in the fall. People think I want to be a lawyer because I've streamed a lot of legal dramas, and they're not entirely wrong. It's true that I have seen The Good Wife *more times than I care to admit, and basically I want to be Christine Baranski in a tie. (I've practiced her take-off-the-glasses-in-court-and-glare routine; it actually works pretty well at the store with customers who want to know why we can't match Amazon's prices.) But there's more to it than that. It's the idea of law as something engraved, something set down that can be studied and learned, something that's there—at least in theory—for the good of all of us, and to allow us to coexist in society. I know that the law, and those who interpret it, can be deeply problematic but I want to be part of those conversations. Maybe, once I'm admitted to the bar, I'll work for the Innocence Project or Legal Aid. I'm hoping to do some good, somewhere.*

In the meantime, there are worse places to be than Read the Room, even during Moviegeddon, as Raven is not-so-cleverly calling it. It's a place that's normally very calm, except for this week. When I first started working here, I had a little crush on Westley— who doesn't? I mean, look at him; a face like that is totally wasted behind a used-books desk—but once I figured out that he was not only straight but also a little slow on the uptake, I moved on. I do like him as a colleague; he's quite considerate and is always willing to take a front desk shift if one of us needs a break. But mostly

I like gazing at him from afar. He is very pretty to look at, but it's also fun to watch the female customers getting all silly over him. The other day, I eavesdropped as a woman went up to him and asked for help finding a book that I'm 98 percent sure she made up on the spot, just so she could write down her number for him when he didn't find it on the computer. I asked Westley about it and he just shrugged, like this sort of thing happens to him all the time. Must be nice.

And then I noticed, just yesterday, that one of the film crew members was gazing at Westley: a man, midtwenties and quite cute (dressed like he was about to appear on the set of Bridgerton), *whose job seemed to involve hanging around near some costume racks, though he occasionally helped out with moving light fixtures or shelves when someone yelled for assistance. (These people are the bane of Julia's existence; she seems to have agreed to the movie not realizing that there would be heavy, potentially floor-scratching equipment involved, despite the fiasco with the commercial.) The guy kept trying to engage Westley in conversation, which is difficult to do even if you're not flirting with him—Westley's just not much of a talker—and I felt bad for him. So when I was tidying up my assigned section (I'm currently handling History and Self-Help), I tried to catch his eye.*

"Hi," he said. "Cute store you have here. Very camera-ready. Very dusty chic."

I wasn't sure whether or not to be insulted, particularly after how much time all of us had been spending dusting the shelves, on Julia's orders. "Ha!" I said. "So what's your job?"

"I'm a costume assistant," he said grandly but sardonically, letting me hear the capital letters. "Which doesn't mean much. I just help out with whatever, outfit-wise. Has it been fun for you guys at the store?"

"It's something different, I guess," I said. "The customers are kind of into it." This was starting to seem like a real conversation, so I took a deep breath. "I'm Andrew."

"Sydney," he said, offering a hand. "Delighted. Have you worked here for a long time?"

I know a halfhearted pickup line when I hear it, particularly when it's one I want to hear. "A few years," I said. "It's a nice place. I hope the owner's been helpful during the shoot."

"The lady with the spiky gray hair? The one who always looks like she's about to shoot laser beams out her eyes?"

"Yes, that's Julia." It was actually a pretty good description.

Sydney shook his head. "She's kind of intense," he said. "Everyone's trying to be as low-maintenance as possible, but there's no way to shoot in a bookstore without disturbing some of the books, know what I mean?"

I did and nodded. Julia's kind of fanatical about the appearance of the store, even when we're not actively shooting anything. If she had her way, the shelves would be tidied every hour, and I think in her dreams she has some kind of electronic system that beeps loudly whenever a book is out of its proper alphabetical slot. Alejandra likes to talk about the glory of discovery, and how it can be quite meaningful for a customer to find a book that's out of place (because, she reasons, that's the book they're meant to find; Alejandra has a sort of spiritual approach to bookselling, which we've all decided to find charming), but Julia's not buying any of it. She wants everything perfect.

"So," Sydney continued, "what's the name of the guy at the desk in the back? The one in the flannel shirt?"

Westley's flannel shirts annoy me, partly because it's summer and who wears flannel shirts when it's hot out? (Perhaps I'm not one to speak; I wear blazers all the time, because I think they make an outfit look nicely polished. Nobody else dresses up for work at Read the Room. But I like looking a bit distinctive, and I've learned you can get great jackets at thrift stores if you go to the ones in fancy neighborhoods.) Anyway, I think somebody once told Westley that he looks good in flannel shirts; he has quite a collection of plaid ones, in soft colors. He looks like a Seattle poster boy in them—seriously, put him on a calendar and everyone would move here, despite the rain. "That's Westley," I said. "He's the only one of us on the staff who looks good enough to be cast in the movie."

"Oh, I wouldn't say that," said Sydney, looking at me appraisingly, which was highly unnecessary but I appreciated it all the same. "Do you happen to know if he's single?"

"Yes, he is," I said. Sydney is not the first gay man to ask me this question, in hopeful tones; I have had to disappoint quite a few Read the Room customers with my next words. "And straight, too. Sorry."

"Really?" Sydney looked over at Westley's desk again, where he was sipping a coffee and frowning at something on his screen, in that cute way he always does. "Huh. Well, maybe I know someone who might like to meet him. A colleague of mine. She's in need of . . . well, something like that." He raised an eyebrow in Westley's direction.

"Well, good luck with that," I said. "See you later."

"Hang on," said Sydney, sighing a bit as he turned his head away from Westley's direction. He looked at me and started to smile. "I don't suppose you'd have coffee with me sometime? Or have I completely screwed things up here?"

"No," I said, returning the smile slowly. I've never gotten Westley's leftovers before, but hey, why not? "My next break is at three. Want to meet me in the café? To talk about something other than Westley?"

"I'll be there," Sydney said. "See ya." He grinned one last time and walked away, whistling a tune that might have been from Cats. I chose to ignore that fact. Did I say that the moviemaking in the store was annoying? Some days it isn't so bad.

20

Westley

I t was strange, Westley often thought, that people both love to buy books and love to get rid of them. It seemed to happen in cycles. Every January, a pile of pristine-looking cookbooks would make their way to the used-books desk at Read the Room, many of them with a handwritten message on the title page saying something like "Merry Christmas! Here's to some delicious meals! XO." Mysteries, read avidly throughout the winter months (particularly those of the cozy variety), would arrive in large numbers in the spring, as people cleared out their groaning shelves. Bestsellers—long family sagas, popular showbiz biographies, romance—showed up in the fall, sometimes smelling a bit mildewy, like they got left overnight in a tote bag alongside a damp towel and maybe just a hint of sand. And all year round, certain trendy books—the ones at the very top of the *New York Times* lists, the ones everyone seems to be talking about for just a few days or weeks—turned up regularly, their pages still crisp but their usefulness over.

Westley himself, despite his love of reading, didn't own many books. He liked to keep his belongings to a minimum, easily fitting into one bedroom or a borrowed car's trunk, and once he'd finished a book, he usually didn't see much need to keep it around. Only a few true favorites, like his childhood copy of *The*

Wonderful Wizard of Oz and a few more recent books like *A Gentleman in Moscow* and *Deacon King Kong*, stayed with him, awaiting a moment of delicious rereading. But between his Read the Room staff discount and the credit he received for returning books, the store basically acted as a lending library for him. Once a month or so, he'd bring in a small pile of books and would purchase—with little or no cash—another small pile. It made him feel wealthy. Enough books, he thought, was all that you needed.

Making a movie involved a great deal of standing around waiting for things to happen, and as work seemed to have ground to a halt this Wednesday afternoon, Westley took the opportunity to go online to look, not for the first time, at Duke Munro's website. *Shivering Timbers* had stayed with Westley, and he'd realized uncomfortably that part of the reason was that, forest fires aside, it reminded him of his relationship with Bridget, in the way the two characters seemed to have an immediate, vivid spark. The difference was, of course, that the fictional relationship had a happy ending. The main male character in the book, Will, seemed a bit like Westley himself: a man who didn't talk much and wasn't entirely sure of himself but who fell hard for Verity "the way a noble oak falls after a touch from a brave man's saw." Westley hadn't had any luck finding evidence of other books by Munro, but he wondered if they were out there somewhere, and if they might also give him that strange sensation of finding a bit of himself on the page.

It seemed odd to Westley that this author, who clearly had talent and was filling a rare manly romance niche, was so obscure. Munro's website had the quaint look of having been made by someone in the early days of the internet; its colors were oddly flat and it had too many words, rendered in a font that looked both sensible and unintentionally retro, and not enough pictures. But it did have an email address under "Contact Duke": dukemunro@hotmail.com. Westley wasn't even sure if Hotmail addresses still worked—he hadn't seen one in a long time—but he had nothing better to do while the crew argued lengthily about camera angles, so he clicked on it and began typing.

TO: dukemunro@hotmail.com
FROM: westleybooks@freemail.com
SUBJECT: Your novel

Hello, Mr. Munro—you don't know me, but I work for the Seattle bookstore Read the Room and recently discovered your novel, *Shivering Timbers*. I really enjoyed it and am wondering if you have written other books? Your website looks like it hasn't been updated for a long time, so I don't know if this will reach you but thought it was worth a try. Anyway, thanks for the good read.

Westley wasn't normally in the habit of writing directly to strangers, but this one seemed like a shot worth taking. He'd dreamed now and then, during his time at Read the Room, of becoming a sort of bookstore superhero by finding some obscure novel, maybe by a local author, and helping bring it to prominence. But as soon as he clicked Send, his attention was distracted by the ongoing drama of the movie (aside from the movie's actual scripted drama). Kelly Drake and Donna Wolfe were having a brief, highly vocal exchange, causing Donna to flounce out the front door in a huff calling someone on her cell, while Kelly pouted attractively over in Science Fiction. An assistant hurried over to Kelly with a bottle of water that the actor elaborately refused, while Gayle, the makeup person, hovered nearby, ever-present powder brush at the ready.

Donna breezed back through the front door, her jaw set. "Let's continue," she told the assistant director, Erica, who looked terrified as usual. "Kelly, please take your place."

"I'm sorry, Donna," said Kelly, as if speaking to a small child. "I need to leave today. I can't shoot all these little scenes before I go. Have an extra do them, or I can do them when I get back. But I'm getting on a plane at two o'clock and you can't stop me. That commercial pays more than ten of your movies and I need the money. I'm buying a house on Queen Anne. It has air-conditioning." (Queen Anne Hill, Westley noted with interest, was a very expensive Seattle neighborhood, one he'd never dreamed of living in; commercials must pay quite a lot.)

Donna closed her eyes, speaking through clenched teeth: "You are under contract. You are not allowed to leave this production. If you do, I will sue you."

Kelly, it appeared, was not a graduate of the University of Washington School of Drama for nothing. "So sue me," he said, letting the words hang in the air. "I've got a plane to catch." He collected his leather backpack from his stunned-looking assistant, waved a hand in the air, and marched out the door in a performance easily as good as anything he'd ever done on camera.

Everyone was silent—Julia, for one, looked like she'd swallowed a fly—as if a play had suddenly gone off-script and nobody knew where the prompt book was. Donna and Erica seemed briefly frozen in time. Westley, fascinated, had to fight the temptation to burst into applause. But he quickly became aware that Donna had broken the pause and was staring directly at him in a way that felt unnerving.

"You," she said, very deliberately, like she was thinking something out. "Behind the counter. The handsome one."

"Uh, me?" said Westley. Donna had not spoken to him directly since the first day of shooting. Occasionally she would point in his direction and murmur something to an assistant, who would come bounding over with some vague and not at all helpful instruction like "let us see your silence," or "make your eyes catch the light" or something, but mostly she ignored him. He had felt that she considered him like a book on a shelf, just part of the scenery.

"Yes. You. You can take Kelly's part."

"What?" said Westley.

"What?" said the assistant director.

"What?" said Julia, looking like she'd now digested the fly and moved on to something unexpectedly spicy.

"WHAT???" said Raven, who had been quietly watching from a corner and could not contain her dismay.

"Yes," said Donna slowly, no longer looking at Westley but gazing off into the distance, picturing something or someone. "He's the right height. We don't need to see his face. Kelly's right: We've finished most of his scenes here and he's shot the rest in the studio. We can use *him*, and shoot around him, and dub Kelly's voice in. We just need a body, and this one will do."

"Um, I'm not an actor?" Westley volunteered, a little peeved at being referred to as "this one" and "a body." Nobody paid any attention to him. Donna and the assistant director were strategizing in low voices. Raven shot dark looks at him from across the room. Westley remembered, fleetingly, his high school drama teacher, who likely would have told him to seize the opportunity. He wasn't sure if this was what she had in mind.

21

Laura

Laura had never in her life left an anonymous note for anyone. Since childhood, she'd had a sense that such an act couldn't possibly turn out well; she hadn't even kept a diary, or a notebook, fearing that someone might accidentally discover it and read her innermost thoughts. (The fate of *Harriet the Spy* may well have played a part here; Laura had read and loved the book many times as a child but couldn't make it through the last third, or even think about it, without a feeling of dread that seemed to swell in her stomach. How horrible to have people find your private notebook and know what you thought of them, as if they could read your mind! Luckily Olivia wasn't yet quite old enough for *Harriet the Spy*; Laura didn't think she, or her stomach, was quite up to reading it aloud.) After more than a week, she still hadn't responded to A's latest note, and wasn't sure where to begin. It was a little weird that A knew about Laura's job—was it stalkerish? Or just sweet?

"Hel-loo-oo," sang out Sydney tunefully, interrupting Laura's reverie. "You look like you're in another world. Wake up. The vintage director lady is here, ready for you."

"You mean Donna Wolfe?"

"The very same. I think she's wearing eighties Saint Laurent today. I offered her a beverage and she looked at me like I was a stain on silk. Didn't even recognize me from toiling away on her production, long hours for little pay. I'd be offended if I wasn't such an easygoing chap."

"You are the opposite of easygoing," said Laura fondly; she saw Sydney as the entertaining if high-maintenance little brother she hadn't known she'd always wanted. But she was nervous for this session. As promised, Donna Wolfe's assistant had arranged a second appointment after the badly botched first one, and Laura had once again scoured every corner of the store in search of outfits. Having now seen Donna in person, she had a more specific idea of her client's rather unique taste, which seemed to meet at a dramatic intersection of vintage clothing collector, slightly pretentious art teacher, and power businesswoman. She wondered, while making her selections, why someone with such strong opinions didn't just do her own shopping. But Laura had a few clients like this: women who loved fashion and had definite opinions on what they liked but just didn't have the time or energy to shop for those specific garments. That was fine as long as they were good at explaining what they wanted—which Donna Wolfe, unfortunately, was not. Laura reviewed the rack of garments, making sure everything looked perfectly pressed and fresh, refreshed her lipstick in the office mirror, breathed deeply, and marched into the waiting area.

Donna Wolfe, wearing a faintly musty-looking brocade pantsuit and carrying a walking stick that she seemed to be using a little too elaborately, was standing, looking impatient (though it was hard to judge her expression behind those habitual dark glasses) and rummaging through her enormous leather tote. "Good morning, Ms. Wolfe," Laura said. "I'm so glad you returned. Please follow me to the dressing room."

After seating Donna in a cushiony chair—Laura's offer of a beverage was, like Sydney's, brushed away like an annoying bug—Laura moved in front of the rack. "I'm sorry we didn't see eye to eye last time," she said. "Since then I've been carefully studying your style, and I think we might have found some things to your liking." Donna often turned up at gala events in Los Angeles and New York, and Laura had spent some time online examining what she chose to wear on such occasions, which tended to be dark, dramatic, and like something you might have found in a trunk in a very posh attic.

"I hope so," said Donna. "I have very little time today." Her phone was beeping regularly, like a heart monitor in a hospital. "Please proceed."

Laura smiled automatically; she'd had experience with rude customers before, and at least Donna represented an interesting world. Making her strongest presentation first, Laura lifted from the rack an utterly simple black silk column gown, with long sleeves and a plain neckline. "I imagined this," she said, "with some very large statement jewelry. I know you have a remarkable collection of vintage pieces. This dress is simply an elegant background . . ." She looked at Donna, who was looking at her phone. Laura couldn't quite make out her expression, but above the sunglasses her eyebrows rose as if trying to depart her face.

"Ms. Wolfe? I'm sorry, do you need a moment?"

Donna sighed heavily, pressed something on her phone, then looked up, gazing at the dress for a split second before turning away from Laura, lost in her own thoughts. "Indeed. That will be fine. Please order it in a size eight, and I'll send my assistant over so it can be hemmed and fitted. She is my exact size."

"But . . . don't you want to see the other garments I've pulled for you?" Laura asked, in disbelief that it could be so easy (and dismay that she'd put in so much time).

"No. This will be fine. I'm afraid I must go. Thank you for your help." And just like that, she was gone, too distracted to remember to use the walking stick.

Sydney watched Donna's retreating form. "Well, that appointment lasted maybe ninety seconds, tops," he said. "Why do you think she was so particular last time, and so easy this time? And is that a regular rich-lady thing, to have an assistant who is her exact size? Do you think that's in the job description?"

"I don't know," said Laura, puzzled and faintly amused. "Something was on her mind. I wonder what." She was accustomed to imperious clients, but there was something theatrical about Donna that was fascinating, like there was a spotlight shining on her that only Donna could see. Maybe people in movies were more dramatic than everyone else; maybe it wasn't always clear to them which side of the camera they were on.

Sydney returned the black dress to the rack. "I think you're right, like you always are," he said. "This will look good on her. It matches her glasses, and it'll make her look like an extremely chic witch. Which is appropriate."

"Don't talk about our clients that way," Laura admonished, smiling. "So . . . how is the movie shoot going? Is it fun?"

"Well . . . I will say yes," Sydney replied dramatically, which was how he said most things. "I met someone. He works there. He's cute. We're going for sushi tomorrow."

Laura paused, mid-keystroke at the computer where she was ordering the dress for Donna. "Oh wow, really?" she said, as casually as she could manage. "Um, what does he do there?"

"Whatever it is they do at bookstores. You know, sells books. Why?"

"Just curious, I guess," Laura said, careful to not look at Sydney. "I was in there the other day. There . . . was a cute guy at the used-books desk. Is that who you mean?"

"Oh, you mean Timothée Chalamet's flannel-loving older brother? I wish!" said Sydney, eyeing Laura with elaborate casualness. "No, I checked him out for sure, but word on the street is that he's straight. My guy works up front. He's sweet. Terrible dresser—he wears tired old blazers that are way too big for him—but I can work with that."

Laura, instantly relaxed, beamed at Sydney. Read the Room really was full of stories. Tonight, after Olivia was in bed, she would reply to A's note.

TO: All Read the Room Staff
FROM: julia@readtheroom.com
SUBJECT: News on movie shoot

Good morning, everyone. Just wanted to confirm the news that some of you may have heard: Our very own Westley now has an expanded role in *Shelf Consciousness*, due to the unexpected absence of actor Kelly Drake (as many of you may know if you were present during the unfortunately loud conversations regarding that absence). I am told that it will not take very much time, as most of the scenes involving Kelly were already shot. But please do help out Westley if you can with his duties, as he may not have as much time to do his work in the next few days.

Thank you all for your patience with the movie process. Reminder: Do NOT help the movie staff to move books or shelves, and notify me IMMEDIATELY if you see them doing so. We had an agreement on this matter. I continue to be unable to reach the production manager, who left me a vague voicemail suggesting that I chill out. I don't think he understands that he is not in charge of the store. Please continue to be vigilant.

Julia

22

April

There really wasn't anyone in April's life whom she could tell about the anonymous correspondence, which felt odd; it was the thing most occupying her mind these days. Maybe it would have been something she could have told her mother, once upon a time. Grief had ebbed over the years, but this was still an open wound—that she had lost her mother right at the age when they could have been adults together, enjoying each other's company. She had a photo of her mother in her apartment, young and laughing. Though the two of them had certainly had their share of disagreements when April was growing up, she preferred to remember her mother as she was in that picture, forever happy.

Or maybe she could have told Janie, back when Janie was more emotionally available to her. April didn't blame Janie a bit, or at least told herself she didn't, and often wondered how on earth a person was supposed to attend to a partner, multiple small children, a job, and a home without completely falling apart. April had no partner, no kids, work that wasn't particularly demanding, and an apartment that she didn't own, and yet even for her, life sometimes felt completely overwhelming, with just too many things to remember to do. (She had a vague feeling that her renter's insurance policy needed updating but couldn't find the energy to figure out how.) Her friendship with Janie was in a different phase now, but she firmly believed they'd return to each other eventually.

Ideally, it wouldn't take too long. She loved Janie's children, and enjoyed buying things for them and making a fuss on their birthdays, but why was it so difficult for a person with kids and a person without kids to be friends? Would it get better when the kids were older? April knew that her life was less complicated than Janie's, and therefore it made sense that she would be the one to be more flexible, but it still irked her. And then it irked her that it irked her. April was determined to be a good person about it all. In fact, she was going to send her a text right now.

Hey! Miss you! Would love to get together sometime; I actually have something I'd love to talk to you about. I might have met someone. ♥

She received no answer.

There was always Ben, who returned her texts promptly, if grammatically questionably. But telling Ben anything personal was usually a mistake. April remembered, years ago, confiding in her brother after she and Josh had broken up. Ben had asked a lot of questions and had seemed at the time genuinely concerned and sympathetic—and then April found out, a few months later, that he'd turned the whole story into a monologue for his acting class, and that members of the class wanted to ask questions about her objectives. "I thought you'd be flattered," Ben had said when she'd confronted him at the time. "Usually nobody listens enough to have any questions. Obviously, I really sold it."

In any case, there was no one with which to discuss the fact that L (Logan? Lee? Liam? Ludwig?) hadn't written back after a week. Sure, he seemed pretty busy—that movie being shot over at Read the Room seemed to have taken on a life of its own. (Visiting the store now was a strange experience; it seemed like a brighter, less-real copy of the Read the Room that she knew.) But if he was really interested—and wasn't he, since he'd written back so quickly after the first note?—it seemed to April that he wouldn't have waited this long. Turning to the pile of second-hand mystery novels she'd bought at Read the Room before the weekend began, she was determined not to push. This needed to flow at whatever speed felt right. She could wait. She could read. Books always made time for her.

A text lit up her phone. Janie? No, it was that unknown number again, and it made April sad to think how thrilled she was for a half-second to think it was her friend.

Why won't u come back. The kids miss u.

This had been going on for some time; April had initially thought it was some sort of scam, but lately she'd wondered if there was some real drama behind this story (other texts had made reference to a car, a possible affair, and some sort of tax fraud; really, it was practically a novel). April had never replied before but she suddenly felt for the person sending these messages. Maybe it was time to put a stop to it. April typed a response.

I'm sorry, but you are texting this to the wrong number.

April did not believe in using abbreviations in texts, like "u" for "you," and always typed in fully punctuated sentences—unlike Janie, whose infrequent texts were sometimes almost impossible to read, just a murky soup of consonants and emojis.

The reply was quick.

Is that u Henry? I know it is! Come home and we just wont say anything about the car.

April wondered what exactly Henry had done with the car, and why the person texting him had such an intimate knowledge of his life and yet didn't know what his correct cell number was. Knowing that she shouldn't engage (why not just block the number?) but unable to stop now that she had started, she texted back.

Not Henry, just a random person at this number. You have the wrong number for him.

Back came the answer, in just a few seconds.

OK Henry. Have it ur way. Just come back NOW pls.

April blocked the number. This story had suddenly become real, and she didn't feel she needed to know its ending.

23

Westley

Duke Munro, oddly enough, had written back to Westley very quickly, calling him "my brother" and telling him that yes, he'd written two other novels (which he called "humble yarns") but they were out of print. He'd signed his email "'Til the creek runs dry, Duke." Westley wasn't at all sure that this person was for real—could this oddly folksy persona be part of an elaborate identity de plume?—but he was interested enough to make a mental note to do some searching on the store's book database for those other books when he had a few minutes.

It would be a pleasant-enough distraction to what was becoming a bigger and bigger problem. Kelly Drake had left the movie and Donna Wolfe had decided that Westley could be his stand-in— Westley thought that was the expression she used, but he hadn't really been consulted so it was hard to know—until Kelly could return. Apparently, they could film Westley and later dub in Kelly's voice; there were camera angles that would obscure Westley's face. The two men were of similar height and build, but even at that Westley couldn't see how this could work, and why it wouldn't just make more sense to wait for Kelly to come back. He'd asked Joe, the production manager, that very question, and Joe had responded with a lot of garbled words about production costs and below-the-line expenses and set shooting dates, none of which made any sense. In any case, Westley was stuck. He could refuse, he supposed, but then he'd be responsible for delaying the movie and causing financial problems for the production, and thus for the store. Joe had managed to make that much abundantly clear. Ah well, he was getting a bit more money for this—they'd added a small bonus to his contract as an extra—so he shouldn't complain.

"Hey, Leonardo DiCaprio, do you have anything ready for shelving?"

It was Raven, with her habitual sarcasm dialed up a few extra notches; she was smiling, rather too broadly. Something was clearly bothering her; maybe, Westley wondered, she was feeling bad because she wasn't in the movie. This was exactly why Westley was reluctant to take on a larger role in the film: He had worried it would cause resentment among his colleagues, whom he liked and whose goodwill mattered to him. Though Andrew and Alejandra seemed content enough to watch the proceedings and had cheerfully congratulated Westley on his role, Raven obviously had some issues with it, and even Julia often seemed like she wished the entire film would just go away. She was now referring to it as "Westley's movie" at staff meetings, which annoyed him to no end. Really, there were only supposed to be a few more days of filming in the evenings and then it would all be over. It wasn't that big a deal.

"Yes, these ones," said Westley, sliding a stack of books over his desk. "I'm going to get a coffee. You want anything?"

"Don't you have an assistant to do that for you?" Raven asked, deadpan.

This did not seem worth answering. Westley navigated the maze of bookshelves and made his way to the café, where the weekday barista, Oscar, nodded at him and made his favorite coffee (latte, extra foam) without Westley needing to ask. Westley had noticed that often in life, people would do things for him without him needing to ask. He vaguely knew that this was because of his looks, which seemed quite unfair, so he tried to be extra polite (and to tip as well as he could afford) to make up for it.

Alejandra was sitting in the café on her break, a plate of nearly finished pastry and a notebook with scribbled handwriting in front of her. She was gazing into space, but broke out of her reverie as Westley approached, closing the notebook quickly. "Hey," she said. "The scones are good today. Lemon raspberry."

The café, Charlotte's Web, operated as a parallel universe to the bookstore: It had a separate owner and its own staff, rules, and regulations. Read the Room employees used it as a break room, buying pastries with their discount and wondering what it might be like to be slinging coffee and baked goods instead of books. Each group of employees eyed the other with curiosity, the way you wonder about a closed society, but kept to themselves; you rarely saw a romance, or even an in-depth conversation, between the aproned and the nonaproned. Rumors flew among the bookstore staff about the current pastry chef, who arrived at an absurdly early hour, made meltingly buttery scones and muffins, and apparently was going through some sort of identity crisis in which he was considering becoming a cobbler.

"Oh, so Sergio's still baking? He hasn't left us to make shoes yet?" Westley said.

"Apparently not. Though I guess for shoes you don't have to get up so early? Want to join me?"

Westley sat down opposite Alejandra, who broke off a piece of what remained of her scone and handed it to him. "Thanks. How's the writing going?" he asked her, believing this was the sort of question you asked writers.

"It's OK," she said, clearly not wanting to engage with the topic. "It's fine. How do you like being a movie star?"

Westley sighed. He was getting this question a lot these days. "Well, I'm barely going to be visible in the movie, so it's hardly like being a movie star," he said. "I kind of wish I'd never gotten into it. It's just a lot of standing around, really."

"Well, I think it's exciting," Alejandra said. "I've never seen a movie made close up. Did you see how last night Donna Wolfe made the lighting guy reposition all the lights, over and over? And it looked exactly the same every time? I guess she can see things that we can't."

Westley had seen it; in fact, he had been standing in the bookstore aisle throughout the entire drama, wondering if he would be allowed to move but concluding that it was safest to stay put. (He had gotten yelled at previously by Fedora for straying from his mark.) "I guess so," he said. "She's kind of demanding."

"I think she's amazing," said Alejandra. "I love her outfits. And I love how she knows exactly what she wants. She's got Julia totally stressed and it's fun to watch." It was true that Julia had been especially on edge lately. She'd had to admit defeat in her crusade to prevent the crew from moving the books and the shelves, every act of which seemed to cause Julia actual physical pain. Westley was not the only one to regret agreeing to the movie. He had spotted Julia in the book storage room, muttering some sort of calming meditation through gritted teeth.

"Do you think this movie's going to be any good?" Westley asked. "I mean, we haven't seen the screenplay or anything, but it does seem sort of weird. A bookstore portal into the inside of a book? Is that what it is?"

"I think it sounds kind of great," Alejandra said. "That's why we read books, right? To disappear into other worlds? The screenplay's just taking that idea and running with it. It's creative."

Westley looked at Alejandra's closed notebook, for the first time wondering what it might contain. "Are you writing something like that?" he asked.

"Not really. I guess it's also a fantasy. But I don't want to talk about it." She smiled shyly. "It's like trying to describe a person you haven't actually met yet. Too soon."

"I understand," said Westley, who really didn't, but who was suddenly and pleasantly realizing that Alejandra was nice to talk to. "Um, have you been a writer for a long time?"

"Oh yes," said Alejandra. "Always, really. Do you write at all? Is that why you work here?"

Westley was taken aback by the question; it wasn't the sort he usually got. "No," he said. "I love to read, though. I'd love to read whatever you're writing, sometime."

"Maybe sometime," Alejandra said vaguely.

The conversation paused. Maybe Westley had overstepped; maybe this wasn't what you were supposed to say. "I guess I'd better get back to my desk," he said. "Julia warned me that some professor died and we're getting her entire library of used books today."

"I should get back too," said Alejandra, taking one last bite of scone and gathering up her notebook. "See you later."

Westley looked down and saw that he had forgotten to drink his coffee.

24

Laura

It was odd to feel so lightheaded. Laura couldn't remember the last time she'd felt all tingly and excited, as if something wonderful was waiting for her somewhere, around a corner that she couldn't quite name. She had finally responded to the note, after taking maybe too long and wondering if A was frustrated with waiting. But this was the next step in an elaborate dance, and she wanted it to be just right. After some consultation with Rebecca, and numerous false starts on the pale-yellow notepaper she'd been saving for an unknown occasion, she finally came up with an answer that felt good, the right balance of light and depth.

She'd dropped it off this morning, after delivering Olivia to school; the bookstore had just opened and felt quiet and a bit unformed, like it was still waking up. Laura felt self-conscious going into Young Adult to hide her note, so she made a quick detour on her way out to the children's section, grabbing the Amelia Bedelia book that Olivia had been eyeing the other day. She wondered why it was that certain books stuck with kids for generations—she remembered reading Amelia Bedelia when she was around Olivia's age and giggling about cutting the flowers and drawing the drapes—and others faded away. A was at his desk but barely looked up and didn't notice her (clearly he was having a busy morning, Laura told herself), and Laura's purchase at the front desk was handled by a young man in a blazer—maybe this was Sydney's new flame?—who seemed eager to get back to whatever he was looking at on his phone.

Mondays were strange days for Laura, whose workweek was Wednesday through Sunday. Ashley had the day off, and after Laura had gotten Olivia up and dressed, packed her Hello Kitty lunchbox, and walked her to school, the townhouse always seemed so very quiet when she returned. There wasn't much to do—Ashley, for all her idiosyncrasies, was good at keeping the house tidy—and Laura often found herself wandering from room to room, looking for somewhere to alight, something to devote herself to. Back from the bookstore this morning, she opened her laptop, paid a few bills, made a shopping list for later (Laura mostly ordered her groceries online to save time, but Olivia loved occasional outings to the supermarket), and wondered about A.

Why would a person, Laura thought, reach out to someone through a note, rather than speaking? Why would a person work for a long time in a store where their job seemed to be just the same thing over and over? Why would a man so good-looking need to resort to anonymous notes to a stranger? None of it made any sense, and the more Laura pondered the situation, the more it seemed to call for drastic action. The whole thing was just so puzzling, and it was hard enough for Laura to get her head around the idea of being involved with another man, let alone one who behaved in such a mysterious way. Maybe Rebecca was right. Maybe she needed to seize the moment. Maybe she needed to raise the stakes a bit: to give him something of herself, more than just her latest note. Clearly this situation needed a bit of a jump-start.

It didn't take long for her to decide what to do. After a quick rummage through her kitchen, Laura swiftly made a batch of chocolate chip cookies—one of the few things she regularly baked, due to the sweet tooth she and Olivia shared; she even had the recipe memorized—and arranged a still-warm assort-ment of them nicely in a Tupperware. Without giving herself time to change her mind, she headed out to her car and drove back to Read the Room, taking what she was beginning to think of as "her" space in the store parking lot.

Ignoring the small group of employees at the front desk, Laura marched bravely toward the used-books desk over on the side of the store, where A sat at his computer. He looked up as she ap-proached, clearly surprised to see somebody carrying not a pile of books but a container of cookies.

"Hi," said Laura, taking a deep breath and putting the Tupper-ware down. "These are for you."

He blinked, looking surprised—as, Laura supposed, he well might. People usually brought weary-looking used books to this desk, not boldly delivered fresh homemade treats. "Um, thank you," he said.

Laura waited for that glorious moment of realization that comes in the final scene of a rom-com, when the two people who've been kept apart by circumstances are finally united, and the music swells and the lighting suddenly looks magical. It didn't come. Nothing came, just awkward silence. The man stared at her, looking like he was hoping that someone, anyone, would come along and bail him out of the moment.

"I just thought you might like them," she faltered.

"They look delicious," he said, looking at the cookies as if it was a welcome break from looking at her. "Wow. That's so nice of you. Thank you again."

This was just too awkward, and clearly a huge mistake. "OK," said Laura, suddenly wanting to be anywhere but in this book-store. "See you later. Bye."

"OK. Bye," said the man, clearly flustered. "Thank you. Again."

Laura spun around and quickly walked out of the store. Back in her car, which still smelled faintly of warm chocolate and nuts, she rested her forehead in her hands, exhaled, and fished her phone out of her bag.

"Hey," Rebecca said. "Just got out of a meeting. What's up? Did you leave the note?"

"Yes," said Laura. "But I think I screwed up! Why am I such an idiot?"

"You're not an idiot," said Rebecca calmly. "What happened?"

"Well, I thought it was time to move things along, so I baked chocolate chip cookies—you know, the ones Livvy likes?—and brought them over to him at the store. But it was a big, big mistake. He looked at me like I was just some strange customer. Or a crazy stalker."

"Oh, wow. I thought you were all about respecting the slow pace of this thing?"

"Well, I was," said Laura, annoyed with herself and with Rebecca's reaction. "But then I wasn't. I think I wanted to make things move faster."

"Rookie mistake," said Rebecca soothingly. "He's the one who initiated this, so he gets to set the pace. You jumped the line and made him all nervous and skittery. He's got a plan, and you've thrown him off a bit."

Laura hadn't considered this. Was that face at the book desk an expression of disinterest, or of dismay that things weren't proceeding according to plan? It could have been the latter? "Oh God," she said. "I am so not good at this. I'm out of practice. Maybe the note was never for me in the first place. Maybe I just imagined this whole thing. Why did you let me do this? This is so embarrassing!"

"Hold on. Calm down." Rebecca was always so reassuringly positive. "You're always so hard on yourself. You did not imagine this, and that guy, whoever he is, would be *so* lucky to have you, and your cookies are awesome, and he is going to enjoy them, and once he gets his head around things, I think this will turn out to be a good development."

"OK. If you think so. I'm sitting in the bookstore parking lot right now, mad at myself. Would it be weird to start screaming in the car?"

"Yes. Go home!" said Rebecca. "Relax. It's your day off. I have another meeting and I have to go. Love you!"

"Love you too," said Laura, ending the call. She wondered, not for the first time, how people without friends ever managed to get through the day.

25

Westley

The cookies were not the problem. They were delicious—
sweetly chewy, with pillows of chocolate and a soft hint of
vanilla. No, it was just odd that a random woman whose
name he didn't even know had delivered them—and had then
stood there like she expected something from Westley. He wasn't
a stranger to women bringing him things, by any means; during
his brief career in college, girls were always showing up at his
dorm-room door with offerings of food or flowers or concert tick-
ets, and just last week a friend of Cory's had brought over a cake,
claiming she couldn't eat it due to allergies and then had hung
around for a long time trying to make conversation and smiling a
lot, until Westley pretended he had to leave for work—but it hadn't
really happened at the store, and certainly not from a stranger.

Well, technically she wasn't a "stranger," really. Westley had
seen her in the store before with her little girl; she had curly hair
and a quiet, elegant way of dressing. He remembered both of
them being in just the other day, and that he'd spoken briefly to
her daughter, who was cute and bouncy and seemed quite comfortable chatting with adults. He'd noticed the woman in the
same way he noticed all the repeat customers—vaguely registering her presence, but no more. (Julia encouraged the Read the
Room staff to pay attention to the customers and be especially

welcoming to regulars; Alejandra, in particular, was good at remembering the names of people who came in a lot.) Maybe this
woman had mistaken him for somebody else? Was she asking
him out? Was that how some women asked men out? Did he even
want to go out with a stranger who made random gestures involving baked goods? Did he need to give the Tupperware back?
It all seemed like too much.

Raven walked by, pushing a cart with new books on it, and
paused. "Those look good," she said, noticing the cookies. "Can I
have one?"

"Sure, help yourself," Westley said. "Um, you didn't happen to
see a woman bringing these in, did you? A woman with curly
hair, dressed sort of nice?"

"No. Why? Who is she?" Raven instantly looked suspicious, her
features suddenly becoming more alert. She was known for pouting a bit when strange things happened that she wasn't briefed on.

Belatedly, Westley realized that it was a mistake bringing this
up with Raven, who today was wearing her "Tell the truth but tell
it slant" Emily Dickinson T-shirt under a handmade cardigan in
multiple shades of gray. The buttons looked unevenly spaced, but
maybe it was meant to be that way. "Nobody," he said. "A friend."

Raven raised an eyebrow. "A friend whose name you don't
know?"

This conversation, like so many conversations with Raven,
was not going well. "I met her on the movie set," Westley lied. "I
can't remember her name."

Raven bit into a cookie and munched it. "Tell your movie
friend her cookies are good," she said. "If you can remember
which one she is." She flounced off in the direction of Science
Fiction/Fantasy, to Westley's relief.

For someone who prided himself on keeping things uncompli-
cated, Westley's life seemed to have gotten rather out of hand. He
still had a few more days to shoot the movie, in which Donna
Wolfe kept telling him to "stand like Kelly," which was not exactly
a clear or helpful bit of direction. Every day brought more stand-

ing under hot lights and people yelling at him and sticking powder brushes in his face, and none of it was any fun at all. The movie work had caused him to get a bit behind in sorting the books, which caused Julia to act a bit put-upon. Nobody stepped up to help him, mainly because everyone was busy following the movie-set gossip on local websites and didn't want to take on any extra work. This seemed unfair; it wasn't Westley's fault that Donna had insisted that he go to an intimidatingly stylish hair salon on Fifth Avenue this week to get his hair cut so it more resembled Kelly's, which made him return late from lunch smelling embarrassingly of expensive hair pomade. (The people in the salon, who'd been tipped off that Westley was coming from the movie set, swarmed around him like mosquitos, asking about Kelly Drake and offering him pedicures and facials and some weird hair treatment that he didn't even understand. He had been very eager to leave.) The extra money was handy, but it wasn't enough to justify all this bother.

And now there was this cookie situation. The curly-haired woman seemed nice, for sure, and the cookies were awfully good. Maybe he should ask her to have coffee, next time she came into the store. Maybe ask her what her name was. But would he just be asking her because of the cookies? Maybe he should just rethink his life.

The evening's shooting was about to begin and Westley's bookstore shift (as opposed to what everyone was now calling, annoyingly, his movie-star shift) was nearly over, when a stylish young man elegantly glided up to Westley's counter. Westley had noticed him working on the set and had exchanged a few words with him the other day. He'd thought the man was in the cast, because of his theatrical way of moving and his very dramatic outfits, which Westley had no idea how to describe but, if he did, he would probably have used the word "billowy" a lot. "Hi," the man said, in tones as impeccably arched as his eyebrows. "We haven't really met. I'm Sydney. Might you possibly have a second to chat?"

This was unexpected. "Uh, OK, hi," Westley said. "I'm Westley. You're working on the movie, right?"

"Yes. So to speak. But this is about something else. Do you mind if I just speak frankly?"

It didn't seem like Westley had much choice in the matter. "No, I guess not?"

"Fab," said Sydney. "So. The TL;DR is basically that you are straight and single, right?"

Oh God, Westley thought, Raven's been gossiping again. Though he only understood half of the sentence, he couldn't deny the part that was clear. "Um, yes, that's right."

"Splendid. So, I have a colleague, and she's a dream, and she's lonely, and I think she would love to meet someone like you. What do you think? I mean, I never do this kind of thing, but I think the two of you would be . . ." Sydney kissed his fingertips and flung them into the air.

Everything about this seemed very high-risk to Westley, who did not believe for a second that Sydney never did this kind of thing; he seemed like the sort of person who thoroughly enjoyed rearranging people's lives. Saying yes to things was all very well, but it hadn't done much for him lately. "That's nice of you," he said politely. "But I'm just not looking for anyone right now. Thank you, though."

"Really?" said Sydney, surprised. "I'm telling you, she's a total catch. Looks kind of like J-Law's older sister. And incredibly nice. You'd pass that up?"

Which one was J-Law? Westley briefly wondered. Jennifer Lopez? Wouldn't her older sister be too old for him? In any case, this situation needed shutting down, and quickly. "I don't think so," he said firmly. "Thank you for the offer."

"So that's a hard no?"

"Yes. Sorry."

Sydney shrugged. "Well, your loss. Anyhoo. Nice to talk to you, and I guess I'll see you around. If you change your mind, you can find me at the costume racks. Cheery-bye." He turned and headed off, a graceful spring in his step, leaving a puzzled Westley staring behind him.

26

April

Long before the whole note drama had started, April had gotten into the habit of treating herself to a new book at the end of an especially busy workday. There was something odd about dealing all day with ephemera—houses were real, sure, but when sitting in her apartment, it was easy to think of every element of her job as some make-believe creation, with pictures of things rather than actual things, emails rather than people. Walking to the bookstore let her shake that off, and the ritual of carefully perusing the thickly stacked new-book tables and holding a new book in her hand felt real and grounding: a physical object, now hers, that contained its own world. And now, of course, there was a second reason to go to the bookstore. April had given up on restraining herself from running down there every day; better to just think of the store as a satellite office, one that needed her frequent presence.

Today a woman in an oddly baggy gray cardigan—it seemed, in the way of so many garments April had found at thrift stores and tried to make hers, to be unacquainted with its wearer—stood at the door; April recognized her as one of the regular Read the Room staff. She greeted April with a stressed-out expression and a voice dangerously close to a groan. "Just wanted to let you know that we're closing early tonight, in about ten minutes," she said. "A feature film is being shot here. Sorry for the inconvenience."

"That's OK," said April. "I'll only be a minute." She strolled casually, pretending to be randomly browsing, over to Young Adult. A quick check of the middle copy of *The Hunger Games* found a folded piece of pale-yellow notepaper, which April slipped into her pocket, looking around furtively to make sure no one had heard her tiny gasp of delight. L, whatever his name was, wasn't at his desk, so April spent a quick moment in Mystery/ Crime Fiction, choosing two paperbacks based on elegant cover design and intriguing opening sentences. The anticipation, knowing the note was there but not what it contained, felt delicious, and April dawdled a bit after making her purchase, watching black-clad people expertly running extension cords down the aisles.

"What's the movie called?" she asked, just to make conversation.

"*Shelf Consciousness*," said the sweatered woman, brushing a bit of lint from her voluminous sleeve. "It's a surreal dark comedy, or at least that's what the director said."

"Will it be shooting for long?"

"Just a few more days, but that's too many. It's very disruptive." The woman, whose tone had become confidential, lowered her voice, looking around as if somebody might be listening, though April didn't see anyone nearby. "We hadn't realized how much bother it would be," she said, as if revealing a secret.

"I would think it would be fun to have a movie shoot at work," said April, wanting to hold up her end of the conversation, and feeling pleasantly confident: a cute bookstore guy, after all, was corresponding with her, and she felt oddly lit-up, like a spotlight was on her. "I work alone at home and it's very boring. Is anyone in the store going to be in the movie?"

The sweatered woman laughed, a bit bitterly. "Not most of us. Our used-books coordinator was asked to appear on camera— he's very handsome." Her eyebrows went up, seemingly to indicate great handsomeness. "And now he's filling in for the lead actor, Kelly Drake, who had to go shoot a commercial somewhere. It's all very inconvenient for us."

Well, this was interesting. "The guy who sits over there?" April said, pointing at the now-empty desk with postcards and random bits of paper pinned up around it.

"Yes. He's supposed to be working right now, but he's off having his makeup done." The woman's tone indicated exactly what she thought of this activity. Another customer stepped up to the counter with a stack of children's books, and the sweatered woman suddenly became briskly efficient. Before April could ask what the handsome man's name was, she was quickly dismissed with a "have a nice evening."

So now L was going to be a movie star? And yet he still had time to put notes in books? This was promising. April hurried home, enjoying the warm summer evening and the way that everyone in the neighborhood seemed to be outdoors, soaking up the sun as if the rainy winter had never happened. She could, of course, have unfolded and read the note at Read the Room, or in the parking lot, but part of the game seemed to be letting it play out, allowing the note to shine in her pocket and make her steps light. Once in her apartment, she exhaled happily and gave in.

Hello again A,

I like mysteries too, especially the kind where nothing too terrible happens and people drink a lot of tea. Yesterday I spent a long time trying to decipher a strange noise coming from down the street. I had thought it might be a crime but actually it was my neighbor's dog being given a bath. Not really much of a mystery, but I enjoyed trying to sort it out.

I do love my job, but it seems like yours is kind of similar: choosing things that people might love, weeding out what they might not, helping them find what they truly want. Perhaps we can meet for coffee and chat more? Wednesday or Thursday next week, after 4, could work for me, and I know of a nice café, not

far from the bookstore, which looks as if a discreet crime might have taken place there. It would be so nice to chat with you in person. Let me know if one of those days works for you. I'll look forward to it, mysteriously.
L

L had nice, precise handwriting and the note had a careful tone to it, like it was meticulously planned. This made sense for a man who kept such a tidy desk and stacked books so neatly. But how did he know about April's job? Had he been watching her when she sat in Read the Room's café with her laptop? Maybe he'd overheard her talking to someone about work? In any case, this was obviously the least interesting part of the note: He wanted to meet. And soon.

27

Laura

Laura had learned something thanks to Rebecca's wisdom: The person who initiates the game gets to set its pace. She would be patient. She'd been waiting a long time, and she could wait a little longer. Sitting in a child-sized chair in Olivia's second-grade classroom, waiting for the year-end "graduation ceremony" to begin, she was resolute. A, whom she'd now seen in fairly close proximity when delivering the cookies, was most definitely adorable and seemed nice; surely worth the wait, however long it might be.

It was strange to be feeling a bit of a spark for somebody, after so many years. Long ago, Laura had won over Sam with a big gesture—not cookies, but showing up unexpectedly at his apartment with a bagful of fast-food burgers after she'd heard him say at the party where they met that he had a weakness for quarter pounders. The greasy odor had stayed in her car for ages afterward but it was worth it. Nowadays, Laura worried that the memory of Sam was slipping away from her—that after five years, she was forgetting the little details that made him who he was. Just the other day, she'd had to pause for a long time to remember the name of Sam's childhood dog; Olivia had asked, wanting to name a stuffed animal in its honor. Eventually Laura remembered—Tony, in honor of a beloved neighborhood postman—but the hesitation worried her. She wanted to move on but still keep Sam with her, a quiet presence in her life. Maybe that was asking too much—but maybe the next man in her life just needed to understand that: that there was a place in her heart that would always belong to Sam. The bookstore man, who had kind eyes, perhaps would. Laura blinked, hard. She was a lot better now at not getting teary when thinking about Sam, but it wasn't entirely reliable.

At the front of the classroom, Olivia sat with her fellow second-grade graduates, all dressed in their nicest and squirming in their carefully arranged little chairs. It seemed odd (though adorable) to Laura that a public school would have a graduation for second graders—and downright annoying to have it on a weekday in the daytime, when many working parents couldn't come and Laura had to request an extra-long lunch break—but she was charmed by the sight of the kids looking so proud and excited. Olivia sat next to her best friend, Hayden, who lived next door and who for once seemed not to be endlessly talking. Laura had once asked Olivia if Hayden's constant chatter ever bothered her. "I like hearing him talking. It makes me feel happy," Olivia had said. This had seemed like such a perfect definition of friendship that Laura had teared up a bit . . . and had to pretend that there was something in her eye.

Olivia's teacher, Ms. Beans—whose real name was Ms. Orleans, but some kid years ago had come up with the nickname, and it stuck—stood in front of the classroom, waving her hands and looking affectionately flustered, as grade-school teachers often do. "One, two, three, eyes on me!" she chanted.

"One, two, eyes on you!" the kids replied, with rhythmic enthusiasm, immediately quieting and focusing on her. It was a good trick; Laura mentally filed it away to try at home.

The chatting parents, squeezed into the small chairs or standing in clumps in the back of the room, silenced instantly, remembering grade-school decorum. "Good afternoon," said Ms. Beans, "and thank you all for coming to our second-grade graduation.

The students have worked very hard this year, and have learned about many things: the solar system, fractions, and the dictionary, to name just a few. I am proud of each and every one of them, and I wish them every success as they progress to third grade in the fall."

Everyone applauded politely. Ashley, who was there to take Olivia home after early dismissal as Laura needed to go back to work, nudged Laura. "Shouldn't they be wearing little caps and gowns?" she whispered, giggling.

"I think it's sweet," Laura whispered back. She felt sorry for the parents who couldn't attend; this sort of thing, with an adorable group of dressed-up little kids, seemed a big reason to enter the parenting game in the first place.

"The students will now sing two songs that we have practiced, and then we'll have punch and cake. There is a gluten-free option available," said Ms. Beans. She clicked a mouse on a nearby computer and some musical notes began, which Laura recognized immediately from the uncountable times she and Olivia had sat through *Frozen* at home. (Laura frequently rued the day when Olivia had learned how to operate their Disney+ streaming account herself.) The kids began the verse, singing about the glowing mountains, wandering a little from the melody as if slightly lost in the snow. But they all chimed in strongly with the "LET IT GO!" chorus, shrieking out the high notes with enough force that a few snoozing grandparents were startled into wakefulness and a toddler sibling started crying.

Laura watched as Olivia earnestly sang, remembering every word of the lyrics (if not necessarily in the right order), looking angelically heavenward as if singing to her father. She looked older than she had yesterday; sometimes it seemed as if Laura could practically see Olivia growing, leaving her tiny self behind. Parenting, Laura sometimes thought, was about saying goodbye, over and over—and saying hello to the many people your child would become. Today Olivia was wearing a dress she'd picked out herself, a French-blue dress with a dropped waist that

Laura actually would have happily worn if it came in adult sizes; she looked oddly grown up in it, or as grown up as a seven-year-old with a missing front tooth can be. Laura missed her baby daughter, but every day she seemed to fall in love again with the new person Olivia was becoming.

Watching the children sing would have been a touching moment, except that every student seemed to be singing in a different key, and some of them seemed to have created some special choreography for the performance, waving their hands and swaying their hips in rhythm, or out of rhythm. The kids ended on a big finish—and an enormous, colorful bouquet of wildly different final notes—and the parents burst into applause.

"Thank you," said Ms. Beans, waiting patiently for the cheers to subside. "And our final song is from the musical *Annie*." She clicked again on the computer. Laura knew this song, "Maybe," from watching the movie a few times with Olivia; it was a sad, sweet tune sung by an orphan who hopes that her real parents will one day magically turn up for her. As the kids sang in their scratchy little voices, looking earnest and wistful, the mood in the room changed; the parents, many of whom had been checking their phones and looking harried, became rapt and attentive. A sniffle was heard, then another, and soon several mothers and fathers were weeping outright. By the final line, with the lyric pleading with parents to come and get their baby, all audience decorum had been abandoned as multiple mothers and fathers, caught up in the spectacle, rushed to claim and embrace their children, weeping over them. Laura, a little sniffly herself, was amused by the scene.

The dad next to Laura, who was sitting by himself and wearing a rather nice navy trenchcoat (Laura couldn't help noticing), cleared his throat a bit too loudly, rubbing his eyes. Laura smiled at him and offered a pack of tissues from her purse. "Allergies?" she said.

"Right," said the dad, taking a tissue and dabbing discreetly. "Which one is yours?"

"That's my daughter over there, in the blue dress," Laura said, pointing to Olivia, who was giggling with a group of classmates. "And yours?"

"Harper's right next to her. In the purple beanie. She *always* wears that beanie."

Laura was familiar with this dynamic, remembering a lengthy period when four-year-old Olivia begged to wear the same ruffled red skirt every day, even after the elastic waistband broke and Laura had to find a pair of very small suspenders on the internet. "Well, it's very cute," she said. "My daughter's Olivia. I'm Laura."

"Nathan. Nice to meet you."

Harper spotted her father and came running up, shrieking with delight. "Daddy! Did you hear me sing?"

"I did!" Nathan said, scooping Harper up easily. "You were wonderful! Want to get some cake?" He nodded toward Laura. "Thanks again for the tissue. For my, um, allergies. Can I bring you some cake?"

"No, that's OK, thank you," said Laura, who pretended to herself that she was not fond of supermarket sheet cake. "Nice to meet you!" She waved a hand at him and turned back toward Ashley. Though Ashley had complained about the change in schedule, she seemed to be enjoying herself, and had carefully watched Laura's interaction with Nathan.

"Does this make you think of Sam?" Ashley asked. "I mean, school stuff, and seeing other dads and everything."

Though Laura had never confided anything in Ashley, thinking it best to maintain a fairly formal employer-employee relationship, Ashley knew Laura's backstory; she'd seen Sam's photo, and had often heard Olivia prattling on about the daddy she didn't know. The babysitter had never asked questions before, but then again, it was rare that the two of them were sitting side-by-side without being actively engaged with Olivia (who had now happily joined the line for cake, barely noticing their presence).

Laura smiled; after five years and many such questions from

well-meaning askers, it wasn't too painful to discuss anymore, just a bit wistful. "A little bit," she said. "He would have really loved this. He used to sing to her a lot when she was a baby."

"Do you think you'll ever date again?" Ashley said bluntly. "Maybe give Livvy a stepdad someday?"

So much for the employer-employee relationship. "Maybe? Sure? Someday? I don't know," said Laura. "It's been a long time." Motivated by she knew not what—the cute kids, the emotion of the moment, the prospect of cake, *Frozen*—she blurted out, "But there is actually someone I have my eye on. He works at that bookstore where you sometimes take Olivia for story hour, Read the Room."

"Oh my God," said Ashley, eyes widening delightedly. "That is *so* awesome, Laura! I love it! Have you gone out? What's his name? What's he like?"

Laura hadn't anticipated questions but was touched by Ashley's excitement. And it actually felt good to talk about it. "I don't know his name," she admitted. "We haven't gone out, and I don't really know anything about him except that he works at the bookstore. There's just something going on between us. It's kind of hard to explain."

Ashley looked like she would like an explanation, but a happy Olivia ran up to them, clutching a paper plate with a rather large piece of cake on it. "Can you really eat all of that?" Laura asked her.

"Yes!" said Olivia indignantly. "I'm not cake intolerant."

On Laura's burst of laughter, Ashley gazed at Laura intently, silent questions on her face.

28

Westley

I t felt good to be at home, Westley thought, now that work was such a mess of complications. At home, nobody yelled at him and nobody acted huffy. His housemates, Cory and Jillian, expected nothing, other than that he pay his share of rent and not leave a mess in the kitchen or bathroom, and they didn't ask him a lot of questions about the movie, because he still hadn't told them about it. He'd wondered if they might read something about it on a local news site, but luckily both were preoccupied with working multiple jobs—Cory was a theater musician who doubled as a DoorDash deliverer; Jillian was a hairdresser and occasional Uber driver, which helped her save for her dream of opening a salon for exclusively primary-colored hair—and seemed oblivious.

On this Saturday night, with the movie mercifully not needing him, they were both out, and Westley had the house to himself—a rare treat, and one he took full advantage of by moving his laptop into their sparsely furnished communal living room. Though the shared house was perfectly adequate, Westley was often all too aware that it lacked the sort of detailed coziness he'd see upon occasionally visiting a co-worker's home for a party or watching a movie about thirtysomethings with life problems. His home had nothing hanging on the walls, nothing decorative anywhere, just very functional and cheap beige furniture—most of which had been left by the previous tenant—and not much of that. It was a placeholder of a home, like the role he played in the movie, filling in until the real thing came along. Whatever that was.

Parking himself on the worn futon couch with a beer, he logged in to his email. It had been a few days since he'd heard back from Duke Munro, and the email had stayed with him; Munro seemed like somebody entirely comfortable in his own skin. Westley hadn't had any luck locating either of Munro's previous titles: *If a Tree Falls* and *Fires of Love* didn't seem to exist in any of the usual used-book searches or on the public library website, so they had to have been self-published. He typed a reply.

TO: dukemunro@hotmail.com
FROM: westleybooks@freemail.com
RE: Your novel

Hello, Mr. Munro, and thank you so much for writing back to me. As I mentioned before, I am a local bookseller and I really enjoyed *Shivering Timbers*. In all honesty I don't understand why it's out of print. It seems like a book that would find a wide audience, particularly here in the Northwest. May I ask if you still live in the area? And are you by any chance working on a new book?

Sincerely,
Westley

Without thinking too much about it, he clicked Send and off it went. Duke Munro, surely, was having a more interesting evening than Westley was; perhaps he was gathered with friends at some rustic-looking village pub, raising a glass and telling stories of his youth as men in plaid shirts gathered round. Westley didn't like telling stories of his own youth, as they typically involved people making a fuss over him. Needing something to do, he logged on to Netflix and found that Donna Wolfe's latest film, *Twelve for Dinner*, was available to stream. He'd seen it before, when it came out a few years ago, and hadn't liked it very much, but it seemed wise to watch it again—mainly to look closely at the actors and try to understand exactly what it was that Donna was looking for. Though he understood that Donna and the crew weren't really looking for him to act—he was, after all, just a placeholder—maybe studying the movie might give him some ideas that would make them yell at him a little less.

Two hours and a second beer later, Westley felt that he didn't know much more. The film was like some postmodern novels he'd tried to read: It seemed to assume a great deal of prior knowledge and wasn't about to help fill you in; you watched it, or read it, feeling perpetually behind. And the tone and plot made no sense to him—was it supposed to be funny? Were the party hosts vampires or cannibals, and did it matter? What happened to the guests who didn't get bitten; did they just take their packed-up leftovers and go home? Was all that blood, presented in the form of gravy, clever or just disgusting? Did people really understand this movie, or did they just pretend they did because it seemed sort of cool? (Westley suspected the latter.)

He'd been carefully watching the lead actor—somebody named Edwin Landers, whose IMDb credits mostly showed movies set in depressing dystopias—but learned little. Landers seemed to have a very nonshowy way of interacting with the camera; entirely at ease with it, entirely unaware of it, but watching the performance, somehow, you liked him. You didn't sense that he was acting, but that he was just being himself and the camera happened to catch him. Not every actor on screen was able to do this—some of them seemed too arch, too aware—but he had an ease that drew your eye to him. Maybe that was the trick to acting: not acting. This seemed like an odd conclusion and Westley was pondering it and pondering another beer (it was the weekend, after all), when a key turned in the front door and Cory came in.

"Hey Westley. Wow, you're in the living room! You're never in the living room."

Westley quickly closed his laptop. "Hey. Yeah, just thought I'd do something different. How was the show?"

Cory shook his head. "ABBA music, man. People eat that stuff up. Mystery to me." Cory was a bass player, tall and thin like his instrument. Though he preferred to play jazz, lately he'd been subbing in a theater orchestra pit for a local production of *Mamma Mia*, which paid well despite his grumbling about the music. Now and then Westley would hear him humming "Dancing Queen" in the kitchen, but it seemed best for housemate harmony not to say anything about it.

"You want a beer?" Westley said. "Take one of mine, and maybe bring me another?"

"Sure. Thanks." Cory brought two beers into the living room, handed one to Westley and sank into the faded armchair by the window. "I think Jillian's staying over with her new boyfriend tonight. How about you? Don't you have a new lady friend these days?" He winked.

Westley was embarrassed, and privately vowed to practice his lines—well, his line—somewhere else in the future. "No, not really," he said. "Been busy with work."

"You've been at that bookstore forever, right?" Cory said, sipping his beer. "Shouldn't you own the place by now? You planning to stay there awhile longer?"

"I don't know," said Westley. "I like it there, but someday I'd like to make a little more money. But I don't know what I'd do. I like being around the books. It feels right."

This was now officially the longest conversation Westley and Cory had ever had; it was rare that they were both in the same room for so long. Though they got along perfectly well, they seemed to be living mostly parallel lives, rarely intersecting.

"Yeah," said Cory, "it'd be nice to make enough money to have my own place. No shade on you; you and Jillian are great housemates. But I always thought I'd be on my own by now. Things just got too expensive."

It was true; Westley had recently taken a look online at studio and one-bedroom apartments in the area, thinking it might be time to strike out on his own, and was horrified at the numbers he saw. He wondered how his colleagues managed it. Maybe they all had housemates as well, or supportive parents or independent wealth. (Andrew in particular—all those blazers!—seemed like somebody who might have some money behind him.) The small additional payment Westley was getting for appearing on camera in the movie wasn't enough to put him where he wanted to be financially: in his own place, not politely sharing a makeshift home with near-strangers. It seemed a distant dream.

"Hey," said Cory, snapping his fingers. "Just thought of this. Are you named for that guy in *The Princess Bride*?"

Julia

The best thing I ever found in a book was an anniversary card, a little cheesy but very sweet, with a photo on the front of two bunnies nestled inside a top hat and the message "Another year making magic together" printed on the inside. The person sending it wrote an effusive note in sprawling handwriting, beginning with "I love you with all my heart, my darling" and signed "Your own Sandro." It just seemed like a tiny picture into somebody's relationship; playful and affectionate and adorable. My wife, Nora, and I give each other cards occasionally, but we're a little more emotionally reserved. She is definitely my happily-ever-after, even if I wouldn't phrase it quite that way.

I probably shouldn't have ever agreed to the movie shoot. It was a weak moment. I was worried about finances; expenses at the store have risen sharply, including the monthly rent, right after I gave all the employees an annual raise (I don't know how they manage in this expensive city working in a bookstore, so I try to help them as best I can), and I was panicking a bit about how to pay the bills. I should have known that the universe usually provides, though sometimes it comes in strange disguises.

Weeks ago I got an email on the general store address, from a location scout saying that the movie was being shot very soon and Read the Room would be perfect for just a handful of scenes. (I learned later that they'd actually had another local bookstore lined up—the Book-Up, a perfectly nice store but not, I think, as well curated as our selection—which had fallen through when one of the owners, a married couple, ran off with the UPS delivery person, so now they're facing both divorce and supply-chain issues.) Anyway, I thought it might be fun for the staff and some nice publicity for the store, and the amount they offered to pay for just a few weeks of shooting was enough to take care of my most worrisome bills. And I believed them when they said it would only be a couple of days and nothing in the store would be disturbed.

Well, now I know not to believe movie people. They've disrupted many of the shelves, chipped the wood floor with their camera and tracks, and even stolen Westley as a stand-in for the lead actor. Nora keeps telling me to calm down, that everything will work itself out and I should try to relax. This only makes me more stressed. I just keep repeating the dollar amount to myself, to remember why I'm doing it. It's a blessing, disguised as an incredible nuisance.

I guess I've always seen the bookstore as the calm center of my life. Not that Nora isn't the center—we're been together thirty years now, and her smile still makes me feel as if I'm young again—but I'm someone for whom work is important. That little store, with its book-jacket prints on the walls and its laden shelves, was my place out in the world, and I wanted it to always be perfect, so that everyone who walked in would suddenly feel happier, like everything was in order and made sense.

I've worked here for a very long time—I started as a bookseller but dreamed of owning the store someday, because other than Nora, nothing makes me feel more like home. I bought it fifteen years ago thanks to an inheritance from my grandfather, whose picture still hangs by the front counter; customers are always asking if he's the guy from Everything Everywhere All at Once—*they're always so disappointed when I say no—and every day I'm grateful to be here.*

Recently I've noticed that I'm the oldest person at Read the Room by probably a couple of decades at least—I'm sixty-one, and I embraced my gray hair long ago. It doesn't really bother me, except when I have to remember not to leave voicemail messages for staffers under thirty (why? Don't their mothers ever call?), or when I need to have Andrew or Alejandra explain to me what the latest social media platform is and how it's different from all the other ones. A lot of them do seem kind of the same? But I do try to stay up to date on such things, so we can promote store events, and have put Andrew in charge of "content." Authors regularly come to the store for readings; we don't have a lot of space but have carved out a corner of the store for a few rows of folding chairs.

I didn't know what to say when the assistant director of the movie—I can never remember her name, but she's the one with the pretentious hat—came to tell me that Westley would be standing in for Kelly Drake. It irritated me to no end that she told me, rather than asked me. Westley of course is an adult and can make his own decisions, but I did feel that my approval was needed for him to take on such a significant role. His primary responsibility is to do his job here, and I hope he knows that I am aware that he took a long lunch the other day to go get an expensive haircut (which, I'm sorry to say, really does look quite good). I should probably discuss this with him but I had hoped to get the message across with an appropriate glare.

Anyway, I just keep telling myself that all of this is worth it, that it'll keep the store going for at least a while longer. It was my dream to own this store, and maybe eventually one of the employees will buy it from me. (Though how any of the current ones would ever afford it, I don't know. Maybe Andrew, after he becomes partner in a law firm.) But in the meantime, I just want the doors open and to put books into customers' hands, and to see kids smile when they enter, and to stand behind the front desk and watch a room full of readers. The store's not very profitable even in the best of times, but that's not why I bought it. It's absolutely worth dealing with all this movie nonsense, if it means we can just keep going.

29

April

He wanted to meet. He was suggesting an actual meeting, on an actual date in an actual café. This meant that April's plan, initially the craziest thing she'd ever done in her life, had actually worked: She'd reached out to a person, and he was reaching right back, just as she'd hoped. It was all a bit overwhelming. Strange; whenever April was in the store and tried to catch his eye, he hadn't really responded (though, of course, he didn't know who she was). But that was OK; the attraction was definitely there on the page, and maybe the bookstore had rules about fraternizing with customers while on duty. Or maybe he was just shy. In any case, this was a big step forward, and April had spent a fair bit of time composing a reply that conveyed what she thought of as an appropriately breezy tone.

Hi L,

I love the idea of the "Café of Discreet Crimes"; perhaps somebody has set a novel there, once upon a time, or a classic noir film. I'm guessing it smells faintly of cigarettes, even if they haven't been allowed there for some time. So yes, let's do it! Tell me the café's real name, and where it is; and how about next Thursday, the 6th? Or suggest another day. Late afternoons on most days work well for me. My work hours are flexible and I usually start early.

Looking forward to sharing some mysteries—and maybe solving one or two. I'll be carrying a Dashiell Hammett novel, just so you'll know it's me. Can't wait.
A

But now there was another problem, one not answered by the advice columns April enjoyed reading online: What does one wear to meet the object of one's epistolary crush for coffee? Unfortunately, as April had been working from home for some time, her wardrobe had suffered; it was now mostly comfy leggings and long sweaters, the latter swapped out for lightweight button-up shirts in warm weather. These outfits were perfectly fine for working in an apartment that was by turns drafty or uncomfortably hot (cute Seattle vintage brick buildings, as April knew too well, tend to have neither well-sealed windows nor air-conditioning), but maybe she needed something new, nothing fancy but something that looked as if a little more effort had gone into it. She gazed into the mirror, vaguely unsatisfied—she looked perfectly fine, and was pleased with her current haircut, but her clothes suddenly seemed so generic, so boring, so not what she wanted to express. Even Tango Lady, with whom April had exchanged pleasantries in the lobby the other day, had a distinctive personal style; dark nipped-waist dresses with flowing skirts, like she was a punctuation mark come to life. Surely, a woman like April, who was brazenly carrying on a clandestine correspondence with a handsome stranger, should dress . . . well, April wasn't sure exactly how, but not this way.

Shopping online was an option, but time was of the essence here and it was always so hard to get the feel of a garment from a screen. And going downtown to a department store seemed like a fun outing; it was something she hadn't done in years, and she wasn't sure if her Waterton's credit card, an account proudly opened back when she was still in her teens, even worked anymore since it had been so long since she'd used it. With optimism and a faint sense of adventure, she hopped on a bus downtown on a gray Saturday afternoon, excited to have an event that merited a new outfit. April found herself smiling at the other people on the bus—mostly elderly people with small shopping carts—as it creakingly made its way up the hills and around the corners. Maybe each of them had a secret too, something they'd dared to try.

As far as April was concerned, Waterton's had always been around. She'd loved it since childhood, remembering expeditions there with her mother many years ago. They'd shop for clothes and have lunch in the store restaurant on the lower floor, where April was always allowed to have a small ice-cream sundae, topped with a cherry and served in a silver dish beaded with condensation, for dessert. She thought of her mother, young and pretty, riffling through the office dresses on a rack with a serious expression, a faint line between her brows, now and then pulling one out to hold it up to herself. "What do you think?" she'd ask April. "I love it," April would always say—until she became a teenager and started to make snarky remarks, at which time the expeditions began to slip away. She'd thought that she didn't want to go shopping with her mother anymore, but now remembered the trips with a genuine ache. Funny how something you thought you didn't care about at the time can become, with the passing of years, unexpectedly dear.

Entering the store, April noticed that it smelled the same way it always had: of perfume and crackling-new paper shopping bags, and that the shiny surfaces of the handbag department still sparkled in a way that seemed almost otherworldly. Deftly avoiding a few smiling cosmetics salespeople wielding spray bottles, she rode the escalator to the second floor and arrived in the womens wear department, which seemed much bigger than it had in the past and a little overwhelming. A very tall saleswoman in an alarmingly chic outfit—an aggressively neon-green jumpsuit, which she wore with the breezy confidence it required—approached. "Can I help you find something?" she asked, her jumpsuit seeming to strobe in the elegantly subtle light.

"Oh, I'm just browsing," April said automatically, not sure that someone in such an outfit could understand fashion for mere mortals. (Did this woman even own a pair of leggings? Were leggings even available at this store?) "I'm not sure exactly what I want."

"We do have some slots available today with one of our personal shoppers, if you'd like some individual help," the woman said. "There's no charge."

April instinctively began to say no, but then paused. Maybe this would be a good idea, to have someone expose her to something that she might not have chosen herself. Left alone, she would probably pick the same nondescript things she always wore. It was time to break out of her box. She could afford to buy something nice; she never went shopping and had plenty saved. "Yes," she said decisively. "Sure. That sounds great. Thank you."

"Lovely," the jumpsuited woman said. "Please come this way."

April followed her to a corner of the store, where behind a glass door marked "Personal Shopping" was an elegant room with several velvet-covered couches and numerous half-doors presumably leading to dressing rooms. The jumpsuit woman briefly disappeared into a back office, from which moments later emerged a curly-haired woman in a sleek beige pantsuit. She walked up to April, smiling and extending a hand.

"Hello," she said. "I'm Laura Barry. I'll be helping you today."

"Hi, I'm April. April Dunne. Nice to meet you," April said, shaking Laura's hand and laughing, a bit nervously; she hadn't expected things to be quite so fancy, and found herself wishing she'd worn something nicer. Of course, that was why she was here.

"And you! Thanks so much for coming in. What can I help you find?"

This wasn't an easy question. "Um, I don't really know?" April said. "I guess what I need is something for a really casual blind date. But I've never had a shopping appointment before. How does it work?"

"Oh, it's easy!" said Laura. April liked how this woman had a casual friendliness to her that seemed very much at odds with the chic formality of their surroundings; it made the whole experience more appealing. "It's a free service, and you're absolutely not required to buy anything I pick out for you. And I'm not just saying that; it's true. Of course we'd like you to buy something, but it has to be right for you. We don't want you bringing it back, or never wearing it! So, you and I will just chat a little bit, and you can tell me what you're looking for and what kinds of styles and colors you like, and I'll find some garments for you to try on. If you have a little time, I can pull them while you wait—things are quiet today for some reason and I can do it quickly—or we can make an appointment for another day if that's easier."

"That's OK. I can wait," April said. "I'd like to buy something today. So"—she took a deep breath— "I'm looking for something to wear on sort of a first date. It's nothing fancy at all. We're just meeting for coffee in the afternoon. I just want to look nice because I really like him." This all sounded very embarrassing and high-school-girly; April could tell that she was blushing, just a bit.

"That's so sweet!" Laura said, who seemed genuinely excited at the prospect, like the absolute nicest girls in April's high school circle would have been. "So, this guy must be someone you know already? But you've never been out together?"

"Right," said April, quickly deciding that the whole story was just too much to burden this nice saleswoman with. "I do know him; we've met. But this is the first time we're *officially* meeting, if that makes any sense. I want to look nice, but like I didn't make any special effort, you know what I mean? Casual but stylish? Maybe just jeans and a top, but really nice ones?"

A frighteningly trendy young man with a Waterton's name tag who was lounging nearby—clearly it was a slow afternoon—chimed in. "You are *definitely* going to need some better shoes," he said, looking appraisingly at April's feet, clad in a pair of navy-blue Toms that had definitely seen better days.

"I would say ignore him, but he's usually right," said Laura. "This is Sydney, our assistant. If you don't like heels, maybe a flat sandal?" Looking carefully at April, she was clearly making a few mental notes. "OK. I have some ideas. Just sit tight and I'll be back soon."

"Don't you need to know my size?" April asked.

"Nope. I can tell," Laura said. "Just relax. Sydney can get you something to drink if you'd like." She headed out into the store.

Sydney gazed at April expectantly. "Coffee? Tea? Prosecco? Coke? Dubonnet with a twist? Sorry, we don't actually have that last thing."

"Just water would be great," April said. "Thank you. I love what you have on." Sydney was wearing a pair of knee-length purple shorts with a brocade vest, flowy white dress shirt, and silk tie. He looked like a businessman pirate who lived in a hot climate, which was to say, he looked wonderful.

"Oh, this old thing?" Sydney said, handing April a bottle of water. "Thanks. I just threw this together. No, I'm just kidding, it took me forever to figure out that this vest would go with the shorts. I mean, who wears a vest with shorts? But why not?" He raised an eyebrow in a practiced way.

"You look amazing," April said. "I wish I had some clothes that were fun. I work from home so it's hard to get motivated to wear something decent."

"Laura can help you with that," Sydney said. "She's the best. It's like she's got a magic wand that tells her what to put with what. It's awesome to watch her. So tell me about this guy you're meeting. Spill the tea; I love drama. How do you know him?"

"It's weird," said April, realizing that it was nice to be able to discuss this with someone. "I've actually never really spoken to him, but he's been leaving me notes. We're having a secret correspondence. Which is apparently still a thing."

"Oh my God, that is so rom-com!" Sydney said, eyes wide. "I love it. Tell me more."

"It is kind of like a movie," April admitted. "But it's real. He seems nice and he likes books and he suggested we get together for coffee. So we'll see!"

"Promise me that you will not wear those shoes when you meet him," Sydney said with a delicate shudder. He gazed at a pocket watch dangling from his vest. "Yikes. The sunglasses lady's assistant is coming back for a hemming and that dress is not going to press itself. More's the pity. Excuse me!" He sprang— quite literally, looking like a dancer in a pirate ballet—through a back doorway and was gone.

Alone, April gazed at the room, which looked like a posh movie set done in rich neutral shades. What would it be like to work somewhere like this all day? The stylist, Laura, seemed so comfortable in this environment, so different from April's dull work-from-home routine. She envied Laura, whose job allowed her to meet new people every day and make them happier, prettier, sleeker. Like the houses April worked with, but for real, not just virtually.

"OK. Here are a few things to try." Laura hurried back into the room, her arms laden with garments, clearly in efficiency mode. "This is just to give us an idea of what fits and what you like. I thought a simple slim dark-wash jean would work, and any of these colors in a top would suit you. I picked one that's a bit lacy, and one that's very tailored, and one that's kind of arty; so just see what you like best. And we can run downstairs and grab some sandals for you, if you'll tell me your shoe size. That's the one thing I can't tell by looking. And do you think you'd like a blazer or cardigan or some kind of jacket? Or maybe not? It's pretty warm out these days, maybe you're fine without one."

April, who already loved everything Laura was holding, felt happier than she had in a long time.

30

Laura

Laura always enjoyed meeting a brand-new client—to look at what they were wearing now and what it said about them (often what it said was, "I need help with this" and/or "I am just not paying attention"), and to hear about what they aspired to wear. She was always surprised by how few women (she had a handful of male clients, but mostly it was women who came in looking for style advice) felt confident in choosing outfits on their own. Most people, she'd found, had a clear idea of what they liked, but lacked the confidence to just choose that look and flaunt it. Hence the need for someone like Laura, who had a way of listening to someone hesitantly describe how they liked soft blues and full skirts and Audrey Hepburn movies, and then producing the perfect dress. Sometimes people cried in the dressing room, seeing how good they looked. These were always Laura's favorite times at work. She loved being part of a moment of change, even if it was for a near-stranger.

Today's new client had been a lot of fun. She was a young woman, maybe just a few years younger than Laura, dressed in Seattle-casual: leggings, well-worn shoes, a nondescript long shirt, with light brown hair cut in a plain bob (Laura suspected she often pushed her hair behind her ears) and no jewelry or makeup; a serviceable crossbody bag was her only accessory.

But there was a spark to her—her smile, as she greeted Laura, was that of someone who'd be good at cheering you up, or fun to hang out with. Laura didn't usually connect with clients personally; they were just part of the job. But this woman, April, was unexpectedly sweet. Funny how April was also having a blind date—though in her case, it sounded like it was someone she already knew—for coffee? Seattle was apparently full of romantic stories these days. Maybe the frequent rain kept everyone indoors and pushed them toward each other once springtime came?

Anyway, April had enthusiastically loved everything Laura had pulled for her and was astonished at how perfectly all of the clothing fit. (A recent client had been furious when Laura brought out garments in a size 12—she was, the client insisted, an 8, and had always been an 8, full stop—but then ended up hugging Laura when the clothes fit perfectly.) April had ended up buying everything Laura suggested, which meant both a nice commission for Laura and the pleasing feeling of having made a client happy. She hoped April would come back. Laura had never fraternized with a client before, but she could imagine giggling over an after-work beer with April.

Now she had an odd appointment. Donna Wolfe's assistant was coming in so that Donna's gown for the banquet could be altered. A typical client would come herself for an alterations appointment—even Laura's wealthiest clients did not seem to be in possession of a body double—but Donna was not a typical client and had insisted that her assistant could handle the fitting. Laura wondered if part of being Donna Wolfe's assistant was that you had to be her exact size. How would you go about advertising such a qualification? ("Assistant wanted: Must have stellar organizational skills, ability to attend to multiple tasks and deadlines, and be long-waisted, size 8 tall, and 34D"?) The unfortunate assistant, a harried-looking woman named Joanna who was indeed an uncanny ringer for Donna's shape and size, was currently standing on a pedestal wearing Donna's black gown, waiting with visible anxiety as a tailor pinned the hem all the way around. Laura had brought a pair of shoes to suit the gown, which Joanna gamely wore despite them pinching her a bit. (Apparently shoe size was not specified in the job description.)

"Will Ms. Wolfe be picking up the dress herself?" Laura asked. "I'd be happy to help her with accessories."

"No," said Joanna, who had a way of making the tiniest of words sound heavy. "I'll be picking it up. Ms. Wolfe is very, very busy."

"I'm sure she is. How is the bookstore movie going?" Laura asked, trying to make conversation. "It's such a nice shop and it must be fun to shoot there."

"Oy," said Joanna, rolling her eyes. "It's been a trial. Kelly Drake had to drop out of the movie for a few days, so we have this guy who works at the store filling in for him. He's very cute, but he has *no* idea what he's doing. I don't know what Donna's thinking."

"Oh, really?" said Laura, trying to sound casual. "Which guy? The one at the front desk, with the blazer?" Funny how she'd gotten to know the bookstore employees by sight, like characters in a movie that she'd seen many times.

"No, the one who sits at the desk where the used books are. Flannel shirt, jeans, beard. Do you know him?"

"Sort of," Laura said, keeping her tone light and becoming mesmerized with the details of Joanna's hem. "I mean, I see him around. I shop at the store sometimes." Very casually, and not looking at Joanna, she added, "You don't happen to know his name, do you?"

Joanna pondered for a second or two, then shook her head. "Sorry, I don't. Too many people working on the movie. I think it's kind of an unusual name, but I can't remember. He seems kind of sweet, but absolutely clueless. Never been in front of a camera before in his life. He's just filling in for Kelly; Donna says we'll dub Kelly's voice in later, so this guy's basically a glorified stand-in."

So now A was in the movies, on top of his bookstore work?

And yet he still had time to maintain a clandestine correspondence? And he knew Kelly Drake, whom Laura had read about as one of Seattle's up-and-coming stars of the future? (Well, she hadn't really read about him, but Ashley had once shown her a picture, wanting Laura to confirm that Ashley's boyfriend, Zach, looked a lot like Kelly. Laura hadn't seen the resemblance at all but had nodded politely.) All of this, except for the "clueless" part, seemed a promising development.

Joanna held the dress's skirt out on both sides, gazing in the mirror. "Are you sure this will fit Donna?" she asked. "It seems a little loose."

"It'll be perfect," said Laura, who had carefully assessed Donna's figure. "It's supposed to be loose. The silk glides over the body. It's very flattering."

"If you say so." Joanna seemed skeptical. "Are we done here? I have to pick up Donna's dry cleaning, and pick up the new script pages from the production office, and write Donna's speech for the banquet, and find out if her new armchair is ready at the upholsterer's and . . ." Her voice trailed off and she sighed, looking a little defeated.

"And maybe look for a new job?" Laura couldn't help it.

"Well, maybe. If I have time."

"You're very busy," said Laura sympathetically. "Would you like me or my assistant to deliver the dress when it's done? We can bring it to the bookstore if Ms. Wolfe is going to be there; it's nearby, so it's no problem at all. I can put a rush on the hemming job and it should be done by end of day tomorrow."

"Would you?" said Joanna gratefully. "I'd appreciate it. She's going to be there shooting every day this week, late afternoon into evening. Thank you so much!"

"It's my pleasure," said Laura. She meant it. It was a favor—she didn't usually deliver things personally—but one with an ulterior motive.

31

Westley

Westley just couldn't get Duke Munro off his mind. He hadn't yet heard back from his last email, but this wasn't surprising; Duke seemed to be the sort of person who maybe wasn't on email that much, who lived maybe somewhere far out in the country, in a house that smelled cozily of wood-burning fires. Maybe he sat alone most days, writing books on an old typewriter, whistling to himself as he happily typed; maybe he rarely checked his email, not really caring much what happened in the outside world. But he clearly was someone who had known passion once, like Westley had. Bridget would probably have loved Munro's book, and Westley wished, as he so often had, that things had worked out differently, and that he and Bridget could have had a future, in which they loved and laughed and read books together. He'd found himself thinking about her more, since reading the book, but reminded himself firmly that not every love story has a happy ending, and that he was only going to find one if he got himself out there and met somebody nice. Soon.

Nonetheless, it was time to stop fantasizing—Westley had been catching himself daydreaming at work way too much lately—and go to Staff Tea. Staff Tea took place on the first Sunday of every month, half an hour before the store opened (which was, thankfully, later on Sundays), and was Julia's idea of a team-building exercise, among the small number of staff who were more or less full-time. The group would sit around a big table at the not-yet-open café, which smelled deliciously but frustratingly of the day's baked goods that weren't yet available for sale, and everyone would have a cup of tea (brewed up by Julia in the tiny closet that was grandly called the "staff room") and share something unique that had happened to them on the job the previous month. Though Staff Tea was never particularly exciting, Westley didn't mind it; he appreciated that Julia meticulously made sure that the half-hour was considered part of a regular shift that day, and sometimes the stories were entertaining. Today he suspected that everyone's tale would have something to do with the movie, which had moved past being a thorn in Julia's side to being a full-bodied dramatic tragedy, to be told in tones of mournful regret.

The staff had assembled at the café's central table, blowing on mugs of hot tea and trying to stifle a few yawns. "Good morning, everyone!" said Julia from her place at the head of the table. "Thank you all for coming in early, and I hope everyone's managing OK with the disruptions this week. There are only a few more days of filming that remain. I have had a meeting with Joe and spoken to him *quite severely* about not moving any books without checking with a staff member. Let's hope he heard me this time. And they have promised to touch up the part of the floor that was scratched by the lighting equipment. And there will be *no* more smoking outside the front door anymore. I was very clear on that as well." Julia paused, slightly out of breath; the litany had seemingly worn her out. "So! Who would like to share first today?"

"I'll go," said Alejandra. "Yesterday I had a customer come in and ask if we could match Amazon's prices. That was number thirty-nine. We're getting close to another round of pastries!" (There was a yellow tablet behind the front desk where staffers kept track of this frequent question from customers. Every fifty customers, Julia would buy the staff treats from the café.)

"That's not very interesting," said Raven.

"Yeah, yeah, I know," said Alejandra. "But he said he seriously wanted to know, why should he shop at our store if it's more expensive than online. I had sort of practiced something new to say: I said he was certainly free to shop online if he wanted to—nobody was going to stop him. But that no online store was going to offer what he was experiencing right now: the scent of coffee, the rainbow of actual books on actual shelves, and the opportunity to have a conversation with a real human being. Poetic, right? And then I smiled really nicely. He not only stayed, he bought five books."

"Did he ask for your number?" said Andrew archly.

"No! Are you kidding? He was like sixty years old!" Alejandra giggled.

"Very well done, Alejandra," Julia said as the staffers politely applauded. "That's very appropriate, but let's please remember that sixty is not old. Who's next?" (Julia was, Westley had realized in the past, a generation older than everyone on the full-time staff. What would it be like to still be in the bookstore at sixty? Actually, now that he thought of it, it seemed possibly nice.)

Andrew spoke up: "A customer came in earlier this week with a dog on a leash. I asked her if it was a service dog and she said no, so I said I was sorry but only service dogs were allowed in the store and that she would need to tie the dog outside. She said she had been reading Flannery O'Connor short stories to him every night and wanted him to pick the next selection."

"Did you let the dog stay?" asked Raven, who was always concerned about rule enforcement and had been known to tattle to Julia when she saw a bookseller turn a blind eye to uncovered drinks, unauthorized animals, and unruly children.

"I'll confess I told her she could bring in the dog if she was quick about it. The store was practically empty. They chose a book really fast. That new Tana French mystery. She said the dog likes suspense."

Julia frowned. "I'll let that slide just this once, but please remember that only service animals are allowed in the store. That's the rule. Westley? Do you want to share something about the movie?"

Raven rolled her eyes. "Yes, Westley. Tell us what it's like being a movie star."

Westley registered her irritation, which had been a constant since the movie began. "It's no big deal," he said. "There isn't really anything to tell. You wear what they say and stand where they put you and move when they tell you. And it's not like my face or voice is going to end up in the movie, really. I wish they'd asked somebody else."

"But isn't it fun knowing that you're standing in for Kelly Drake? And being directed by Donna Wolfe?" Alejandra asked. She was the only one on the staff who could recite Donna Wolfe's IMDb credits by heart.

"I guess," said Westley. "But it's not like I even met Kelly, really. I'm just a placeholder. I haven't even read the script." Suddenly he felt like changing the subject. "Can I share something else?" he asked. Julia nodded. "I found this really good book the other day," he said. "It was in a donation pile. Sort of a romance novel, but from a male point of view and it really surprised me. It's from a publisher that I haven't heard of, and it must be either self-published or out of print as I can't find it listed anywhere, but I think customers would really like it. The author is local, or at least lives somewhere in the Pacific Northwest, and I wonder if maybe he would come into the store to read?"

"Why would we want someone to come in and read if their book is out of print?" said Raven. "What's in it for the author, if he can't sell any copies?"

"Well, maybe we could encourage a local press to republish it. It's really good. It might be good publicity for the store."

Julia pursed her lips, clearly remembering what had happened the last time she was told something would be good publicity for the store. "Well, I suppose we could think about it," she said, trying to be fair. "Maybe try to contact the author? What's the book's title?"

"It's called *Shivering Timbers*."

Eyes widened around the table. "I know, I know," said Westley. "The title's a little satirical. It works, I swear! It's a romance set in a remote firefighters' base. Very Northwesty." Everyone looked skeptical. Westley went resolutely on. "Seriously, it's good! The author's name is Duke Munro, and he seems really colorful and interesting, and I think a romance from a male point of view is an underrepresented genre. We're having a bit of an email exchange." Maybe sharing this at Staff Tea was a mistake.

"Well, we can talk about that later, once this movie business is done," Julia said. "Anyone else have something to share?" She had picked up on Raven looking at Andrew in a way that implied that she had a bit of dirt on him, as was Raven's way. He was trying not to catch her eye. The two of them never got along very well, mainly because Andrew was less invested than the others in keeping the peace, and would occasionally pick fights with Raven, seemingly to help pass the time.

"I'll go," said Raven, who clearly didn't want to wait any longer. "Just sharing that there's been a, shall we say, development between someone on our staff and someone on the movie." She continued to gaze at Andrew, who adjusted his lapels self-consciously. "Maybe that person would like to share?"

"Argh," said Andrew, or something like it. "Are we in high school? Anyway, yes, I did meet a nice guy. He's working in the costume department. Not that it's anyone's business. I didn't realize Staff Tea was for airing our personal lives."

"He's the guy who was wearing a cape yesterday!" said Raven breathlessly, wanting to make sure she had credit for breaking the story.

"Ooh, I saw him!" Alejandra said, excited. "I love the way he dresses! I wanted to ask him where he found that scarf thing he was wearing."

"It's called an ascot," said Andrew, annoyed. "And it wasn't a cape. It's a *cloak*. Men wear them. Anyway, his name is Sydney, and he's nice, and we've gone out a couple of times, and he thinks Westley is really cute, so thank goodness you're straight, Westley. And that is the end of our staff conversation about my personal relationships, thank you all very much."

Westley felt himself turning a bit red. He tried hard to keep his own personal life separate from work; not that he had much of a personal life these days. Did everyone else at the store have a busy personal life, full of drama and intrigue and romance? He was sure that Julia didn't, at least.

"Anyone else?" said Julia, trying to move things along. "Raven, would you like to share something from your *own* experiences?"

Raven drummed her fingers—stained various shades of blue, as usual—on the table. "No, but I'd like to know how much the store is making from the movie, and whether that will be passed along to the staff who have had extra work to deal with during the filming." (Raven hadn't actually been doing any extra work, as far as Westley could tell, but this was typical. She always had an eye out for a side hustle.)

Julia clearly didn't like the question. "I'm afraid I'm not able to discuss the financial arrangements. That's a private matter. But all of you full-timers are still getting your full salaries, even when we close early."

"Well, is it a lot of money?" Raven persisted. (Appropriately, because she was wearing her "Nevertheless, She Persisted" T-shirt today.)

"I don't have anything to share about that," said Julia with an air of weary finality. "Please understand that the money, whatever it is, is going toward keeping the store on solid ground. Anyway, the work is almost done, and we just need to continue cooperating with the movie staff and helping them with whatever they need. Nobody is getting rich off this. It's an independent film, and there aren't large amounts of money involved."

"Well, there seem to be an awful lot of people running around, getting paid by somebody," Andrew said. "Kelly Drake had a hair *and* a makeup person for just him."

"No wonder he looks so good," Alejandra said.

"He does look good!" said Raven. "Do you think the hair and makeup people might want to style our staff as well, if they're not too busy? That might be good for business!"

Staff Tea was quickly deteriorating. Julia looked horrified. "Again, please do not bother the movie people," said Julia, making a "that's all" gesture with her hands. "I think it's time we got the store opened. Thank you again for coming in early. Let's have a great day."

32

April

April had reluctantly agreed to go on a blind date. Not with L, alas, who hadn't yet responded to April's latest note suggesting they meet Thursday (this didn't worry April, as she knew he was busy with the movie and his work), but with Simon, a friend of Janie's husband, Ryan, whose restaurant had helped cater their second baby's christening. Simon was, Janie swore, a great conversationalist and a really interesting guy. (Apparently every unattached man Janie knew, oddly enough, was a great conversationalist and a really interesting guy. Ryan, oddly enough, never seemed like much of a talker—April had rarely gotten any sort of conversation out of him—so maybe that was Janie's highest priority in a fixer-upper.) This particular Really Interesting Guy was, April had been told, the manager of Mad Hatter, a quirky and well-known restaurant downtown that April had never been to, as it was the sort of pricey place you didn't go to on the spur of the moment. April had tried to stop accepting Janie's offered blind dates (she was still recovering from 24-Hour-Pajamas Guy), but this casual Sunday-night dinner seemed like a good idea, as it would enable her to road-test a new outfit and get in a little first-date banter practice before actually meeting L. So she had texted Simon (in a series of messages meticulously stage-managed by a very excited Janie) and arranged to meet him at Mad Hatter at seven. He had assured her that he was off-duty that night and would enjoy introducing her to the restaurant's cuisine. April wasn't at all sure about going out with someone who non-ironically used the word "cuisine," but she was determined to keep an open mind. She'd waved to Tango Lady, who was gazing out her window as April left the building, and got an almost-wave back—really more of a dramatic wrist-flick, as if accompanied by music.

Stepping out of her Uber, April was charmed even by the Mad Hatter entrance, a door that featured an elaborately carved top hat as a door knocker. Inside, it felt like a magical cave, with the kind of soft lighting that makes everyone look a little glowier, and mural-painted walls featuring abstract shapes of hats. At the front desk, a top-hatted host greeted her with a warm if somewhat rehearsed "Good evening."

"Good evening," April said. "I'm here to meet Simon Rudnick?"

At this, the host seemed to take rather more interest, looking at April more carefully. "Oh, of course," she said. "He's just in the back. Let me take you to your table, and he'll be right with you." She smoothly collected two menus and glided off through a maze of tables, April following as they made their way to a cozy corner booth, lit by a candle.

"This is one of our best tables," the host said, motioning April to sit. "I'll let Simon know you're here."

There was something curiously theatrical about the restaurant, not in a bad way. April was wondering if the waitstaff, in their natty vests, sometimes burst into song and if it would be rude to order a drink immediately when suddenly a man appeared in a dark suit and angular dark-framed glasses. "April?" he said. "I'm Simon. It's so nice to meet you."

"Likewise," said April, relieved that Simon seemed, at first glance, reasonably cute and pleasantly normal, maybe even a little bookish. "I've heard a lot about you from Janie. So you've known Ryan for a long time?"

"Yes, we were in college together," said Simon, sliding into the booth opposite April. "We were both waiters here, years ago, and I became the manager after a sort of weird romantic dust-up happened."

This sounded intriguing. "What do you mean?"

"Well, the previous manager, who was a friend of the owner, was having a fling with the pastry chef, who was the owner's fiancée, and the owner found them together and it was *very* dramatic," said Simon, who clearly enjoyed sharing a bit of gossip. "All three of them ended up leaving the restaurant. We got a new owner a long time ago. Would you like something to drink? I've already ordered a couple of glasses of sparkling wine to start; I hope that's OK with you?"

"Oh, that sounds great," said April. In truth she was mildly irritated that he hadn't asked her what she wanted, but reminded herself that this wasn't the time to be rigid. She could already see a server headed over with a small tray and a sour expression, which seemed at odds with the restaurant's elegance. The server, a tall, slender woman with her hair twisted up in a tight bun beside which a tiny boater hat was secured with a dramatically large hatpin, placed the glasses in front of them, putting them down slightly too heavily. April's splashed up a bit, leaving a small puddle on the table.

Simon suddenly seemed uncomfortable. "Hi, Brooke," he said. "Maybe you could wipe that up?" he asked lightly, seeing that she had made no attempt to right the misstep.

Brooke stared in response. "Oh, I guess I could," she said coolly. Still staring at Simon and elaborately avoiding April's gaze, she took a napkin from her apron pocket and dabbed indifferently at the spill, without actually looking at it. "Will that do?" she said in a tone implying that she didn't care much.

"OK," said Simon quickly. "Thank you. We're good now." Brooke turned and stalked off, and Simon, looking around the room, caught the eye of a suited-and-hatted man and beckoned him. "I'm so sorry," he said to April, holding up a finger as if asking for a quick time-out. To the suited man, not quite as quietly as he seemed to have planned, Simon hissed, "She was *not* supposed to wait on this table! Please arrange for another server for us!" The suited man nodded and hurried off.

April had the strange feeling of having inadvertently walked into somebody else's drama. "Everything OK?" she said.

Simon pressed his fingers into his forehead and sighed heavily. "This is embarrassing," he said. "But I may as well just be honest. Brooke and I broke up recently. It didn't go very well, and obviously she still works here so it's a bit awkward. I tried to arrange for someone else to cover this table but something must have gone wrong. But that was the assistant manager and he'll sort things out. I'm so sorry."

"Oh, I understand," said April, wanting to giggle but feeling that it might have been rude, and wondering why on earth Simon would bring a new date to the restaurant he worked in with his ex? "No worries. We all have baggage. Not your fault. Maybe we can get an appetizer?"

"Of course! How about a sampler plate?"

"Perfect."

A different server arrived at the table. To Simon's request for the appetizer, she nodded, but as she left the table, she turned her head toward April and gave her what could only be described as a sneer, teeth briefly bared and nose wrinkled. Apparently "cuisine" was not the only thing on the menu for April tonight.

"Um, did you see that?" April said, not quite successfully stifling a giggle this time. "I'm going to guess that this new server is maybe also a good friend of your ex?"

Simon sighed heavily. "Yes, she is. Maybe we should have eaten somewhere else."

The meal progressed, rather like one in a farcical comedy in which innuendo rather than food is thrown. Apparently Brooke had many allies in the restaurant: A breadbasket was deliberately put out of April's reach; a salad was served to her without any dressing; a busboy took her wineglass away while still half-full; and her dinner plate was put down with such force that half the pasta on it slid across the table. At this point, she had to give in to laughter—what else could she do?—but Simon was turning red with anger and embarrassment.

"How long did you go out with her?" April asked. "And how many friends does she have? This is really quite an impressive show." Really, she hadn't seen anything this dramatic since that HBO series where Hugh Grant maybe killed someone and Nicole Kidman wore a lot of coats.

"Too long," Simon sighed. "Way, way too long. How about I take you someplace else for dessert?"

April, who was already planning on devouring a pint of Häagen-Dazs at home while texting Janie with the details of the date (and planning how exactly Janie could make this up to her), thought it best to put the evening out of its misery. "I think tonight's kind of done, don't you?" she said as nicely as she could. "I do appreciate the dinner. At least the part of it that I got. Maybe we can try again sometime . . . at a restaurant that doesn't have so much drama?"

"Maybe," said Simon in a tone that made clear that they wouldn't be trying again anytime soon; obviously the rejection had hurt his feelings a bit. But that was fine with April. Simon was nice enough, but there were no fireworks. He'd probably be happier peddling his cuisine—which was good, at least the amount she sampled that wasn't spilled—to somebody else. And really, if this was what practice was like, she'd rather proceed directly to the real thing.

33

Laura

T he silk dress, meticulously hemmed and steamed so that its fabric flowed like water, was safely encased in a Waterton's garment bag and carefully laid out on the backseat of Laura's car (after she had brushed away the crumbs from some stray goldfish crackers and made sure that there were no leaky juice boxes in the vicinity). She didn't usually do personal deliveries of clothing purchases—generally customers were expected to pick up their items after alterations, though a courier might be hired for certain very high-end shoppers—and had planned to ask Sydney to deliver it, as he was working on the movie set. But it turned out Sydney had a dinner date with his bookstore guy; he'd taken more trouble than usual with his attire today, showing up at work in a striped silk blazer and green paisley ascot with the British accent dialed up by half. Laura was happy enough to take the excuse to visit the bookstore again. She had another note to drop into *The Hunger Games* and planned to sneak a peek at A (Andy? Alex?).

The Read the Room parking lot was once again full, with movie people milling in and out of the front door. The harried-looking woman with spiky gray hair, whom Laura had seen in the store before and who always seemed a little stressed, stood by the door. "Good afternoon," she said to Laura. "Just letting customers know that we're once again closing early, due to the movie disruption. In about fifteen minutes."

"That's fine," said Laura. "Is Donna Wolfe, the director, here, do you know?"

"I think she's over there," the woman said, pointing toward the back and noticing that two black-clad people in a corner of the store were busy removing books from a shelf. She gasped. "Excuse me!" she said to Laura, racing off with the cry, "DO NOT TOUCH THE BOOKS!"

Holding the garment bag high so it wouldn't drag on the floor, Laura walked over to where Donna Wolfe was standing, talking to a small group. "Excuse me," she said as Donna finished the conversation and looked over at her. "Ms. Wolfe, you remember me from Waterton's. I'm delivering your gown."

"Ah," said Donna, gazing at Laura through her dark glasses. Or maybe she was looking elsewhere; it was kind of hard to tell. "That was good of you to bring it. Could you please hang it up somewhere?" She lost interest in Laura quickly, turning away. "All right," she said to someone unseen. "I'm going to need to see all those new script pages *now*."

Bookstores are not typically full of convenient places in which to hang a full-length formal gown. Laura looked around and headed to a corner of the store, where a makeshift dressing area with clothing racks had been set up. She recognized Maverick, Sydney's friend (they had a distinctive ear tattoo and were wearing multitudes of safety pins on their clothing), who was looking at a tablet and gazed up when Laura approached.

"Hi," Laura said. "Maverick, right? I'm Laura, Sydney's coworker from the store? We all went out one night a while ago?"

Maverick's face, initially puzzled, quickly cleared. "Oh, right! Hey, Laura. Are you looking for Sydney? He's not here. He has a hot date with that bookstore dude who looks like he's on *Suits*. If *Suits* specialized in ill-fitting ones."

"No," said Laura. "I'm delivering a gown for Ms. Wolfe. Could I hang it here?"

"I don't know anything about a gown. Is it a costume?"

"No, it's Ms. Wolfe's personal garment. It just needs to hang somewhere. Is this OK?"

Maverick shrugged. "Sure, sure. Nobody told me a gown was coming in, but that's OK. Jane Eyre is a 14 and her résumé says size 6, but sure, I'll make it work. Whatever."

This seemed like a little more drama than Laura had time for. "OK. Thank you. I'll just hang it right here," she said. Maverick nodded, so she hung the garment bag on the end of the rack and headed for Young Adult, where indeed the three *Hunger Games* copies still sat in a row. Looking around furtively, she slipped a folded piece of paper into the middle book.

Realizing that she should probably notify Donna Wolfe's assistant of the gown's arrival—otherwise she didn't entirely trust Maverick not to dress somebody in it and insert it into the film— Laura looked around for Joanna, and instead saw A, emerging from the dressing area wearing jeans and a flannel shirt, similar to what he normally wore but much higher quality, to Laura's trained eye. He looked uncomfortable. "Is this OK?" he asked Maverick, who said "Splendid" and elaborately bowed.

A, embarrassed, turned around and caught Laura's eye. He seemed to recognize her. "Oh, hi," he said. "That was you who brought the cookies, right? They were awesome."

"Glad you liked them," said Laura. "Is this your costume for the movie?"

"Yes," A said. "Not like it's really a costume, though. I'm just a stand-in."

"I wonder why they have you in those jeans," Laura said out loud but really to herself. "A straighter cut would be better on you, and these ones look sort of obviously expensive, which is not what I think a character who works in a bookstore would be wearing. And I think a soft blue plaid in the shirt would be better with your eyes than this mustardy color . . ." She broke off, seeing A staring at her, puzzled. "Sorry," she said. "I have a lot of thoughts about clothes. Never mind. Is it fun being in a movie?"

A sighed, clearly not fond of the topic. "Not really," he said. "I thought it might be fun? But it's basically a lot of standing around. I'd rather just do my job."

"You must be very busy," said Laura, speaking deliberately as she wasn't sure what to say next. It was nice to be talking with A, but it seemed like the conversation should be going somewhere, and it wasn't moving past this awkward small talk. "Not much time outside of work?" she asked, hoping she was bringing a delicately mysterious nuance to the question.

"I guess not," A said in what seemed to be a fairly nuance-free way. A woman hurried up to him, hairbrush and can of spray in hand. Someone else yelled "Places!" A looked overwhelmed. "I'm sorry, excuse me," he said. "Better get back to it."

"I guess you'd better," Laura said, trying not to sound relieved.

"Uh, sure," he said, turning away and submitting to the hairbrush.

This had not been an entirely satisfying encounter; clearly he was shy (and how charming was that, for someone who looked like him to be shy?), and there were too many people around, and he was distracted by all the movie stuff. But at least it was an encounter. And soon they'd be connecting for real, outside of the store, when they could converse freely. She hoped he'd pick up the note soon. Things were starting to move more quickly.

Hi,

How about next Thursday, the 6th, at 4:30 p.m.? The café I have in mind is the Tough Beans coffee shop on 15th and John St.; I've always thought it looked a bit like a set from a noir movie, a place where seedy transactions might go down; maybe a place Raymond Chandler might have set a story or two. The coffee's good too. See you then.

L

34

Westley

Monday was Westley's day off this week and he was grateful, more so than usual. During less-stressful times, he never knew what to do with his days off and would actually have preferred working; he typically spent these days taking long walks, half-watching TV shows streamed on his laptop, and deciding between the three nearby takeout places where he'd get his dinner. (He'd recently been horrified to realize that he was alternating three evening meals—lamb kebab, cheeseburger, chicken shawarma—each of which provided enough for the next day's lunch as well—so precisely that he knew what day it was based on the meal he was eating. Clearly it was time to mix things up a bit.) Lately both Jillian and Cory were gone a lot—Cory had a new gig that was keeping him away, and Jillian had apparently met somebody—and it felt like a treat to have the house to himself. He was happy for the solitude, and for a day when the most sociability he planned was to get coffee up the street, where the barista would wink at him and give him an extra shot, as baristas tended to do.

Today's barista was the usual weekday guy, all tattoos and forearms, and Westley's latte was done to foamy perfection. He put a cap on the cup and headed for the door, bent on his usual day-off routine of taking a long walk with his coffee, when

Westley spotted a man slumped at a table, staring at his phone. The man looked like he hadn't showered for a while; his clothes had a limp, lifeless look and his hair seemed flattened by an impromptu nap. Nonetheless, something about the way the man was sitting had an air of self-conscious importance—as if he was aware that people were looking at him and wanted to give them what they were after—and Westley knew immediately who this was: It was Kelly Drake.

Westley stared, and Kelly looked up from his phone, scowling attractively in a practiced way. "Do I know you?" he said.

"Hey," said Westley. "You're Kelly, right? I'm Westley. From the bookstore. They've got me standing in for you in the movie." Something didn't seem right about Kelly sitting here. "Aren't you supposed to be off shooting a commercial somewhere?"

"Oh, for God's sake," said Kelly, "keep your voice down." He motioned for Westley to sit down, looking around elaborately to see if anyone recognized him. Nobody did—the coffeehouse was quiet and the few patrons seemed far more interested in their own phones—but it seemed important to Kelly to make the effort.

"I thought you were out of town," Westley said. "Isn't that why I'm standing in? Aren't you coming back?"

"Well, obviously I'm not out of town," Kelly hissed. "I needed to get out of that movie for a few days. Donna was making me crazy and I had another project I needed to look into. I'll come back this week and make nice."

"So you just made up that whole thing about a commercial?" Westley asked, irritated by the lie but nonetheless impressed—obviously Kelly was a better actor than he'd originally thought—and feeling enormously relieved at the thought of Kelly returning to the production. He was tired of how working on a movie scene seemed to be a great deal of flurry for a very small moment.

"Yes. I made my agent go along with it. Donna will never know. We'll just say the commercial got canceled," Kelly said. "Besides, I'm busy launching a limited series. It's independently funded. It's called *Rain Delay*, and it's sort of a film noir set in Seattle. I play a detective named Jeff Delay. And I'm producing. I think it'll be big. I hear premium cable is interested, maybe Max."

"Oh, wow," said Westley politely, despite not really understanding most of what Kelly had said. Kelly was staring at him in a way that was making him a bit uncomfortable.

"What's your name again?"

"Westley. With a T."

"Like in *The Princess Bride*?"

"Yes, like that." Westley had occasionally considered getting a T-shirt that said "Yes, like in *The Princess Bride*," but it seemed a bit heavy-handed.

"How would you like to be in my series?" Kelly said. "Just a small part. You just look so . . . Seattle."

Westley had no idea what looking "Seattle" might mean and wondered if he'd just been insulted. "I don't think so," he said. "Acting isn't really working out for me. I don't think I even like being in front of cameras."

Kelly laughed, as if Westley had told a good joke. "Right! No, seriously." He rummaged in his wallet and handed Westley a card. "That's my agent, Ramona. Call her. Tell her I sent you. Seriously. It'll be fun."

Westley took the card and put it in his shirt pocket. He had no intention of calling that number. Acting was for people who were more certain of where they belonged. It was odd, though, that Kelly seemed so different here, like a faded version of himself. Maybe actors were just different without lights shining on them. "I don't mean to be rude," Westley said hesitantly, "but are you OK? You seem . . . not quite yourself."

Kelly laughed, the sort without any merriment in it. "This is me without the hair and makeup. I can't be bothered to put myself together every day. Too much work. And this way, nobody recognizes me."

This seemed a bit of a stretch—as far as Westley knew, Kelly Drake was not quite at the level of fame at which he'd be recognized in a random coffee shop—but he nodded.

"I guess I'll see you at the store, then?" Westley said.

"Sure. Bye."

Westley was clearly being dismissed. On the sidewalk outside the coffee shop, he paused. There was something odd about seeing Kelly Drake looking so non-Kelly-Drake-ish, out in the world. He looked strangely familiar, somehow. And suddenly Westley realized why: Kelly looked exactly like the description of Will, the handsome firefighter in *Shivering Timbers*, Duke Munro's book.

Raven

The best thing I ever found in a book? A twenty-dollar bill. Ha. I wish. I've never found cash in a book; I don't think anyone out there is using currency for a bookmark, though it would be a nice treat for me if they were. I mostly just find the usual junk: bookmarks from other bookstores, New Yorker *subscription cards, library hold slips, grocery lists. Once I found a photograph, old and faded and yellow and faintly sticky, of three kids in a wading pool, laughing as they splashed water on each other. I wondered if there was a way to figure out who they were, but eventually I had to toss it; it seemed like an impossible task to track them down.*

I'm really not angry all the time. People think I am, but I just have that kind of face; Resting Bitch Face is what people call it. I'm just not a smiler. If you want me to smile, you'll need to actually say something funny, or do something that genuinely makes me happy. And not enough people do that. Particularly at my workplace, Read the Room, where everyone falls all over Westley because he's so good-looking, or Alejandra because she's pretty and cool and supposedly a science fiction writer (but seriously, has anyone actually read her work? Maybe she's terrible. I mean, who knows?). Nobody really pays any attention to me, and I swear I'm the one who's holding the entire operation together. Julia is theoretically in charge—I mean, she is the owner—but she's too easily panicked. I'm the one who always knows exactly what's going on, at any given time.

I got the job at Read the Room about five years ago; before that, I was waiting tables at a sleepy café, sick of being told to smile by my customers and wondering what I would do with my life. An English degree, specializing in women writers of the nineteenth and early twentieth centuries, doesn't really prepare you for much, but I loved it. It didn't occur to me that working in a bookstore was something I could possibly do—that seemed like the kind of job people in movies have, almost too pretty to be real—but one day I saw a "Help Wanted" sign in the window (seriously, that's how Julia finds employees; she thinks that fate sends the right people to her door) and just like that, there I was: a full-time bookseller. I would never tell anyone here, but I absolutely love my job. There's something about this place that makes me feel instantly calmer, like the books are surrounding me with reassurance.

Being around books was something I always dreamed of growing up; my single mom never had money for extras. I didn't think books were extras but we disagreed, so I grew up haunting the library, checking out the same books over and over because they were friends that I'd missed. It still seems unreal to me that I work surrounded by books, and that I can even buy them with my staff discount. I'm extremely strict with myself about this—two paperback books per each every-other-week paycheck, no more—but it still feels, to the kid I once was, like an unheard-of dream. (That kid's name, by the way, was Karen. I changed it legally when I was eighteen. I mean, do I seem like a Karen to you?)

My yarn business is another dream, just something that I thought would be fun that I do from my studio apartment. I've always loved to crochet—my mom taught me, with scrap balls of yarn that we'd find at the Goodwill—but I always found the colors too cartoonishly bright. A few years ago, I had the idea to buy some fabric dye and transform some white yarn in my sink into a really pretty soft blue. It turned out beautifully and before I knew it I had an Etsy page and a kitchen filled with plastic tubs and liners. I'm not making much money but I've got a few loyal customers and I love thinking up things to do with the yarn. I've made myself some jewelry and knitted a sweater from a pattern (it didn't turn out exactly as nice as the picture, but it's not like I work in a place where people dress up). I'm now thinking about a very old-school crocheted swimwear line, like what you see people wearing on beaches in 1920s photographs. I haven't told anyone about this idea, as they'd probably try to talk me out of it. I think I'm just more visionary than most people.

I wouldn't say I have a lot of friends at work. What I do have is an awkward situation: Westley and I had a bit of a thing behind a bookshelf at last year's staff holiday party. We'd both had too much to drink (and I felt awful the next day; that cheap Chardonnay is nasty), and I mean, come on: Who wouldn't want to make out with Westley? He's quite a decent kisser, if you're wondering. It was all entirely consensual and instantly regretted—well, by Westley at least, who eventually jumped away from me as if I was radioactive. We've now agreed to treat each other with respect, blah blah blah, and never to discuss it again, but it still hangs in the air, like the faintly mildewy aroma Read the Room gives off no matter how much we clean it. I actually like the smell, though I only notice it now if I've been away for a while. Westley, for the record, smells pretty good too. Sometimes I imagine how things might have gone differently—a story in which Westley and I fell in love—and it passes the time. He's nice, really.

There are a lot of not-so-glamorous elements to working in a bookstore. You have to do cleaning as part of your shift every day—there's no janitor to do things like sweeping, mopping, and dusting, though we do have someone come in a few times a year to wash the windows—and Julia makes us all spend a lot of time checking the shelves to be sure they're properly alphabetized. I think Julia was born in alphabetical order. She's always saying, "What if a customer came in for a specific book and couldn't find it because the shelves were out of order?" Well, the customer would just come to the desk and ask us and we'd figure out how to find it for them, right? But she's the boss.

The customers are, for the most part, my favorite part of the job. Sure, there are a few diehard Amazon users who think we don't see them furtively photographing book covers with their phones for convenient online ordering later. But most people who come into Read the Room are there because they love books and bookstores, and I enjoy helping people find what they're looking for, or telling them what they're looking for when they don't really know. Sometimes I wonder if certain authors, like Alice McDermott and Brit Bennett and Emma Straub, should be paying me a commission, for the many hands into which I've pressed their books. But hey, I don't do this for the money. I do it because I think I was meant to be in a bookstore. It's where I feel like myself. It's my home.

35

April

April sat in the coffee shop, feeling oddly self-conscious and breathlessly excited, like she was about to read a final chapter in a book full of twists and turns. She'd signed off work early and exchanged pleasant nods with Tango Lady in her building lobby, whose raised eyebrows indicated approval of April's new outfit (slim jeans and a faintly vintage-looking black shirt with broderie lace, casual yet more sophisticated than anything April had ever worn). It was not quite 4:30, but she'd arrived early to be sure to not keep L waiting, realizing that she didn't have his cell number and couldn't text if she was running late. It seemed so strange to not know how to contact someone; maybe she should have asked for his number? But that would break the whole old-world vibe that they had going, with this correspondence. Anyway, too late for that now. Here she was at Tough Beans with her copy of *The Thin Man* carefully placed face-up on her table, sipping a cappuccino and trying to calm down the rapid beat of her heart. (Admittedly, the cappuccino—probably the strongest one she'd ever had, which practically lurched out of the cup and hissed at her—wasn't helping.)

In a city that had become too full of chain coffeehouses, Tough

Beans was an old-school place—maybe that was why L had chosen it. April hadn't been there before, though she knew it was famous in Seattle lore: an independently owned café that had been around forever, operating under various names (legend was that Theodore Roethke used to write poems at the back table), serving coffee out of thick white mugs that held faint shadows of beverages past, with patrons sitting at a mishmash of perpetually wiggly wooden tables and chairs seemingly sourced from long-ago garage sales. The only food item Tough Beans served was brownies; thick, dense brownies that the owner cooked up every morning in the back room and left sitting on the counter all day under a big glass globe. It was kind of brilliant, April thought; the chocolate aroma merged with the coffee to create a delicious wall of scent, and she imagined that if you sat there long enough drinking strong coffee and eating chocolate, you'd be so buzzed that you wouldn't need to sleep that night. Which is how many of the patrons looked: like they'd been at Tough Beans for a few days solid, making their way through some sort of existential crisis. April, feeling pleasantly stylish in her new clothes, didn't quite fit in. Nonetheless, she had to restrain herself from beaming at the other patrons; it was a beautiful day, and something momentous was finally going to happen.

It was 4:34. L was late. Well, it was only a few minutes, and traffic was notoriously bad at this time of day, and buses weren't always on time, and it didn't mean anything bad if someone wasn't as particular about punctuality as April was. Who knew how far away he lived? Maybe it was silly for her to have arrived so early. She needed to not obsess so much about timeliness. Everything was fine.

Suddenly April's phone flashed with a text and she was momentarily startled; how had L known how to reach her? But no, it was Ben.

Hey sis! How you? I got the bookstore movie gig!!!!

April replied automatically:

That's great! Congratulations.

She expected that this might not be the end of the exchange, and sure enough, it wasn't:

Wondering if you can maybe spot me another grand?
Unexpected bills, and they cut my hours AGAIN at the deli.
You're the BEST xoxoxo

April sighed and replied.

Call me tomorrow.

Maybe L also had a brother who drove him crazy. But at this point all she really knew about him was that he was definitely late. April watched idly as an elderly couple entered, maneuvering their walkers to the counter and being heartily if sarcastically greeted by the barista, who clearly knew them well and carried their coffee—regular drip, nothing fancy; they hadn't even needed to tell the barista what they wanted—for them to a table. They sat, sipping their coffee, not talking to each other but seeming not to need to. Maybe that was what love meant: sitting and drinking coffee with someone and not needing any words. The sun was slanting in through the west windows, catching in the cracks on the tables, blurring the faded posters on the wall.

Five p.m. came and went, with April trying to interest herself in reading the news on her phone, and trying not to constantly glance at the doorway every time a new customer came in. But nobody looked like L, and nobody paid any attention to her—and with every new non-L person through the door, April's shoulders seemed to drop just a little lower. The dregs of her cappuccino had long ago turned cold. She didn't want another.

April made herself sit at the table until 5:30, but by that point, she could no longer deny it: L wasn't coming, and that was that. It had been stupid not to get his number. Maybe the whole thing was just stupid. Maybe it really was just a game to him, nothing more. Maybe meet-cutes don't happen in real life; at least, not in hers. She carried her empty mug to the scratched plastic bin under the window, took one last whiff of fading chocolate, and left the café. The late-afternoon sun seemed a little less bright, but she nonetheless blinked hard upon stepping outside, to ward off a very unwanted tear.

36

Laura

I t hadn't been a problem for Laura to get approval to leave work early to go meet A at Tough Beans; she was one of the highest-seniority people in her department and rarely asked for extra time off. She suspected Sydney thought something was going on, as he'd given her a rather knowing look as she waved good-bye for the afternoon. One of these days she would tell him the whole story, but for now she preferred to be mysterious. Though abbreviated, the workday had seemed long, and Laura's stomach had been flip-flopping a bit all day in nervously happy anticipation. She didn't care to count how many years it had been since she'd met somebody new for a date (for that was surely what this was?), and she tried not to think about how that person had been Sam, but it was exciting, in a teenage-y way. At minimum, she'd be having coffee and exchanging small talk with a very handsome man—who would probably be a lot more relaxed than he was in the bookstore, as he wouldn't be on the clock. And maybe it would lead to something more. To Laura's surprise, the anticipation really did feel good. Maybe it truly was time.

Laura slid into her car and, automatically, checked her phone before starting the ignition. A missed call notification from just moments ago and a text from Ashley popped up.

Call me!!! ASAP! Please!

Fingers trembling, Laura pressed Ashley's number instantly. Though a bit of a worrier in general, one thing Laura had never allowed herself to contemplate was the possibility of something terrible happening to Olivia; somehow, she just couldn't bring herself to imagine it. The world, she was certain, could never be so cruel as to take both her beloved husband and her precious child, could it? Laura's heart seemed to stop and breathing seemed impossible until she heard Ashley's voice.

"Laura!" said Ashley, picking up instantly on the first ring and sounding urgent, which wasn't like her. "Don't panic! Livvy is fine!"

"Oh, thank goodness," said Laura, gasping a bit and feeling as if sudden storm clouds had parted. "You scared me!" The world seemed lighter once again. Of course Olivia was fine. Of course she was.

"I'm really sorry!" said Ashley. "I didn't mean to upset you. But I do need you to come home right away because I can't stay with Livvy. Zach had a skateboarding accident and he's in the emergency room and I need to go." Ashley sounded upset, in a way that Laura found touching. It was hard to imagine someone having tender feelings for Zach, but what was that expression? A lid for every pot?

"Oh, I hope he's OK," Laura said. "But I have an appointment. Can you drop Livvy at Hayden's? I'm sure his mom wouldn't mind."

"I tried. They're not home," Ashley said, her voice catching as if she might burst into tears. "I'm really sorry, but I have to get to the hospital. Apparently Zach had a concussion and some sort of amnesia and he thinks he's fourteen years old. So I need you to come right away. Please!"

Laura thought privately that Zach often seemed as if he was fourteen years old, so perhaps nothing was amiss. But Ashley sounded like she was practically out the door already, and a seven-year-old absolutely couldn't be left alone. Rebecca was on a busy trial and surely couldn't drop everything. There wasn't time to find another sitter, and nothing else to be done. "OK, OK," Laura said. "I'll be there in just a few minutes. Hang on." Damn it, she thought, picturing A waiting and waiting for someone who never came. But emergencies did happen, and surely he knew that she had a child—of course he knew, he'd seen her with Olivia in the store—and hopefully would understand that an unavoidable family situation had cropped up. Driving home as quickly as legally possible, Laura sketched out another note in her head. Never mind coffee; it was time to extend a dinner invitation.

Arriving home, Laura barely had her key in the lock when the front door swung open and Ashley flew out, looking tearful. "Thank you!" she said. "I have to run!"

"I hope Zach is OK!" Laura called after her. "Let me know!" She entered, closing the door behind her. Olivia was perched on a stool at the kitchen counter, a plate of sliced apple in front of her (causing Laura to feel a moment of gratitude that Ashley, even in the throes of personal crisis, had made time to assemble a healthy snack). She looked at Laura, wide-eyed.

"Hi, sweetie," Laura said, dropping a kiss on top of Olivia's head and tousling her curls. "How was school today?"

Olivia was not in the mood for small talk. "Is Zach going to be OK?"

"I'm sure he will."

"Ashley Two was *crying*," Olivia said solemnly. Clearly this had shaken her; she'd never seen her easygoing babysitter upset before.

"She was just shocked," Laura explained. "People get emotional when they're surprised like that. I'm sure he's going to be fine. Ashley will let us know as soon as she can. Don't worry."

"But how do you know he's going to be fine?" Olivia persisted.

Laura paused, trying to find that tricky balance of being honest yet positive. "Well, you're right. I don't really know. But he's young and healthy and he's at a hospital where they'll take good care of him, so it seems likely that he'll be fine. And sometimes what we do in life is look on the positive side. If we don't know what's going on, it's always best to assume good news."

"Why?" Olivia was ignoring her snack now.

"Because it just makes everyone feel better," Laura said.

Olivia pondered this, eventually nodding.

"OK," said Laura. "Finish your snack and wash your hands. We're going out to get some pizza. And on the way, we're going to stop at the bookstore. There's something I need to do there."

37

April

Maybe L was for Loser. Or Lonely. Or Lame. April was trying hard not to let being stood up get her down, but she was losing the battle. It was just so strange—L had seemed so engaged on paper. What kind of person sends nice messages hidden in YA books, but then fails to show up when it counts? Had the whole thing been his idea of a joke—to play along with this weird note-writing person, and then laugh when she ended up sitting in a coffeehouse alone? Was somebody watching at Tough Beans, and was she about to become the subject of some sad viral video?

Maybe she'd completely misjudged him. April, trying to work in her too-quiet apartment, kept playing the previous afternoon over in her head, wondering how to make its ending turn out differently. It was hard not to feel a little humiliated. Though nobody at Tough Beans had seemed to pay the slightest bit of attention to her, wasn't it a bit pathetic to get dressed up in a nice outfit and then wait for someone who never showed? She'd felt so good when she arrived, so chic and confident and ready to embark on a potentially fascinating journey, and now she just felt small and mousy, like somebody nobody noticed. Somebody who'd maybe been too easily fooled. Somebody who'd taken a leap and had found no one there to break her fall. Somebody who, upon returning home and being told by Mr. Jackson in the hallway that she looked nice, mumbled something unintelligible and hurried inside her door to let go and cry.

A knock interrupted her thoughts, forcing her up from her chair. It was Ben—of course it was, who else would come over unannounced?—beaming and carrying a tired supermarket bouquet wrapped in crinkly plastic, along with a lumpy-looking duffel bag.

"Oh, hi," April said, walking away from the door. He bounded in, putting down the bag and handing her the flowers. They looked about as weary as she felt.

"Hey!" said Ben cheerfully. "Those are for you. I wanted to thank you for the money."

"Well, you shouldn't thank me by spending it on me," said April. Although, to be fair, he clearly hadn't spent much.

"I'm so stoked for the movie gig!" Ben said, seeming not to notice April's low spirits. "I'm going to be an extra in the bookstore scenes. It actually pays! It's just a couple of days, but it starts tomorrow!"

"That's great," April replied mechanically, not really registering his news; she was in no mood to hear about good fortune. "I'm busy working now. Thanks for stopping by."

"What's the rush? You don't have time to talk to your brother, the famous actor?" said Ben, opening the door of April's fridge and frowning at its contents.

"I'm just kind of busy," April said. "And no, I don't have any of that expensive juice you drink."

"It's acai berry juice. It's very good for your gut. You should try it," Ben said. He finally looked at her. "What's wrong? You look like Dad after a bad golf game."

"My gut is fine. It's nothing," April said. She knew well not to share details of her personal life, as Ben was incapable of keeping things to himself. Not long ago, she'd given him advice about a girlfriend and then days later, said girlfriend turned up on April's doorstep, accusing April of "interfering" in their relationship and complaining about Ben's sexual technique (a topic that April's advice had not remotely alluded to and which she did *not* wish to hear about, thank you very much).

"Oh, come on," said Ben, taking a can of Diet Coke from April's fridge and popping the tab. "Something's bothering you. Maybe I can help." Ben had once played a therapist in a community theater production and felt that it gave him some expertise, not to mention some appropriate lines to parrot.

"It's nothing," said April against her better judgment but suddenly finding that she was welcoming the chance to talk to someone, even if that someone was Ben. "I just tried something and it didn't work out. It's OK." Suddenly it was as if a latched cupboard door had popped open, spilling out its contents like a waterfall. "There was a guy at the bookstore that I liked—you know, the store down the street, where the movie is. He works there. I left him a note one day, and we wrote notes back and forth for a bit. It was fun. But then we made plans to meet at a coffeehouse yesterday afternoon and he never showed. So now I don't know what to think. Maybe he was just having fun with me."

"Doesn't sound like much fun," Ben said, gulping his soda. "So who's this guy again?"

"Well, that's just it," said April. "I don't know his name. I could have asked somebody at the bookstore, I guess, but it just seemed like a fun game to be having this anonymous correspondence."

"Like *You've Got Mail*," said Ben unexpectedly.

"How do you even know that movie?"

"Kelsey made me watch it." Kelsey was the girlfriend of the uncomfortable conversation; they were still, unfortunately, more or less together, and April now tried to avoid being alone with her, or even thinking about her. "So this guy is Tom Hanks and you're Meg Ryan, right?"

"You are so not helping," April said. "Do something useful and get me a Diet Coke." He complied. "So, I just don't know where things stand and I'm embarrassed to go back to the bookstore and see him, after he stood me up like that."

"But he doesn't know who you are, right? So why would you be embarrassed to see him? Why would you take this personally at all, when he's never actually met you?"

Every now and then Ben made a good point, like those proverbial stopped clocks that are right twice a day. April paused. "Yeah, OK, that's true. He doesn't know who he stood up. But he still stood me up."

"Did he have your cell number?"

"Well, no, like I said, we haven't had conversations in real life."

"So he could have had a legit emergency and had no way to tell you."

"I guess," April said. She hadn't really let herself consider this possibility. "But how often do people have real emergencies, the kind that mean they can't show up where they said they'll show up?"

"All the time," said Ben. "I had one the other day. The power went out at my apartment, and I wasn't able to get to a meeting with a guy who's maybe going to cast me in his web series."

"How does losing your power mean you can't get to an appointment?"

"Well, I couldn't charge my phone," Ben said, as if explaining to a child. "So obviously I couldn't go anywhere, because my phone wouldn't work and nobody would be able to reach me."

"But nobody could reach you if your phone was dead, whether you stayed home or went out."

"Exactly," said Ben, sipping his Diet Coke.

"You're an idiot," said April. But she was starting to feel a little better. "Maybe he did have a real emergency, or a delay. It was kind of stupid to not get his cell number. Maybe I should just go talk to him and give him the chance to explain."

"Do it!" Ben pumped a fist in the air. "Go there! Fling yourself into the unknown! Speak to the anonymous guy! Seize the day!"

"And I should follow your advice . . . why?" April asked, smiling in spite of herself.

"Because I know that if this guy went out with you, he would be one lucky dude. You're awesome. You should give him a chance to experience that awesomeness."

"You're only saying that because I sent you money."

Ben held out his arms, palms open and empty. "Nope. I'm just saying it because it's the truth. And I don't say it often enough. Give the dude a chance. You deserve to have something amazing happen."

April was touched, and a little flustered; except for a brief period after their mother's death, when he would call her every day just to check in and try to make her laugh, Ben was rarely this sweet. Perhaps it was worth putting up with him. "OK," she said. "OK. I'll do it. Maybe tomorrow. Thank you." She gave him a quick hug. "But I need you to leave now because I have work to do."

Ben pointed at the bag on the floor. "I need to use your laundry room," he said. "I'm out of underwear."

38

Westley

Filming on Monday was finally finished, and Westley was relieved; the lights were getting hot and he was tired of keeping his mind blank, which seemed to be the easiest way to avoid looking at the camera. Things were ending early today. Westley didn't know why, but he wasn't going to question it; Kelly was back, and the movie seemed to be proceeding smoothly, finally, though one of the new extras was spending a lot of time staring at Westley, and at one point walked up to him and said, "Seize the day, man! Go for it!" and pumped a fist. Westley had no idea how to respond to this, so he nodded and tried to look busy.

After Fedora yelled "Wrap" and Westley was rearranging the books on his desk to better resemble his real job rather than the movie job, he sensed somebody looking at him. It was the harried-looking woman who had the unfortunate job of being Donna Wolfe's assistant; Westley didn't know her name but recognized her, though he'd never seen her separately from Donna before. She had the appearance of being held together by something very tenuous, like a sort of house of cards in human form. "Excuse me, Westley?" she said. "Do you have a minute?"

"Uh, sure," said Westley, surprised that she knew his name, as they'd never spoken before.

Her next question was even more surprising. "Are you by any chance free this evening?" she asked. "And do you own a suit that is acceptable for a formal event?"

"Um, what?" This was not at all what he expected. "I mean, I guess so. And not really. I mean, yes, I'm free, and, yes, I do. Own a suit. But it's really old and not very nice. I don't know if it still fits." He paused, took a breath, began again. "Can you tell me why you are asking? I'm sorry, but I don't even know your name."

"It's not for me," the woman said, managing to look simultaneously amused and stressed. "I'm Joanna, by the way. Ms. Wolfe's assistant. She has a gala event tonight at the Olympic Hotel downtown, and she wondered if you might like to accompany her."

This conversation was just getting stranger and stranger. "Huh. Hang on. Donna Wolfe is asking me *out*?"

Joanna made a noise that might have been a laugh, if given sufficient oxygen. "No, no. Not like that. She just thought that, since you are in the movie, you might like to escort her to an event. You would meet some members of the press. It would be a chance for some visibility for you."

Westley was puzzled. "Why would I want visibility? I'm just a stand-in. I work in a bookstore."

"It's of course up to you," said Joanna, who didn't appear to be terribly invested in this errand. "But Ms. Wolfe thought you might enjoy it. It's a gala dinner and you would hear Ms. Wolfe's speech. If you need a suit, the wardrobe department could provide you with one."

Westley opened his mouth to say no. But then he thought of another quiet evening at his house, eating takeout and trying to stay out of his housemates' way, and of how he kept urging himself to try different things, and heard himself saying, "Sure, why not? What time?"

"Cocktails begin at eight. Maverick, in wardrobe, has been alerted that you might need to borrow something to wear. Here is your ticket for the event. Ms. Wolfe will meet you in the Olympic Hotel lobby at 8:10 sharp." Joanna handed over the ticket and quickly turned on her heel and walked away, on alert for the next crisis.

Three hours later, Westley—outfitted in a sleek black suit,

which a grumpy Maverick had produced from a rack and pinned in a few nonvisible places, and with his hair meticulously slicked back by Inez the hair person—stood in the elegant Olympic Hotel lobby. He'd felt rather self-conscious on the bus, where people kept looking at him and elaborately getting out of his way like he was some sort of royalty, but taking a car downtown was expensive. Donna Wolfe, in a shiny black gown, was standing next to a large potted palm and an overstuffed sofa as if she'd been posed there for editorial purposes, swiping on her phone with a slender finger. She looked up as Westley approached. "Ah," she said. "You."

Westley wasn't quite sure how to respond to that, though it wasn't actually a question. "Yes," he said awkwardly. "It's me. Thank you for inviting me."

Donna Wolfe—Westley still found it difficult to think of her without using both names—ignored his words. She slipped her phone into her clutch purse. "All right," she said. "We'll walk in together. There will be a few members of the press. Do not answer any of their questions."

Across the lobby, Westley could see a small crowd gathered around the entrance to what seemed to be a ballroom, with high ceilings and elaborate archways like a castle. A makeshift red carpet had been placed over the lobby rug, and some sporadic flashbulbs fluttered. To Westley, who had not been to any sort of formal event since his senior prom (an awkward, stressful evening in which his date ended up crying because her fantasy of Westley asking her to marry him on prom night didn't materialize), it all looked unexpectedly glamorous. Donna Wolfe, whose trademark dark glasses seemed to coordinate perfectly with her gown, slipped her hand through the crook of his arm and purposefully steered him toward the entry. Though other guests seemed to be stopping at a table manned by well-dressed people with lists and clipboards, she bypassed that checkpoint entirely, waving imperiously and sailing toward the small group of photographers, towing Westley as if he were cargo.

Only a few flashbulbs clicked; this was Seattle, after all, not

Hollywood. "Hey Donna!" one of the photographers called. "Who's your hot date?"

Donna Wolfe, acting as if she hadn't heard, glided through the doorway, and Westley, made a bit red-faced by the question, was swept along with her as if on an unavoidable tide. The ballroom was glittery and vast, with candlelit tables and a small army of black-aproned servers, one of whom approached with a tray full of champagne flutes. Donna Wolfe took one, nodding to Westley that he should do the same.

He hesitated. "It's all free, right?"

Donna Wolfe, looking pained, nodded.

This was definitely the swankiest room Westley had ever been in, and the most well-dressed company he'd been with; he was accustomed to the casualness of the bookstore, really the only place where he felt at home. The beautiful ballroom felt like a place for somebody else, someone more confident. Westley, tieless because Maverick had thought an open shirt (also borrowed, and distractingly silky) would "offset the suit's formality," was uncomfortably aware that he was still wearing his work sneakers. Maybe that was why people were looking at him, maybe wondering why Donna Wolfe was showing up with some schmuck who didn't even own dress shoes. Because they really were looking at him, in a way that made him nervous. Coming here was a mistake. Maybe Donna Wolfe wouldn't mind if he left early.

Moving through the crowd as if fully expecting it to part for her—which, surprisingly, it pretty much did—Donna Wolfe maneuvered Westley through the room, pausing in front of a distinguished, arty-looking man in a stylish suit that fit him far better than Westley's borrowed one did. "Ah. Paolo," she said. "I thought you'd like to meet this young man. Regarding that project we talked about."

Paolo, who smelled of an extremely pungent yet not unappealing cologne—it was like the scent of a very masculine garden—stared at Westley, who smiled back uncertainly. The smile was, quickly and dramatically, returned.

TO: All Read the Room Staff
FROM: Julia@readtheroom.com
SUBJECT: Movie shoot ending (finally!)

Hello, everyone. I am VERY happy to report that the end is in sight, and the final days of filming will be at the end of this week. I have so appreciated everyone's patience with this process. I have learned a great deal about the movie business, particularly about what movie people mean when they say there will be "no disruption," and will remember that knowledge going forward. I have also learned to truly value the peaceful atmosphere of the store when it is not a movie set, and will treasure that going forward, as I hope will all of you.

A reminder that even though we have had much commotion in the store in recent weeks, everyone's duties remain the same. Today I found a copy of Colson Whitehead's *The Underground Railroad* in the Travel section, and George Eliot's *Silas Marner* in Memoir & Biography. Please be sure to check the shelves in your assigned sections daily!

One of the extras yesterday—the one who was dismissed for "stealing focus," whatever that is—asked me a strange question about leaving notes in books. (Specifically: "Like, if someone liked someone and left a note in a book, someone would find it, right?") I have no idea what he was talking about, but it seemed like a good opportunity to remind you that our customers should find nothing in our books except pages and printed words.

Thank you again for all your patience during this ordeal. I look forward to Read the Room returning to its tranquil self. When the movie opens in theaters, I will organize a staff outing.

Julia

P.S. I have been notified by Mel, the café manager, that Sergio the pastry chef has indeed left this week to study shoemaking, and has been replaced by a man named Sébastien, which is pronounced the French way (he is in fact French and worked as a baker in Paris). Mel hopes the bookstore staff will let her know what they think of his baking, and is offering each of us a free pastry this week. Heaven knows we all deserve one.

39

Laura

Zach, it turned out, was fine. He did not have a concussion, Ashley happily reported, just a scrape on his head after his skateboard became entangled with a dog's leash, causing a dramatic head-first spill. (The dog, Ashley was quick to add, was uninjured, though its owner had a few choice words on the matter.) The doctors in the emergency room had asked Zach his age and he had answered "fourteen," but he was speaking metaphorically, believing himself to be young at heart. Once the medical staff, with help from Ashley, realized that this was Zach's personal credo and not an indicator of traumatic injury, he was sent home with a bandage and a warning to be more careful while skateboarding, however old he might actually be.

"So he's totally OK!" Ashley told a rapt Olivia and a somewhat less rapt Laura, who had just arrived home from work. It wasn't that Laura wished Zach any ill fortune, but it had been annoying to have to cancel her coffee with A, and she might have been more sympathetic if it had been a real emergency, not some silly skateboarding mishap.

"Well, that's a relief," said Laura, making herself smile. "Tell Zach we're glad to hear it."

"I hope it wasn't a problem that I had to rush off. I really appreciate that you came home early," Ashley said as Olivia ran upstairs to inspect the stuffed animals in her room, which she always suspected of moving around by themselves while she was elsewhere.

"Well, I kind of had a date that afternoon that I had to cancel," said Laura, trying to sound casual. "With the bookstore guy I told you about."

Ashley's eyes grew wide, "Oh nooo! I'm so sorry!"

Laura quickly reassured her. "It's OK, emergencies happen." Ever since Laura had confided to her about A's existence during the second-grade graduation, Ashley had been somewhat invested in this non-relationship, often asking about it and offering not-very-helpful advice that Laura had no intention of following, such as maybe sending A a really sexy selfie. (Ashley couldn't seem to get her head around the fact that Laura couldn't send any sort of selfie even if she'd wanted to, as she didn't know A's cell number or even his name. This analog state of affairs seemed utterly unthinkable to Ashley.)

"Oh, but you should have told me!" Ashley said, distressed that this nonromance seemed to be going awry. "I could have found somebody else to watch Livvy!"

"No, you were stressed and upset and you needed to go right away. It's totally fine," said Laura, even though it wasn't really and it had taken her a full twenty-four hours, and a long conversation with a soothing Rebecca (who had numerous suggestions about what Laura should wear to the dinner date) to get her irritation about the sudden cancellation under control. "Actually, I left him another note and said I wanted to buy him dinner this weekend to make up for it. So the stakes have been raised. In one way, you kind of helped me to move things along."

Ashley beamed, thrilled to be a part of the rom-com playing out in her head. Laura could practically see her composing it as an Instagram story. "Did he say yes to dinner? Where are you going?"

"Hang on. He hasn't said anything yet. I'm waiting for a reply."

"You're not still doing this by writing notes? And leaving them in a book at the store? Really?" Ashley stared, mouth agape, un-intentionally providing an unappetizing view of her well-chewed organic gum.

"Yes. I'm trying to respect the rhythm of the thing," Laura said. "If we meet at his work and talk about the notes, the whole thing fizzles, right? He's really committed to the long game."

"Your generation is so weird," Ashley said. "So you're just waiting for him to leave you another note? Someday?"

"Yes. It'll be soon. Maybe tomorrow, or the next day."

"OK," Ashley said. "OK. You do you, Laura. But I just have to say something."

"What?" said Laura absently, riffling through a pile of mail.

Ashley paused, as if wanting to get her words just right. "OK. Maybe it's not my business, but I've been working for you for a long time, and I've been thinking for a while that it would be so great if you could meet someone. I know you loved your husband and you miss him, but you've been lonely for too long and you're kind of amazing and you're such a great mom and you have so much to give, I know there's someone out there for you, and maybe it's this guy, whoever he is, and maybe Livvy would love for you to meet someone."

Laura was startled; Ashley's habitual incredibly long sen-tences didn't usually end with a gut punch. "Has she said any-thing about that?"

"Well, no, not really," Ashley admitted. "But you know how much she loves weddings and stories where people live happily ever after. Wouldn't you want her to have a nice stepdad someday?"

"Slow down," said Laura, holding up a hand. "Let's just do a date first. Way too soon to talk about stepdads." It was odd; she probably should have been annoyed at Ashley being so presump-tuous, but really all she felt was gratitude.

"So, um, what book is it that you leave the notes in at the store?" Ashley asked, a little too innocently.

Laura laughed. "Like I would tell you. You'd go over and look for the note. I'm doing this my way."

"When you do have dinner," Ashley said, moving on to a more important topic, "what are you going to wear?" Unlike Ashley One, the current Ashley loved Laura's closet.

"I don't know. Nothing fancy," said Laura. "Maybe jeans. What do you think?"

"Hmm," said Ashley. "We'll discuss when the time comes."

40

Westley

There was no filming in Read the Room today, and the store felt strangely quiet and undefined, like a parade route after all the floats and marching bands have gone by. Westley wasn't sure if the movie was done or not. Julia had said she thought the location shoot was finished but the production office had stopped communicating with her, and Westley had noticed that making a movie didn't seem like a linear thing, more a series of non-chronological steps with no set boundaries. But he was happy to be back in the bookstore—after the strange evening at the hotel ballroom, where he had received an entirely surreal offer that he didn't even know what to think about, being at Read the Room felt pleasantly grounding. And for all the staff, it was clearly a relief to not be dealing with movie chaos for the moment; Julia, in particular, was happily flitting about straightening books and humming to herself. The curly-haired woman with the little girl—the one who'd given him cookies the other day; he probably should have asked her name—had come in, browsing a bit over in Young Adult and then taking her daughter to pick out something in the children's section. Westley had given her a cheerful wave, and she'd waved back with an odd expression, like she was apologizing for something. But he was very much behind in his work, with books piling up alarmingly during the movie shoot, so couldn't give it much thought. Women were always looking at him with odd expressions. He was used to it.

Alejandra passed his desk, and he called to her. "Come here a sec, Alejandra. I want to show you something."

"What's up?"

Westley had marked the page in *Shivering Timbers* with a sticky note. He opened it and pointed to the beginning of a paragraph. "Read this and tell me if it makes you think of someone."

Alejandra looked puzzled and a little anxious. "I'm kind of busy right now," she said. "Science Fiction/Fantasy is a real mess after that Boy Scout troop came in. Can we do this later?"

"It'll just take a second. Here, just read this paragraph."

Will was tall but not in a way that you'd make a fuss about, with eyes deep and dark as a lake at midnight. He was the sort of man who looked like he would know what to do with a hammer, but who would also be at home pouring red wine at a book-club meeting. His wavy hair, the color of shadows in a forest, seemed tousled yet arranged by the hands of gods, and he had a way of listening to you like the rest of the world had fallen away.

Alejandra finished the paragraph and looked up expectantly. "Sounds like . . . I don't know? Someone we know?"

"No. I mean, yes, sort of," said Westley.

"I really have to go, but um, he sounds kind of like you?" Alejandra blurted out, hesitantly and clearly embarrassed.

Westley was horrified. "What? No! I mean, think about if this book were a movie. Like an actor."

"Oh, it's totally Kelly Drake," said Alejandra, recovering quickly. "I mean, it's obvious. The hair especially. What is this book?" She flipped over the front cover. "*Shivering Timbers*? Oh, this is the one you were talking about at Staff Tea?"

"It's really good," said Westley. "Maybe I'm crazy, but I think it could be a movie. You should read it."

"Well, OK," said Alejandra. "It looks like it's a romance?"

"It is," Westley said, "and it's got a sense of humor about itself. It really stayed with me, and I'm not usually into romance books. I think you would like it."

He handed the book over to her, a little awkwardly; their hands touched and Alejandra giggled momentarily, a bit too quickly. "I'll read it," she said. "For sure."

Julia, feather duster in hand, suddenly appeared next to Alejandra, who was vaguely startled; Julia at times seemed to have uncanny powers of apparition. "What's this?" she said, looking at the cover. "I haven't seen this book before." Julia also had remarkable powers of memory; she seemed to know the title of every book that had passed through Read the Room's doors.

"It's nothing," said Westley. "Just an old book I found. Alejandra's going to read it."

"Well, I hope you enjoy it!" said Julia, so cheerily that Westley wondered if she was about to burst into song. "So! I just came by to tell you that I'm treating all the staff to a coffee drink of their choice today. As a little thank-you for putting up with the Recent Disturbance." (This was how Julia was now referring to the movie, with implied capital letters.) "Just tell the café server that it's on my tab. Enjoy!" She trilled the final word and walked away, making a few dramatic gestures with her duster.

"Someone's cheerful," said Alejandra.

"I'd better get back to it." As Westley turned away toward his desk, she quickly slipped a folded piece of paper into a book at the top of one of the piles. She walked away, cheerfully humming a tune not unlike Julia's.

Westley turned back to his piles of books, sighing over a stack of dated-looking and dog-eared science fiction that had the faint odor of onions and garlic, when he noticed a young woman approaching his counter. She was blond and pretty, like the sort of college girl Westley remembered from his brief academic career. "Hel-lo," she said, almost as if she were saying it to herself. "Wow. You really are good-looking."

There was a part of Westley that admired unfiltered people

like this—he was someone who always thought rather than spoke, and then quite often thought better of speaking—but it still made him uncomfortable. "Hi," he said, deciding to ignore her comment. "Can I help you?"

"Yes," said the young woman, sounding forthright, like she was getting ready to deliver a speech she'd prepared. "My name's Ashley, and I'm here on behalf of Laura, the woman you were supposed to meet for coffee the other day. The one who had to cancel because of an emergency."

Whatever Westley was expecting the woman to say, it wasn't this. "Laura?" he said. "I think you're mistaken. I don't know any Lauras and I didn't have any plans to meet anyone for coffee."

The woman shook her head vigorously, blond locks flying. "Oh, no," she said. "There's no mix-up. Laura's the one you've been sending notes to. I'm her little girl's babysitter. She told me all about it."

"The one I've been *sending notes to*?" It wasn't unusual for Westley to feel that a conversation had taken a leap and left him behind, scrambling to catch up, but this was something else entirely. He was quite certain he'd never left a note for anyone; that didn't sound like him at all. "I'm really sorry," he said, "but I just don't know what you're talking about. You really must have me mixed up with someone else."

Ashley closed her eyes for a second, breathing hard, then snapped them back open. "Millennials," she said. "You're all so weird. Anyway, OK, play your game that way if you want. I don't care. Not my business. But just know this: Laura is amazing, and you would be so lucky to go out with her, and you should go have dinner with her and maybe, you know, fall in love or something. I mean, she would seriously be the best thing to ever happen to you. Anyway, I feel sort of responsible that you couldn't meet Laura the other day, because my boyfriend had a skateboarding accident and I had to leave Livvy, she's Laura's daughter and she's seven and really adorable. I know Laura felt really bad about missing coffee with you, but she came hurrying right home because that's the kind of person she is. And—" She broke off, seeing that Westley was holding up a hand, like he was desperately trying to hail a cab to take him out of the conversation.

"Hang on," he said, trying to stay polite but increasingly frustrated at the effort of climbing over Ashley's wall of words. "Just stop. Go back. I'm really sorry but I need to say again that I have absolutely no idea what you're talking about."

Ashley looked exasperated. "OK," she said. "Fine. If that's how you want to play it. I just wanted you to know that there's another human being at the other end of this game you're playing, and she's amazing. That's all. I have to go pick up Livvy from school. Bye."

She turned around and marched out the door of the bookstore, leaving Westley staring after her feeling utterly confused, the way he felt after watching the ending of *True Detective*. Was time really a flat circle? Had he connected with someone named Laura without noticing somehow? Was there someone named Laura in his past whom he'd forgotten about? Surely Ashley was just confused, but there was something in her forthrightness that Westley admired: She'd had the nerve to approach a stranger and say something, however crazy. He turned back to the books, relieved that they, at least, couldn't ask him any questions.

Leaning over the used-books counter, he slid a few stacks aside to have room to put his head in his hands. Things seemed overwhelming, even more so than usual. Did everyone feel perpetually out of control, he wondered, like their lives weren't their own? He wished he could, like the character in the movie, disappear into a book, into someone else's story.

Andrew, passing by, noticed Westley's despairing posture. "Hey man," he said. "You OK? Your busy life of book-sorting and movie stardom got you down?"

"Don't start," Westley said. "I'm not having a good day. Something really weird just happened." He looked up, holding Andrew's eye contact, suddenly aware he had someone to talk to. "Have you ever been in a relationship with someone but you didn't know it?"

"No," said Andrew, without hesitation. "As a rule, I always meet the people I get involved with. Like Sydney, the costume guy from the set. He's adorable. We're having fun. We might go away for the weekend. Thanks for asking. Oh wait, we're talking about you. So, who's the person you don't know you're seeing?" Andrew had a tendency to be sardonic that Westley usually found off-putting, but today it was welcoming; the edgy distance that Andrew brought to this strange experience felt good.

"It's not that," said Westley, reddening a little. "Some blond woman I've never met in my life just turned up at the counter and told me that I've been sending romantic notes to someone named Laura. She wanted to tell me that Laura is awesome and I should meet her."

Andrew took all of this surprisingly in stride; Westley remembered that Andrew talked a lot about being a lawyer someday, and maybe he'd practiced never giving away his own reactions. Andrew tilted his head to one side, hands raised and fingertips pressed together.

"Is there a possibility that you're trapped in a romantic comedy?" he said archly. Westley glared at him. "Too bad. That would be fun. OK then. There are only a few other possibilities. Number one: This woman has you mixed up with somebody else."

"I don't think so," said Westley. "She came right up to me, and very specifically mentioned me and my job. She didn't seem at all confused about that."

"OK. Number two. You are indeed carrying on a relationship that you don't know about. Have you by any chance been taking Ambien? I hear the sleep-emailing when you're on it can be pretty extreme. Maybe sleep-dating is a thing."

This sounded alarming. "No," Westley said. "I'm not taking anything. And I know I haven't talked to or written to anyone named Laura and said I'd go out with her." He was, indeed, certain of that. Ever since a debacle in high school, when a girl who might have been named Jessica thought Westley had invited her to a party when he actually hadn't, Westley had tried to be more meticulous in his communication.

"Well, OK," Andrew said, warming to the subject; Westley saw that Andrew was enjoying presenting his arguments as a lawyer might. "Assuming there's no mental illness on either side of the equation—there isn't any, right?—clearly you've done something to indicate to this Laura person that you're interested. And then she told a third party—this woman who came to see you—and that's where we are. So you need to talk to Laura and get yourself on the same page."

"But how do I talk to her if I have no idea who she is?" Westley said, feeling that he had tumbled down an Alice-in-Wonderland rabbit hole, with no way of climbing out.

Andrew brushed some imaginary lint from his lapel. "I wouldn't worry about that," he said. "I feel fairly sure she'll find you."

41

Laura

Ashley was acting oddly, like she wanted Laura to ask her about something. Normally the babysitter was in a rush to head out as soon as Laura got home from work, eager to catch up with Zach and whatever his latest podcast ideas were, but today she was hanging around, watching Laura organize dinner for herself and Olivia and looking like she had a secret that she couldn't wait to spill. Laura knew that Ashley wasn't very good at keeping secrets (these days Laura knew everything about Ashley's circle of friends, including their hidden tattoos, true hair color, parental dramas, misbegotten love affairs, and gynecological challenges), so it was just a matter of time until the shoe dropped.

It wasn't too long of a wait, once Ashley ascertained that Olivia was engrossed in watching *Frozen* yet again and wouldn't overhear. "So!" she said to Laura, as if the word was exploding from her mouth from some pent-up place. "I went to your bookstore yesterday. And I met your bookstore guy."

Laura wasn't entirely surprised; she'd been wondering for a while about the wisdom of sharing this story with Ashley. Ah well, it was done, and maybe the damage could be limited. "Oh, now he's *my* bookstore guy?" she said as good-naturedly as she could. "What do you mean, you met him? Did you actually talk to him?"

"Well, not really," said Ashley, not looking at Laura. "But I saw him. Laura, you were holding out on me! He is adorable! He's almost as cute as Zach!"

"Oh, I wouldn't go that far," said Laura, who privately thought A was *much* better-looking than Zach, and not just because he was a bit older; Zach had a blank-slate quality to him that Laura assumed you needed to be quite young to find attractive. "But yeah, he's pretty nice looking. And he seems nice. Doesn't he?"

"Absolutely!" enthused Ashley. "And I think he's a little younger than you, Laura? You cougar!"

"Oh, you think so?" said Laura, a bit embarrassed. "I thought he seemed like he was in my ballpark. I'm bad with guessing ages."

"Oh, he's totally in your appropriate range! Don't worry!" Ashley said. "But yeah, he does seem totally nice. So you guys are really still just leaving notes for each other? You haven't talked at all?"

"Well, we have talked a little bit," admitted Laura. "Just in the store, pleasantries, you know. He's pretty committed to the game. We're not really supposed to meet until we meet. It's like a movie or something."

"He *is* committed, for sure," murmured Ashley.

"Why would you say that? You didn't talk to him, did you? Please tell me you didn't say anything to him. I'd be so embarrassed. I think the idea is that this is supposed to be a secret between us, and I probably shouldn't have told anyone." Laura was surprised by how much it bothered her to think of Ashley stepping into the middle of the situation and probably exploding it.

"Oh, no, not really," said Ashley breezily. "Just, you know, bookstore stuff, 'Can I help you find a book?', that sort of thing. Nothing real." She seemed eager to move the conversation along. "So, when's your dinner happening? Did he say he was coming?"

"Saturday night. Yes, he's coming," Laura said, her tone indicating that she was not going to entertain more talk on the matter. She hadn't exactly gotten an RSVP from him, but things had gone on long enough and surely he was planning to be there.

Laura changed the subject, hoping to distract Ashley. "So, I'm thinking about getting a new couch. Something colorful. Maybe a red or a pink? Or maybe a stripe or a print? What do you think?"

Ashley, who had in the past made comments about the nondescript-ness of Laura's weary beige sectional, widened her eyes. "Um, that would be a yes! Red or pink or purple or whatever! I love it! It would brighten the room so much."

"I know," Laura said. "Time for a change. I've been putting it off too long."

42

April

April felt that she wasn't very good at confrontation. Even blocking that anonymous texting person, who refused to believe that April wasn't Henry (who had done something mysterious with a car), seemed an indication of being afraid to step up and find out. That whole situation was almost certainly a scam, but there was the tiniest chance that it was real, and that it might have been a good story. Now she'd never know what happened with the car. Anyway, too late now.

But here was another chance to confront, on a more personal level. On the short walk to the bookstore, April tried to psych herself up by channeling Sophie McBride, the Picket Fence CEO, who seemed like someone who would know exactly what to say in this sort of situation. Not that this sort of situation likely came up often in Sophie's life. Sophie was always giving inspirational talks on the Picket Fence employee network, about knowing your worth and valuing yourself and asking for what you want. April hadn't paid much attention to those talks, thinking they were for people who thought in cliché, but now the confidence with which Sophie delivered those words seemed welcome. Had anyone ever stood Sophie up? Probably not, as she seemed to have no shortage of husbands. (The current one was a high-up editor at the local daily paper; rumors scurried that she'd married him to control Picket Fence's press coverage. Which hadn't actually worked; just the other day there was a story about how one of Sophie's interns was threatening a lawsuit after being forced to make Sophie's coffee extra hot; she was claiming compensation for third-degree burns and coffee stains on her knockoff Manolos. In response, Sophie's office had put out a statement saying that the intern had watched *The Devil Wears Prada* too many times.) But if somebody did stand her up, surely Sophie simply would not tolerate it.

Regardless of Sophie, April had gone over the situation in her head many times since being stood up just over a week ago (during which time she'd stopped checking for notes at Read the Room, as the game seemed over) and had decided what to do. Perhaps L truly had had an emergency, as Ben suggested, in which case April would be glad to hear about it and would be as magnanimous as she could. But late last night, she concluded that no matter what, this note-writing game needed to be replaced with real life. It was time to get real. She tried to channel Tango Lady, walking tall and tossing her head, as if she was not to be messed with, as if there was sophisticated choreography or a clever script to follow.

Read the Room looked quiet, without any movie activity today and just a few customers sprinkled throughout the store, peacefully browsing. The employees at the front desk seemed unusually cheery, particularly the older woman with the spiky gray hair, who practically sang out a greeting to April. April nodded to her but marched purposefully over to the used-books desk. There was L, looking handsomely preoccupied in his usual flannel shirt and jeans, staring into space with a perplexed expression. It took a little time before he noticed April at the counter; clearly, he was caught up in his own world. "Hi," he said, not really registering her presence. "Do you have some used books for us to look at today?"

"No," said April. "I needed to talk to you. In person."

L blinked, still not entirely there. "OK. Is there a particular book you need me to look up for you?"

This wasn't going quite as April had planned. Then again, she hadn't exactly planned it. "No, thank you," said April, taking a deep breath. "I'm the one who's been writing to you. I just need to say that this note-writing has been fun and everything, but I think it's time that we should just talk. You weren't at the café last week, and that's OK; I'm assuming you had some sort of emergency and didn't know how to reach me. At least I'd rather assume that than believe that you stood me up. But maybe you did stand me up, and maybe you had a reason. So I thought we should just talk, and figure out what's going on here."

L, silent, stared at her, looking mystified. He closed his eyes, shook his head a bit in what looked like a please-let-this-not-be-happening gesture, and opened them again. "I stood you up?" he said incredulously. "At a café?"

"Yes. At Tough Beans. Last Thursday." April's tone was in-credulous.

A long pause. "I'm sorry, I don't even know your name." His face cleared, just for a moment, like things were suddenly begin-ning to make sense. "Is your name Laura by any chance?"

"No." April was taken aback. Maybe she wasn't the only woman writing to L? This suddenly felt a bit embarrassing. "It's April."

L, seeming distressed, raised his hands in the air as if surren-dering. "I'm really sorry," he said. "I just don't know what you're talking about. That's been happening to me a lot lately." There was a pause, in which he seemed to remember his manners. "My name is Westley, by the way," he said. "I don't mean to be rude. So who's been writing you notes?"

"Well, *you* have," April said, clinging to the story she thought she knew, as if by repeating it, she could make it make sense. "I left you a note, in a book, a few weeks ago, and you answered. And we've been writing back and forth. And we were supposed to meet at Tough Beans. And . . . you don't know anything about this, do you?" Her voice trailed away, as it was becoming difficult to focus on Westley's face; he seemed to be literally fading away before her eyes.

"I'm sorry," Westley said. "No, I definitely never left anyone a note. Not you or anyone. I've never done that. It just . . . never occurred to me. I'm really sorry."

April blew out a breath, abruptly, as if helping her rom-com fantasy scatter to the winds. It was hard to know what to say, but she pressed on. "So, if you didn't write the notes, who's the guy who's been writing to me? Is someone just having fun at my expense? Who is he?"

"I don't know." Westley seemed completely distracted. "I genuinely have no idea. I'm really sorry you were put in this position, but I only know it isn't me writing to you. I need to go take a walk or something. This has been such a weird day. I hope you find who it is. Excuse me." He picked up his messenger bag and left, shaking his head. An employee with a blue streak in her hair, who appeared to be checking the alphabetization in Self-Help but who April suspected was eavesdropping, jumped out of the way, eyeing April with curiosity.

Standing alone in the bookstore aisle, April felt as if the floor had shifted, that maybe she needed to hold on to something, to find something real. She had prepared herself, a little bit, for the possibility that the bookstore guy might tell her that he'd just met somebody else and was no longer interested in pursuing things with her, or that maybe, when she actually got to know him, he might not be her type. It had never occurred to her, though, that the whole thing could be a misunderstanding. She'd believed, fervently, that the notes were from him, because she wanted to believe it, because life felt happier and more colorful with a romantic story unfolding. But she didn't predict this ending: a fantasy that turned out to be pure fiction.

Though every instinct told April to walk her numb, deflated self out of the store and go home immediately, where her couch was waiting and maybe she could have a good cry in peace, April automatically wandered over to Young Adult; a habit she couldn't quite break. The middle copy of *The Hunger Games* looked like it had been pushed out a bit, like it was beckoning her. She opened it, and out fell a note. No longer feeling the need to keep things secret, she unfolded it and read it right there.

I'm so terribly sorry—there was a family emergency (everything's fine now) and I couldn't meet you. I felt awful about it but there was no way to reach you, as I don't have your number (or even your name!). But could I make it up to you by buying you dinner? How about 7 p.m. Saturday the 15th at Emilio's? I'll make a reservation and I can't wait to see you there. Looking forward to learning your name, among other things.
L

The script had disappeared; anything could happen. The fantasy that April had wanted was gone, and maybe later she'd have time to grieve it, but in her confusion and disappointment she tried to focus on one clear thing: She was absolutely going to be at Emilio's at 7 p.m. tomorrow. Maybe she didn't have a rom-com anymore, but she did have a mystery, and it needed to be solved.

43

Westley

It was raining, the kind of soft, warm June rain that Seattleites accept as inevitable, but that didn't stop Westley from taking a long, long walk, the hood flipped up on his rain jacket. He hoped nobody at work would get upset about his absence. It wasn't easy to learn that he was in the middle of a very strange love triangle that he had known absolutely nothing about, and it helped a lot to go outside and to breathe some air, however damp, and turn things over in his head. While he wasn't quite sure entirely what had happened, he'd made two people unhappy, even though he hadn't meant to, and this was upsetting.

Wesley paused in his walk to gaze at a downtown view: a city full of people moving to and fro, talking to each other and misunderstanding each other and breaking each other's hearts and somehow moving on, every single day. From the hillside where he stood, he could see faraway sidewalks and umbrellas dotting the landscape like tiny flowers. As he gazed out, his phone buzzed from his pocket. He picked it up: It was Julia. Sighing, he answered. "Hey, Julia."

"Westley! Where are you? You should have been back from lunch an hour ago!"

"I'm really sorry," Westley said, feeling as if he had been apologizing a lot lately. "Something came up and I needed to step away for a bit. Personal time." Julia was a big believer in "personal time"; Westley hoped invoking the phrase might help his case.

Not this time. "Westley, you know perfectly well that personal time needs to be scheduled in advance! Please do not abuse the system. We are short-staffed this afternoon and it was inconsiderate to just walk out. How quickly can you get back?"

"Maybe twenty minutes?" Westley said, figuring he could walk fast. "I'm really sorry. I thought things were calmer now that the movie is done."

"That doesn't mean you can just leave your desk and not tell anyone. I'm disappointed in you, Westley." Julia paused, long enough to let the cape of management in which she had wrapped herself fall, just a bit. "Is everything OK?" she asked in a softer tone.

"I'm fine," Westley said, reminding himself that at heart Julia was a good boss and a good egg. "Just needed to be alone for a bit. I'll be back right away."

"Thank you. See you soon."

The walk back went quickly; blocks and blocks of genteel 1920s Seattle houses that all seemed to be peering at him with casual interest, behind their leaded-glass windows and quiet bricks. Inside them, maybe there were people who had their lives figured out, people who had control of their stories. Back at the store, Raven greeted him at the door with a cat-ate-the-canary expression, if the cat was wearing earrings that seemed to be unraveling. "Where'd you go?" she said. "Julia's been looking for you. She's not happy."

"I just needed a walk," Westley said, maneuvering himself around Raven—whom he'd been trying to avoid for several days now—and heading to his desk. It didn't work; she followed him anyway.

"So," she said, "who was that woman you were talking to earlier? The one who said something to you that got you all upset. I heard a bit of it; I didn't mean to but I was shelving nearby. Were you sending notes to her? Really?"

"I don't want to talk about it," Westley said, looking away from her and trying to instantly busy himself with books on his desk.

"But why would you do that?" Raven said. "Why would someone who looks like you leave notes for someone? You could seriously have anyone you wanted."

Westley took a deep breath. "Look. I'm just going to say this once: I am not leaving notes for anyone and even if I was, I don't think that would be your concern. Now can you please leave me alone? I have work to do."

Raven pursed her lips, taken aback by what was for Westley a rather long string of words. "Oh yes," she said. "You'd better get to that." She sounded like she might be near tears but kept on going. "That's way more important than talking to me. You know, you don't work anywhere near as hard as the rest of us. I've seen that. You just sit there, looking handsome. You sometimes forget to check the books. And everyone lets you get away with it. Things just fall into your lap. It must be nice. Isn't it nice?"

"That's not true," said Westley, feeling his face flush with the unfairness of her accusation, and suddenly finding that he had the right words. "Maybe people should ask me how I feel about things? Maybe people shouldn't just assume things about me because of how I look? Maybe people should understand when I say that I'm sorry, and I wish what happened at the Christmas party hadn't happened, but it was a mistake and I'm sorry. I didn't mean to hurt your feelings and I'm sorry! It was really terrible of me and it's bothered me for a long time and I'm sorry! I'm sorry! I screwed up! I'm sorry! I'm so sorry!" Westley stopped, realizing he'd gotten louder than he intended and that he almost felt that he might cry. And that though his words did apply to Raven, she wasn't really who he was talking to. Raven stared at him, not expecting the outburst, something in her expression indicating, unexpectedly, sympathy and understanding. Customers, looking curious, were staring too.

"Okay," Raven finally said softly. "Okay. I hear you. Apology accepted. Anyway, I have work to do. I can't stand here talking to you all day." She turned and, as if to recover from a moment of weakness, made a show of flouncing off, or as much as a person can flounce in ill-fitting Converse high-tops.

Westley watched her go, hoping that the awkwardness between them might be gone now. Maybe she'd just needed to hear a real apology, even if his words were for Bridget, wherever she was.

For now, there was work, and Westley returned to his desk and picked up the book on top of the nearest used-books stack. It was, oddly enough, *The History of Love* by Nicole Krauss, and indifferently he flipped through the pages, to make sure nothing had been left behind.

A folded piece of lined paper, like the sort he remembered seeing in Alejandra's notebook, fell out. The handwriting was lacy and wandering, and he read through it slowly.

Dear Westley,

I'm leaving this note in a book because it seems like the easiest way to get a message to you—and because it's impossible to talk privately here with Julia and Raven constantly around. Just wanted to say that I enjoyed our chat over coffee the other day, and wondered if you might want to continue it, maybe someplace that isn't Read the Room? In case I'm not being clear: yes, I am asking you out on a date. I thought I picked up a little vibe between us? If I'm wrong, or if you're not single, I apologize for the misunderstanding and we just won't speak of this again. But if I'm right, meet me for a beer at O'Neill's at 7 on Saturday night, the 15th. I think we'd have lots more to talk about.

Alejandra

P.S. I know you've been trying to find out about the author of Shivering Timbers. *Well, you work with her. It's me. I had a copy printed up, with a stock author photo; I was curious how people would react if they thought it was written by a man. Duke appreciated your emails.*

Westley looked across the store, at Alejandra standing behind the front desk, her head bent over a computer terminal and her dark hair shining in a shaft of sunlight. As he stared, she raised her head and looked at him, as if sensing his gaze. They both smiled, and suddenly Westley didn't feel worried at all.

SHIVERING TIMBERS
page 295

The smoke whirled around them like a matador's cape, strangely frosty and warm at the same time. Not that it mattered: Will only saw Verity, her eyes glowing in the mist like pale-blue pearls, her face smudged with ash. "You saved me," he said, gasping the words.

"No, I didn't," she said. "You saved yourself. I just reached out a hand."

The fire was out, the sirens were fading into the night, and the other firefighters were putting equipment away, tactfully keeping their distance. Will felt exhausted yet utterly alive, as if somehow the day was just beginning. "Do you want to get some coffee?" he said. "Or some pie? There's a café a few miles down the road."

"I'd love to," Verity said. "You can tell me your whole life."

"I can't wait," Will said.

44

Laura

"Excuuuuse me," said Sydney, stretching out the syllables as if they were a pair of Spanx. "What is this noise I am hearing? Are you *singing*?"

"I guess I was," said Laura, who hadn't realized she was warbling a tune from her high-school musical (it was *Oklahoma!*, and the song wasn't really in her key). She was feeling cheerful and hopeful. It was Saturday, her workday was nearly done and had gone well: She'd actually managed to get her client Harriet, a tech company VP, to try on a pair of non-sneaker, non-Velcro shoes, and to reconsider her habit of carrying necessities around in a plastic Walgreens bag. And she was meeting A for dinner in just a few hours. Nothing was going to get in the way this time. Ashley, a big supporter of tonight's events, was eager to babysit for the evening and had promised there would be no last-minute drama: Zach, busy with his web series, would not be skateboarding today.

Sydney gazed at Laura, carefully reading her face. "Oh my God," he said. "Praise the heavens. You have a date! Is this really a thing? Is this the first date you've had since . . . well, ever?"

Laura couldn't help smiling. "Well, yes, but not *ever*," she said. "If you really want me to spell it out, this is the first dinner I will have had alone in a restaurant with a man since my husband died more than five years ago. Are you happy? And it feels good. It's been a long time. I'm ready."

"You are so NOT ready," Sydney said. "Please tell me you're not wearing that."

"What's wrong with it?" Laura was wearing a tailored beige shirtdress, part of her work wardrobe of classic, neutral pieces.

"She can dress every lady in town, but she can't dress herself," said Sydney to nobody in particular, shaking his head. "This is a *date*, Laura. We are not going to look classic and professional. We are going to look freaking hot."

Laura gulped and nodded. "Okay."

An hour later, Laura arrived at home, wearing the outfit Sydney had convinced her to buy with her store discount: a dress in a deep red with a dramatically asymmetrical skirt, vintage-looking heels, dangly earrings. She couldn't remember when she'd last felt so vivid, so ready to be seen. "Hey, you guys," she called, entering the front door. "I need some feedback here!"

Ashley and Olivia looked up from the table where they were doing a homework worksheet. "Mommy!" said Olivia. "You look so pretty! I like the red dress!"

Ashley nodded, gazing up and down at Laura knowingly. "Nice. Very nice. Super elegant and arty. It suits you. Are you excited?"

"I am," said Laura, whose eyes were shining. "It feels weird, but good. It's been a long wait, but I'm excited for what comes next. Whatever that might be. I'm ready. It's time." She stopped, realizing that she wasn't really talking to Ashley, but to herself. And to Sam, with love. Always.

"Zach says congratulations!" Ashley said, bringing Laura's thoughts back into the present. "He's excited for you. He might work your story into the web series. A whole plotline, you know, about older people who think they're cats, falling in love."

Laura snorted. "I'm not *that* old," she said. "You know, many people would consider me young."

"OK," said Ashley, clearly unconvinced. "What time are you meeting him?"

"At seven. I should go in a minute. You two all set for dinner?"

"Yes. Mac and cheese. Mine is gluten-free. Just go. Have a wonderful time! Stay out as late as you want! How are you getting there?"

"I'm driving," said Laura, who hadn't thought about it.

"Laura! Take an Uber. What if he wants to order a bottle of champagne?" Ashley giggled.

"Oh, stop," said Laura. Ashley was right, though. She took a deep breath. "OK, Livvy," Laura said, "come say goodnight to your silly mama. She's doing something brave tonight."

Olivia came running over; Laura encased her in a hug, inhaling that sweet fragrance of baby shampoo and peanut butter. "Bye, Mommy," she said. "Can I watch a movie with Ashley Two tonight?"

"Yes, if it's something appropriate," Laura said. "Good night, baby."

"I was thinking one of those Nora Ephron movies you're always talking about," said Ashley, giggling. "See you later. Have an amazing, amazing time."

The Uber driver looked a bit like Tom Hanks, which Laura thought might have been a good omen. He wasn't one for chatting, but efficiently drove her downtown to Emilio's, a new restaurant that Laura had chosen for its pretty, white-tablecloth look and quiet atmosphere; it was the sort of place where you could have an actual conversation. She arrived before A and was led to a corner table, where she sipped a glass of water and watched the restaurant's entrance, waiting for A to walk through.

Rebecca texted:

Is he there yet?

Laura replied:

No. Nice restaurant though. You'd approve of the tablecloths.

Rebecca replied:

Don't worry. He'll show. You got this.

Laura wrote back:

Xoxo

Laura took a compact from her purse and checked her lipstick; all looked good. She stared, just for a few seconds, at her reflection in the tiny mirror. What might Sam think, she wondered. Could he see her, maybe? It was nice to imagine that he might be cheering her on, somewhere. "It Had to Be You" was playing on the restaurant's sound system, which seemed almost too spot-on, but lovely. Laura hummed along.

The door swung open, letting in a bit of the summer air, and a familiar face entered the restaurant: It was April, the nice client Laura had helped recently at work. April scanned the room, looking for someone; Laura caught her eye and waved. April, recognizing Laura, had a strange expression on her face, as if she'd finally solved a puzzle. She slowly approached Laura's table.

"Hey April!" said Laura. "So nice to see you! How funny to run into you here! Are you meeting someone?"

"Yes," April said, after a pause. "I'm having dinner with . . . well, it's sort of a blind date. What about you?"

"Me too. He isn't here yet. I'm excited to meet him," Laura said. "Is this the date you were buying the new outfit for? But why aren't you wearing it? I mean, you look very nice! But this isn't the outfit we chose." There was something odd about the way April was looking at Laura, as if she couldn't quite decide whether to cry or laugh, and might elect to do both. "Are you OK?" Laura asked.

April nodded, slowly.

"So, is this the guy you told me about?" Laura asked, filling the slightly awkward silence. "That you kind of knew already, but it was your first official date?"

"Yes," said April, still seeming a little distant, like she was revisiting someplace else, checking off the entries on an itinerary in her mind. "That guy. Our first date for coffee got postponed, because he didn't show up. I thought he'd stood me up and I was a little mad, but we're finally having dinner tonight. I thought I'd give him another chance." She paused, swallowing hard. "I don't see him here, though."

Laura stared at April. Suddenly it felt as if dominoes were falling, but not in the direction she'd planned. "Right," she said deliberately. "Um, tell me again how you met him in the first place?"

"I don't think I told you before. He works in a bookstore, Read the Room, and I left him a note in a book. We've been corresponding."

"With notes left in a book?" The room seemed to be spinning, just a bit.

"Yes," April said. "It's been kind of adorable. I would see him in the store and it was like we had this secret special correspondence that couldn't be mentioned."

"But you've never actually spoken to him," said Laura, a statement more than a question. A shape was slowly forming in her head, while a different one formed in her stomach.

"No. Not really," said April slowly. "Just the notes."

The two women were silent, just for a moment. Laura, frantically playing back in her head the sequence of events with the letters, realized that now it all made sense.

April was watching Laura carefully as she continued to speak. "And you've been doing the same? You answered the notes from me, and thought you were writing to him. You're L. I'm A."

The handsome bookstore guy was just another guy; he'd never written to her, and probably would never have noticed her if she hadn't brought the cookies. There would be no date, and no agonizing over whether she was ready or whether they had anything in common. And, weirdly, what Laura felt in that moment was just the tiniest bit of relief. Maybe, somehow, she'd known all along that it wasn't real; maybe this was a game she'd needed to play, or a part she had to rehearse before actually stepping on stage. This was, maybe, the right ending. For now.

And here, instead of a fantasy man, was an actual person: April, who'd had the courage to reach out to another human being without knowing what she'd get in reply, who was looking at Laura like she was worried about her. "Are you OK?" April said hesitantly. "This is . . . kind of a weird moment. I don't really know what to say."

"I'm OK," said Laura slowly, still putting the pieces of the story together in her head. "Someday this will be a great story that we'll both tell. It's practically a movie."

"It kind of is," said April, beginning to smile. "Actually, I'm glad it's you."

It was strange how the moment was not so uncomfortable; how, though Laura barely knew April, she felt oddly happy to see her. "Do you want to sit down?" Laura asked. "Maybe have a drink with me? We probably both could use one."

"Sure," said April gratefully, swallowing hard and sitting down. "Maybe just one."

Laura caught the eye of a waiter, who hurried over. After two glasses of wine were ordered, the table was quiet for a moment, the women still processing the evening's outcome. Laura broke the silence. "So," she said, "tell me one thing, though. I absolutely love that you did this but—why not just talk to him?"

"His name's actually Westley, as I learned today," April said. "I left him a note in a book because . . . I don't know, it just seemed more interesting than walking up to him and starting a conversation. I love books, I figured he loves books, and it was one of those late-night ideas that I got attached to. I haven't had much luck with dating the regular way lately, so it seemed worth a try."

"That's just so . . . brave," Laura said. She meant it. "I haven't even had the nerve to date. I've been single for a long time, since my husband died five and a half years ago." Strange how that slipped out without her even thinking about it; Laura didn't usually tell her story to people with whom she wasn't well acquainted.

April gasped softly. "I'm so sorry," she said slowly. "I didn't know. That's just awful. I . . . can't imagine how you move on from that."

"Thank you," Laura said, touched. "But I'm all right. It's been a long time, and time helps. I have my daughter, who's wonderful, and I have a really good life. And your notes . . . kind of woke me up a bit." Laura realized she'd never put these thoughts into words before. "It was like my life got lit up, like being seen by a stranger. Maybe I needed that."

"Well, glad to help," April said. "Maybe you woke me up a bit too. I needed a push; I was kind of stuck in my apartment wondering why nothing was happening. This is all just so strange, but . . . nice, really. I feel like I sort of know everything and nothing about you." The table was quiet for a moment, comfortably so. "Are you from Seattle originally?" April asked finally.

"Oh no," Laura said. "But I've been here almost twenty years. My husband—Sam—and I came here after college in Chicago, because we liked the idea of living somewhere green, and back then Seattle was actually kind of affordable. . . ."

Three hours, two appetizers, two entrees, one shared dessert (they both loved crème brûlée, which led to a lively discussion of the movie *Amélie*, which led to sharing notes on their favorite French films), one bottle of wine, two brandies, several cups of coffee, and one meticulously split bill later, the two rose from the table, reluctantly aware that they were the last customers left in the restaurant. The music had long ago been turned off and the staff had begun elaborately tidying up.

"Westley doesn't know what he missed," April said, smiling. "That was a great dinner. And great company."

"No, he doesn't. And I guess he never will," said Laura. "Would you like to come over for dinner next week? I'd love to have you meet Olivia. And I can give you that book I mentioned." (Laura had been horrified to hear that April had never read *The Secret History*.)

"I'd love that," April said.

"Does Friday work?"

"Great."

They walked out of the restaurant into the summer night to-gether, where two Ubers were waiting. Saying goodnight, they hugged before parting. If you were watching from a distance, you'd have thought that they were old friends.

TO: laurabarrysea@freemail.com
FROM: aprildunne7@freemail.com
SUBJECT: Thank you!

Thanks so much for the dinner at your house last night. The pasta was delicious, and Olivia is . . . well, she's you, in smaller form. And I'm so excited for the red couch! Let me know when it comes!

I'm going to the bookstore today and will see if Westley can/will have coffee with me. Like we discussed, I want to explain to him what happened, and apologize for making him uncomfortable. Now that I look back on it, it must have been SO weird for him. I didn't mean for it to be, for sure.

It's so pretty out today and yet all I want to do is stay home and read!

Xoxo

TO: aprildunne7@freemail.com
FROM: laurabarrysea@freemail.com
RE: Thank you!

It was wonderful having you over! And YES I do know the feeling of wanting to stay home and read. Whenever I have a day off on one of Olivia's school days, that's all I want to do. I hope Livvy grows up to be a reader. Did you have a chance to start *The Secret History* yet? I reread it every few years, usually in the winter but really it could be anytime.

Taking Olivia to the new Pixar movie tomorrow afternoon; want to join us? There's usually a LOT of popcorn involved. Text me if so!

Xo

TO: laurabarrysea@freemail.com
FROM: aprildunne7@freemail.com
SUBJECT: Trapped in a book

I had no idea that such a small person could eat so much popcorn. It really was a wonder to behold.

I hope I wasn't being too negative when you asked about my brother. He's actually sort of adorable, when he's not driving me absolutely crazy. Which he was, just yesterday, because he's decided that he looks like Ryan Gosling and could maybe get work as his stand-in, to which I said a) you do not look like Ryan Gosling, and b) having one day of experience in an indie movie does not qualify you to do ANYTHING. (Spoiler alert: His gig in the bookstore movie did not go well.) Seriously, I spend half my life explaining the obvious to him. But he's a sweetheart really. When you meet him, don't tell him I said that.

And thanks a lot–I have now not left the house in three days, because all I want to do is read *The Secret History*. You're off on Mondays, right? Want to meet me at the Read the Room café for lunch to talk about it? I'll be done reading it by then, for sure. I have a theory about the murder that I want to run by you.

Xo

Help! My dad has invited me to some fancy dinner thing
at his golf club, and I don't have a thing to wear!
Please advise!

> Don't panic! I can absolutely find you something!
> Emailing you some ideas right now.

TO: aprildunne7@freemail.com
FROM: laurabarrysea@freemail.com
SUBJECT: Outfit ideas

See attachments; do you like any of these? I especially think the deep-purple
dress would be lovely on you, but if you think you'd rather do pants, let me
know! We have some great wide-legged flowy but tailored pants at the store;
very Katharine Hepburn and I can absolutely see you in them.

Olivia's off to third grade tomorrow and I feel bereft; want to have lunch? And
she wants to see you again soon. She loved all your stories about your brother.
He doesn't really sing as badly as all that, does he?

Hope all the weirdness at work is getting sorted out—keep me posted! xo

---

TO: laurabarrysea@freemail.com
FROM: aprildunne7@freemail.com
RE: Outfit ideas

Love the pants! Maybe a silk shirt too? Something like the one Rebecca was wearing at happy hour the other day? I LOVE her, by the way. That ex-husband was totally not worthy of her. What an idiot he must be.

I can come to the store Thursday afternoon; would that work? Tell Sydney I expect some decent champagne this time.

Work-related weirdness—not really weirdness, but an idea—still developing. Stay tuned.

TO: aprildunne7@freemail.com
FROM: laurabarrysea@freemail.com
SUBJECT: It's here!

Aren't the leaves beautiful today? I love fall so much.

Rebecca LOVED meeting you last week. She wants to do another happy hour soon. How are things with Janie? Don't worry if she's not quick to get back to you; I remember, way too well, how hard it is when you have tiny kids. She'll come around. You're obviously important to her. Just be patient with her. Babies are hard. I don't know how I got through Olivia's infancy. It passes.

The couch arrived! You'd better come over and take a look. It is very, very red. A bit menstrual maybe. But maybe that's what the place needs.

TO: laurabarrysea@freemail.com
FROM: aprildunne7@freemail.com
SUBJECT: Needing advice

I think I have formed an idea. A job idea. Can I run it by you sometime soon? Also thinking about the pros/cons of getting a cat. Please advise.

TO: aprildunne7@freemail.com
FROM: laurabarrysea@freemail.com
RE: Needing advice

OMG. Livvy wants a kitten SO BADLY. I find myself weakening—I do like cats—but it would just be one more thing to take care of. If you got one, she could come visit it! So yes, please get a cat! Does your building allow them?

Have you thought any more about what we discussed? Regarding the job? Do it!

And . . . are we at the stage in our friendship where we can fix each other up? Because I'm about to. He's cute, he's nice, he looks good in a suit (I should know; I fitted him in one), and he loves to read. Call me for details. xoxox

---

TO: laurabarrysea@freemail.com
FROM: aprildunne7@freemail.com
RE: Needing advice

Yes. Yes. And yes. (Yes I'm going to do the job thing, yes I'm going to go look at cats, yes they're allowed, yes we can fix each other up. Except you wouldn't want me to because all the guys I work with are boring. The suit guy sounds nice. Bring him on.) xoxo

TO: aprildunne7@freemail.com
FROM: laurabarrysea@freemail.com
RE: Needing advice

OK, he has your cell number. His name's Justin. Your assignment: get together with him before Thanksgiving. Definitely bringing potato casserole and Rebecca's bringing bread and that fancy wine she likes (let her pay for it, it's expensive), and no, you don't need to do anything special for Olivia, she's not picky and loves turkey. Do you need me to bring extra chairs or anything like that? See you soon! Thanks again for inviting us! xoxo

TO: donna@donnawolfefilms.com
FROM: westleybooks@freemail.com
SUBJECT: Movie Idea

Hey Donna! Thanks again for the photo gig with Paolo; I really appreciate the introduction at the dinner, though at the time I wasn't sure why you wanted me there. I was worried about how the photos might turn out–I'm not a model!– but I saw the proofs and they look great. The lighting is gorgeous, and you were absolutely right about matching the drink to the sweater. Your assistant Joanna told me that a check would be in the mail soon, and I really appreciate it.

Wonder if you'd be willing to have coffee with me? I have a great idea for a movie, based on a book by a little-known author whose work you just might like. Maybe some afternoon next week at the store? Drop by anytime. I'm always here.

45

April

April couldn't remember the last time it snowed just before Thanksgiving. Novembers in Seattle are usually dark and rainy, with the ground never quite drying between storms and a damp, spongelike grayness prevailing, both outdoors and in people's moods. But the prettiest dusting of white had arrived on Tuesday—just enough to delicately frost the trees and hedges but not enough to snarl the city's notoriously volatile traffic. April had spent more time than she should have gazing from the third floor to the transformed streets below, marveling at how beautiful a city street can be when it's outlined in fine-point lines of white. Snow makes a city so soft and quiet, blurring its edges, turning it into poetry.

She hadn't been home so much in recent weeks since starting her new job. There'd been some drama at Picket Fence: Sophie McBride's fourth husband, the journalist, published a bombshell investigative story in *The Seattle Times* about Sophie's third husband, who was swiftly indicted for some creative accounting on Picket Fence's books (and whose published emails to his partner in crime—a feral-eyed Picket Fence employee who bore a resemblance to a slightly younger Sophie—revealed that he was not only amoral but also couldn't spell). The company had abruptly announced a downsizing: Sophie, in the throes of her fourth divorce, had decided to focus more on her standup career, and wanted Picket Fence streamlined, or so she said. April, feeling flush after a very generous severance package as well as some vested stock options, had written to Julia, proposing a job at the bookstore—one in which she believed her modest salary would be easily offset by increased book sales for the store.

She was now a part-time employee of Read the Room (her salary funded by the money Julia had received for the movie shoot; more hours might come later, Julia said, if all went well), and her job involved helping the store strengthen their monthly book subscription service, in which customers signed up for regular mailings or pickups of books chosen by the staff. It was something nobody had much time for before, but April loved crafting emails and social media posts about new and classic books, and quickly created an email newsletter to customers in which she wrote from the point of view of a character in a book looking for a home. It had only been a few weeks, but Julia was already looking a little less stressed: book subscriptions were up and every book that April recommended in the newsletter had a vigorous sales rate. April loved thinking of people reading her words and being inspired to buy a new book, one that might make them feel a bit less lonely, like the world was full of stories just waiting to be read. She'd also proposed a new program, in which randomly selected books sent out to subscribers had a handwritten note in them sharing a favorite literary quote and offering the buyer a discount on an in-person purchase.

Though she was able to work from home, Julia had given her a corner at the store, near the used-books desk. It was nice sitting there, hearing the buzz of people around her, watching them happily search the shelves. Westley was there sometimes. The initial awkwardness between the two of them had faded away, particularly after a long lunch in which they were both able to laugh at the misunderstanding and talk about their favorite books, and it was adorable watching him and Alejandra pretend they weren't in love, for the sake of their coworkers. He was often away, though, working as a sort of muse to Donna Wolfe. April had read an interview online in which the filmmaker spoke vaguely of a new "creative partner," and Raven had breathlessly told her that Westley was appearing in a new print and video ad campaign that Donna was directing for some expensive liquor. Apparently, the ads, which weren't out yet, featured a dramatically lit Westley, necktie askew, moodily gazing up from a book with a drink at his side, as if interrupted during some very compelling reading.

But now there wasn't time to admire the snow, even if the windows weren't already steamed up from the activity in the kitchen. Yesterday April had been busy setting up a makeshift dining area in her living room, extending her own small kitchen table with a card table and extra chairs borrowed from Mr. Jackson (who was spending Thanksgiving weekend at a lake cabin with Tango Lady, whose name was actually Lenore; April had learned all of this while having coffee with the two of them in Mr. Jackson's apartment last week). The china didn't match and the room really wasn't big enough to hold nine people comfortably— two of them would have to sit on April's slightly saggy couch, which would make them a bit low at the table—but April was pleased with the centerpiece of tiny orange pumpkins, fall leaves, and candles. From the kitchen wafted the rich scent of turkey; April had spent the previous week studying the Thanksgiving recipes in *The New York Times*, and the fourteen-pounder in the oven, stuffed with onion and lemon and basted with cider, smelled enticing. It was the first turkey April had ever cooked; she'd never thought that she'd have enough people around to make it worthwhile.

"Are you sure it's supposed to be that brown?" said Ben, bending over to peer into the oven. He and April had been invited to Thanksgiving dinner at the golf club—a tradition their father never missed—but had agreed to a family dinner on Saturday instead. April was delighted to have Ben join her party, particularly since he and Kelsey had broken up in rather spectacular fashion a month earlier, after Kelsey found notes for a monologue Ben was practicing and thought it was a love letter to someone else. The fact that it was in iambic pentameter didn't seem to give her pause. Good riddance, April thought.

"Mom used to cook it like that," April said. "Get away from the oven." She swatted Ben on the behind with a spatula. Anonymous (Nonny), April's cat, jumped back from sniffing around the oven, as did Ben, laughing.

A knock, or more like a low kick, sounded at the door. April opened it to find Laura, her hands full with a large casserole dish covered in foil. Olivia, two nattily dressed stuffed bears under her arm, stood next to her, gazing down with pride at a pair of shiny dress-up shoes; behind them was Rebecca, with a large paper bag April recognized as coming from the way-too-expensive bakery down the street.

"Hi April!" said Laura breathlessly, stepping into the apartment with the air of someone who'd been there multiple times before, as indeed she had. "Happy Thanksgiving! I'd give you a hug but I don't have any hands. The table looks so pretty! Where should I put this? Livvy, say hi to April! Rebecca, the kitchen's over this way if you want to put down that bread."

"Thank you so much for inviting me," Rebecca said to April, hustling Olivia into the entryway and gracefully slipping out of her towering stilettos. "It smells wonderful in here. What a pretty apartment! Oh, and thank you again for the suggestion of that mystery book, *The Stranger Diaries*! I'm going by the store to pick it up on Saturday. I think my book club—the one Laura ditched—might love it."

"Yes, the order came in! It's on hold for you at the desk. Hope you love it!" said April, giving Rebecca a quick hug. "Laura, just find a spot anywhere in the kitchen. And you know my brother, Ben, right? Wasn't Sydney coming with you as well?"

"Oh, he and Andrew are coming together," said Laura, moving to the kitchen and depositing her dish on the counter. "They're still quite inseparable. Did you notice that Andrew has started wearing pocket squares? Sydney said they'd pick up that wine Rebecca ordered. April, come with me down the hall for one sec,

I need to ask you something. Livvy, sweetie, give me your coat; I'll put it in April's room. You can keep the bears with you."

"Olivia, you look so nice. I like your dress," April said, squatting down a bit to greet Olivia at eye level. Olivia, as always, was wearing an outfit rather cuter than April's; this particular dress had an adorably retro look to it, as if chosen by a small Mary Poppins.

"Thank you," said Olivia solemnly. She held up her two stuffed animals. "This is Blueberry and this is Snowberry. They came because they both like turkey. Can I see your kitty?"

"Well, I hope the bears are hungry," April said. "If you go into the kitchen, my brother, Ben, can get them something to drink. And yes, Nonny is around here somewhere! She would love to play with you. Try looking under the couch. That's where all her toys end up." She headed down the hall with Laura to her bedroom, which felt quiet after the sudden noise of guests arriving.

Laura giggled. "Am I safe leaving Rebecca alone with Ben?"

"Ha!" April said. "He's actually kind of scared of powerful women, for all his talk. He'll probably tell her all about this weird web series he just got a teeny part on. Ben's all excited because Kelly Drake is in it. He thinks it's his big break."

Laura quickly closed the door, seeming to be bursting with curiosity. "So, how did it go?" she asked. Laura had fixed April up with one of her clients: a software guy named Justin who'd come in to get outfitted for a gala but told Laura he'd really rather be at home reading. This seemed like a good omen, and Laura had quickly ascertained that he was single, nice, and willing to be fixed up with a stranger.

"He's nice!" April said. "*Really* nice. We're going to a movie tomorrow. I didn't invite him today because that seemed like kind of a big step to come for Thanksgiving? But thank you, thank you, thank you. Best first date I've had in . . . well, maybe ever." It really had been a lovely time. He'd met her at Read the Room and they'd sat in the café and talked about books, while her new colleagues elaborately pretended not to be eavesdropping. Even

Westley had given her a knowing smile afterward. "And . . . how are things going with Nathan?"

Laura had begun dating the widowed dad of one of Olivia's classmates earlier in the fall; he'd contacted her a few weeks after meeting her at the second-grade graduation, having looked up her email address on the class parent list. Like Laura, he was raising a daughter by himself. April had been eagerly following the developments: Laura was taking things slowly but all was going well. Nathan, Laura had reported, was kind and funny and didn't mind Laura offering suggestions on his wardrobe (which wasn't terrible but had perhaps too many half-zip fleeces), and the two girls were getting along wonderfully.

"He's good! He said to thank you again for the invitation today, and he's sorry that he and Harper couldn't come; they always go to his parents' on Thanksgiving. But I'm seeing him Saturday for dinner, and we're taking the girls to the aquarium on Sunday."

April's eyes shone. "I'm so glad," she said. "I can't wait to meet him. He sounds so much better than some loser who would leave you notes in a book."

Laura smiled. "I don't know about that. Maybe that's not the worst way to meet someone."

"Maybe not," said April. "OK. We'd better get back to the kitchen before Ben says something to Rebecca that we'll all regret."

"Maybe we should fix him up with my babysitter," said Laura, giggling. "She has a similar lack of filter."

"Doesn't she have a boyfriend?"

"I think she's about to dump him. She found an earring in their bed that he swears belongs to his mother, and there's no good way for *that* story to end."

In the kitchen, April found a basket for the bread and told Ben—who was, indeed, pontificating about *Rain Delay* ("It's sort of like *The Wire*, but with rain and maybe some zombies")— to put down his beer and get slicing. Ben, glancing at Laura for the first time, raised an eyebrow at April, pointing elaborately at Laura and pantomiming *Who's that?*

April's eyebrows went up even higher. *Way out of your league,* she mouthed, smiling.

"Did you just say something, April?" said Laura, peeling the foil off her casserole.

"No! Nothing!" Mercifully a knock sounded on the door at exactly that moment and April excused herself to answer it. It was Westley and Alejandra, each carrying a pie and looking adorably red-cheeked and bundled-up, like they'd just emerged from a holiday photograph. They really looked, April reflected, like they belonged together. "Welcome!" she said. "Come in and warm up! It's freezing out!"

The moment might have been just the tiniest bit awkward— Westley and Alejandra were at that point in their relationship where they couldn't even remove their coats without some very hot eye contact and arm-stroking—but just behind them hurried Sydney, whose turquoise wool overcoat and feather-trimmed derby hat made a bright spot in the room, and Andrew, carefully carrying a box containing several bottles of wine with elegant labels. "Love it," Sydney said, gesturing to the room with a waving arm and dramatically giving April twin kisses on both cheeks. "Love the apartment, love the table, love it all. Very rustic. Very chic."

"So glad you could come!" said April. "Hey, Andrew! Love the pocket square."

"Sydney's influence, but thanks!" said Andrew. "Hey, Westley! I was online this morning and saw a preview of your Donna Wolfe ad. Very artsy! Totally made me want to drink while reading. I don't know why I never thought of that before."

Westley smiled a little sheepishly. "Thanks. I still wonder why I let Donna talk me into it, but the money was kind of ridiculous."

"He can *finally* get his own place," Alejandra interjected, smiling. "Donna's sort of his fairy godmother now."

"Donna's OK, really," Westley said. "I have a movie idea I'm trying to pitch to her." Though she hadn't known him long, April had noticed that Westley seemed so much more at ease than even a few months ago; something, whether it was Alejandra or being a muse, seemed to have changed him. Maybe it was the salsa classes Alejandra was reportedly dragging him to, or maybe it was just love.

Things always seem chaotic at the beginnings of gatherings, with the multiple arrivals of guests and coats to dispose of and drinks to pour and the conversation alternating between rapid small talk and awkward silences. But then comes the middle, that lovely middle, when suddenly everything finds its groove: Everyone is seated and comfortable, the food is perfect, and the evening seems like it could go on forever, in the very best of ways.

April gazed around the candlelit table wanting to freeze time, just for a moment. She watched as Ben helped Olivia ladle an enormous crimson pool of cranberry sauce over her turkey slices, and Westley held the salad bowl and seemed utterly enraptured by the way Alejandra wielded the salad tongs, and Rebecca and Sydney snickered together over a joke that perhaps made sense only to them, and Andrew helped himself to too many potatoes and scraped half of them onto Sydney's plate, without needing to ask if he wanted them. So many stories, in a room that had been so quiet for such a long time.

Laura had also paused over her plate, looking around the table. April caught her eye and they giggled together. It was amazing how quickly they had become part of each other's lives, after that long, strange, wine-soaked, unexpectedly lovely dinner at Emilio's.

"This is so nice," Laura said to April quietly. "Thank you."

"What's nice?" said Olivia, who had that only-child way of always wanting to know what the grown-ups were talking about.

"Nothing, sweetie," said Laura. "It's just nice to be here."

Outside, darkness was beginning to fall, and the street looked a bit like a winter snow globe, with tiny snowflakes whirling near the streetlight. Inside it was warm, with the candles on the table flicking gracefully with the conversation, giving everyone's face a soft glow. The whole scene felt, April thought, just like a movie, the kind you'd want to watch over and over, always wanting to enter its world one more time.

(Found inside new paperback copy of Elly Griffiths's *The Stranger Diaries*, waiting at the front desk at Read the Room)

Bonjour Rebecca,
You don't know me, but I've seen you in the store and heard your friend—the nice young woman who sits near that handsome guy at the used-books desk—call you by name; may I do so? My apologies that my English is not yet perfect, but I am new to the city and just started baking in the café. Though I do not yet know everyone's name in the bookstore, I heard them talking about leaving this book for you. Is it too forward to say that I would love to get to know you? May I make you a croissant someday?
Avec les doigts croisés,
Sébastien

Acknowledgments

Though writing is by nature a solitary pursuit, getting a book to the finish line requires a vast ensemble. Consequently I have many people to thank.

Appropriately for a book that's ultimately about friendship, my first thanks go to my beloved circle of friends: some of whom read the manuscript and offered helpful suggestions (and didn't mind when I swiped an old boyfriend's name to use in the book); some stood by with positive energy and Diet Cokes and encouraging texts exactly when I needed them. I am enormously grateful for all of it. Much love, thanks, and hugs to Bethany Jean Clement, Janet Ellerby, Sally Freed, Amy Frey, Katherine Frey, Sarah Gage, Lynn Jacobson, Arlene Libby, Marjorie Manwaring, Crystal Paul, Terri Sharkey, and Cindy Thompson. Also sending love to Carla Zilbersmith, who's cheering from her perch on a cloud somewhere.

Thank you to Allison Hunter, my dream of an agent (she's so good at what she does I sometimes wonder if I made her up), and to the entire wonderful team at Trellis Literary Management, especially Allison Malecha, Natalie Edwards, Tori Clayton, and Michelle Brower. And thank you to my lovely London agent, Katie Greenstreet, who has no idea how much fun I've had dropping the phrase "my London agent."

I'm thrilled to be published by Dutton Books at Penguin Random House, and want to first thank my brilliant editor, Maya Ziv, who made the editing process an absolute joy. Also at Dutton, thank you to Ella Kurki, Andrea Peabbles, and Leah Marsh. At Bloomsbury in the UK, the delightful Darcy Nicholson's keen editorial insights were an enormous help.

Thank you to my colleagues at *The Seattle Times*, whose talents inspire me every day; particularly the amazing Features crew. Thank you to editors extraordinaire Janet Tu and Stefanie Loh, whose support of my fiction endeavors was unflagging and greatly appreciated. And thank you to photojournalist/artist Erika J. Schultz for my author photo and its beautiful light.

Thank you to Seattle bookselling legend Michael Coy, who kindly allowed me to buy him coffee and pester him with questions about how bookstores work. (Any strange business practices at Read the Room are my own invention.) Speaking of Seattle bookselling legends, I'm forever grateful to Karen Maeda Allman, who referred me to the Writer to Agent program at AWP23 that set this journey into motion. Many thanks also to Lori Galvin, whose encouragement and suggestions were incredibly helpful early on.

Thank you to everyone at Third Place Books Ravenna, my enchanting neighborhood bookstore (and Read the Room's doppelgänger), and to indie bookstores everywhere. They are—as at least one of my characters says, and I believe—places of magic.

As always, I send love and thanks to my entire extended family of Macdonalds, Monroes, and Malvins. I especially want to acknowledge my now grown-up nieces, Anna Malvin and Ellie Monroe, and goddaughters, Teya Patt and Alix Diaz: Memories of your adorable selves at age seven helped me to create the character of Olivia, and were so much fun to revisit. A special note, with love, to my immediate family: It's my fondest hope that this book might contain something of the warmth of my mother, Sue, the wit of my dad, Jim, the strength of my sister, Linda, and the kindness of my brother, Blaine. The hardest thing about being a debut author later in life is that not all of your loved ones are there to celebrate with you. My brother was able to see an early copy of the book before he left this world in December 2024, and his pride and excitement will be forever in my heart. I wish my dad could hold this book, but I think he knows about it, somewhere.

Finally, my deepest gratitude goes to the person without whom this book would never have existed: the person who believed in me when I didn't, who readily agreed to my extremely irresponsible plan to take an unpaid leave from my steady job—during a pandemic!—to chase a vague fiction dream, who always said, yes, you can do this, just keep going. This book is for Bruce Monroe: my husband, my rock, my song, my favorite bookstore companion, my storybook ending.

About the Author

MOIRA MACDONALD is the longtime arts critic for *The Seattle Times. Storybook Ending* is her first novel.